Ballet for Men in Gumboots
=An Oyster Farmer's Tale =

By
Hailey Roussin-Guillemot

copyright 2014 Hailey Roussin-Guillemot

ISBN 978-0-473-31726-3

For Gwendal. My favourite oyster farmer.

This is a work of fiction. Yep, it's all made up. Any reference to people living or not is entirely coincidental and unintentional. Some of the events described may have happened to people I know in a way that is *similar*, but not quite the same. The story is set in New Zealand but the location is unknown, somewhere between North and South, I think.

The reader may come across new words. These are mostly real words in New Zealand. Let the world wide web be your friend in explaining these, or better yet, get on a plane and get amongst it!

I should also add here a WARNING: most kiwi oyster farmers make frequent use of coarse language. For authenticity's sake I have included a fair bit of it, words like Fuck, and Shit. If you don't like reading that sort of stuff then close your book now.

May all your oysters bloom and grow. =

= Chapter 1 =

Winter was a hell of a time to start a new job thought Jack. It had been this time a year ago he'd started working on the oyster farm, and the thought of getting up in the cold and spending a day in the freezing water was enough to make his balls jump. There was only one way to do it - fast. He swung his legs over the side of the hammock and dropped to the floor. He'd learnt the art of sleeping in a hammock during his time on a fishing trawler in Tauranga, and still preferred it when he slept on boats. The wake from other vessels going in and out of the harbour disturbed him if he slept on the bed, and the foam squab gave him a crick in his neck.

Smell Hound had taken up on the double berth below. Normally he didn't agree with animals getting ideas above their station, but she was getting grey around the muzzle and arthritic in her back legs, so he pretended not to notice. Smell was careful to climb up stealthily after he was in bed and jump down before he woke, knowing it was wrong but unable to resist.

Jack recoiled at the feel of cold wood under his feet. He hit the floor exactly two minutes before his alarm was set to go off. Good old body clock. He suspected his subconscious didn't like to be jolted out of sleep and had trained his body to avoid the annoying foghorn sound his phone played. Even if the hour he got up was changed he would still wake before the alarm.

The houseboat wasn't heated because it was such a small space that cooking usually did the trick, so mornings were the worst before the cooker got going. Nothing prepared you for the moment of leaving a warm bed and pulling on clothes before starting the gas cooker. A rug on the floor just there would have been a comfort, but that would mean shopping for one.

Jack didn't like shops. They were always trying to sell you stuff you didn't need. He only went to the 4square to stock up on food and basics like loo paper and dog biscuits. The local 4square was a five minute uphill walk from the wharf, and it was owned and run by a husband and wife from Vietnam. He liked it there. The wife made excellent sushi on weekdays, and Jack often filled up a plastic takeaway container before work, trying any new combinations laid out in their neat rows. He liked the details of Asian food. There were yellowish slices of ginger, a blob of green wasabi, a fish shaped tube of soy sauce, and a pair of wooden chopsticks. Mr Chin never tried to sell Jack anything. He never asked for your loyalty card or if you had Flybuys. He would nod politely and smile as Jack came in, and wait patiently at the till as Jack loaded his basket. It was a shame they didn't sell rugs. Mrs Chin was never seen behind the counter except to refill the trays of sushi. The job of serving customers was done entirely by her husband, and Jack guessed his English was better than hers, which was saying something.

Over the past year the two men had become friendly. Chin liked to make conversation, though

Jack didn't understand most of what was said, and that probably went both ways. Some men Jack talked to at the pub didn't make much sense either, but they didn't make sense in plain English, which is different from not making sense in pidgin English. It was almost cryptic, like Chin only spoke in riddles or images. Jack liked it that he could buy a basket of boring but necessary items and be given a thought for the day. Apart from the small grocer stocking enough to meet Jack's needs and not bothering him, his originality kept Jack coming back for more little chats.

He was still puzzling over last week's conversation. Mr Chin had cast a glance at the sky and rung up Jack's purchases saying, 'When win brow sout, cat and dog be friends. Brrrr. You share bed, be nice warm. You a dog no cat,' and his small, dark eyes had twinkled with mischief. 'Maybe you like pussy from Vietnam? Vee-ry pretty but wash-out!' He made a claw with one hand and bared his teeth. Jack had laughed, 'Ah Chin, you're a funny bugger. I don't have room for a cat.' Jack smiled and shook his head in confusion. Apart from the 4square the pub was his only other regular stop.

Smell Hound was such a loyal dog that she had waited for Jack to start going grey before letting hers show. Over the last year it had crept in gradually, and now there was a fair show of grey round Jack's muzzle too, but nothing he couldn't hide with a quick swipe of the razor. In the small shaving mirror propped over the galley sink his eyes looked grey this morning. His mother always knew he'd be devoted to the sea with eyes like that; changeable and unpredictable, some days more green, some days blue, but always a muted colour.

It was still dark out, with the first hint of sun over the hills, and mist lifting off the water. Jack opened the door for Smell who trotted down the plank connecting the boat with the shore and went about her morning toilet. Jack finished his coffee and did the same on board. Every week he had to empty his portable toilet down the long drop on the reserve. It was the only job associated with boats that he had zero pleasure in doing, but there was no way round it. Some of the other boat dwellers preferred to make a trip out to the open sea and release their sewerage where the currents would take it further out, but it was a hassle getting the houseboat secured again on the mooring. Jack also considered it a bit dirty; he had to work in that water five days a week. The fish might not mind a bit of final product, but he doubted they ate toilet paper.

He heated a can of beans on the small Bunsen burner, stirring them every thirty seconds, and managed not to burn his toast. He held the slices of bread between the bars of what looked like a large fork. It was an old fashioned thing used for camping, and when side A was brown you flipped it over to toast side B. Not burning the toast required attention, and so did not burning the beans. Sometimes it was a case of one or the other, but today he had it under control. This small achievement put him in a good mood, and he ate his breakfast contentedly at the fold out table.

Wonder what this new bloke's like then. Another one from the boss's rugby club. Last one, what was his name? Shawn or something, stopped coming after three months. Said it was too much like hard work. He wasn't wrong there, it was hard work, damn hard. Most evenings Jack was about as much use as a pair of knickers without elastic.

Pulling on gumboots over his thick socks Jack whistled for Smell Hound. The ute sat idling with the choke out and the heater on high while Jack locked up the houseboat. Plenty of people round here who couldn't say no to an unlocked door. This town was full of empty summer houses, and close enough to the city to make easy pickings for those disaffected citizens who preferred not to do an honest day's work when a dishonest one could be more lucrative. In the last twelve months no one had broken into his boat, but he'd woken one morning to find a piece of garden hose jammed in his petrol tank. The ute was in the car park about fifteen metres away, but he hadn't heard a thing. Thanks to the anti-syphon system the thieves had been prevented from stealing his petrol, but it had cost him three hundred dollars to have the hose removed. Since then Jack brought home sacks of oyster shell and dumped them in the car park and along the path to the boats. The shells crunched underfoot and Smell would bark at anyone loitering after dark.

He waved to old Betty on her boat next door throwing tea leaves over the side. Betty was the unofficial Houseboat Mother. She had no children, and loved her role as Chairwoman of the houseboat community. She was the first to greet newcomers, sign them in, take complaints, and organize events. She kept a close eye on who came and went, so the boats should have been safe, but Betty was a busy woman. Most days she was out and about.

'Have a good day, Jack!'

'And you!' Jack called back, jumping into the warm cab. He backed onto the road, adjusting his position on the seat for comfort. This was his favourite moment of the day. Everything was fresh and all possibilities existed. Smell rode on the back, sheltering in her box. She didn't do it often, but when she dropped one you sure knew about it, and mornings were the worst. Jack fed her at night so the gas came out in the morning, because feeding her in the morning meant one of them would have to sleep outside at night.

Smell got her name one morning when she was a pup. Jack and his mate were on their way home, sorely hungover after a big party the night before. They'd gone about 10km down the road when Jack sniffed the air and said, 'What is that smell?' The guy beside him took a big sniff of the air, and seconds later they were both winding down their windows at incredible speed, and throwing up all down the side of the car before they could pull off the road and get out. Still dry-heaving on the roadside, Jack turned his head towards his mate who was in a similar position. 'That is the foulest smell ever to come from man or beast.' There was another gushing noise from his companion. Hands on his knees he turned to Jack wide-eyed,

'Well don't bloody look at *me*!'

'Well, it wasn't *me*! A man would have to be awful crook to make a smell like that.'

'You look crook enough.'

'I was doing ok until a moment ago.'

'Then it had to be-'

'-the dog!' they chorused.

'Yep, no doubt that is the smelliest dog alive,' said the bloke, wiping his mouth with a sleeve. Back in the car with all the windows down Jack looked over his shoulder at the puppy lolling across the back seat and said to her, 'I think we just found you a name. You're the Smell Hound.' The men had managed to laugh and shake their heads though it hurt to do so.

Jack looked at the numbers on the boxes. Not far now. Ross had told him the new worker would be at his gate, and sure enough he could see a pair of short, stocky legs poking out of black stubbies and a big grin looking his way. He looks alright, thought Jack. Should be able to keep up with shoulders like that and legs like tree stumps. The word 'burly' came to mind. He pulled over and leaned across to open the passenger door. 'You Ryan?' he called.

'Yeah. Gidday. You must be Jack.' They shook hands as he climbed in.

'Here, shut that door and put your hands under the air vent,' Jack said. 'You must've been waiting a while to get hands that cold.' His bare legs were covered in goose pimples, and his thigh was tattooed with writing. Jack read it while he waited for Ryan to stash his bag at his feet and put his seat belt on; it said:

> Big cats bite
>
> but a little pussy
>
> never hurt me

'Yeah, didn't want to be late for my first shift,' Ryan replied.

'So, you a mate of Ross then?'

'I've known Ross awhile. We played rugby together for ten years. I guess you could say that brings two men as close together as they should be,' he said with a laugh. 'What's he like as a boss?'

'Not my place to say. I wouldn't want to spoil your fun in finding out.'

'Fair enough.' Ryan smiled and relaxed into his seat. A minute later they pulled into the petrol station. 'Here, I'll fill the tank while you go and pay,' Ryan offered. 'I don't know if Ross mentioned it, but my car's not too reliable on the gravel road. If you're happy to take me to work I'll pay half your gas bill on paydays.' Jack nodded that this was an acceptable plan. Ryan got the tank filled while Jack grabbed some milk and paid inside where the lady on the till said, 'Fresh meat?' and nodded in Ryan's direction. 'Ross sure gets through em eh? What're we up to? Must be third one in a year. Not everyone got *your* abilities, Jack,' she added meaningfully. He was slightly puzzled by that. It wasn't like Ross to sing his praises, and there was a definite leer on her face when she said it. He thought about what abilities she might suppose he had and suddenly cringed. Of course, word gets around a small town fast. He knew it had been a mistake to accept that last beer on Saturday night, but it was Merv's birthday, and he was shouting the drinks. Most likely the whole town'd be talking about him leaving the pub with that Lara. What a mistake. Jack smiled sheepishly and made for the exit. Luckily there were no other customers in the shop to witness his embarrassment. He pushed these thoughts out of his mind and decided Monday morning was not the time for thinking about it.

Ryan bought three cans of fizzy caffeinated drink and three tepid pies. He gobbled two of them in less than five minutes. It wasn't a pretty sight. Even Smell Hound who was looking intently at those pies from behind the cab looked disgusted, and not only because she could count (pies specifically), but because she could eat them with more manners than that. 'God, I was starving. Not used to early starts. I don't normally eat breakfast because when I get up it's lunchtime.' Ryan erupted a mighty contented belch and showed himself to be quite at ease. Yup, they all start out this way. Poor bastard. Wait till five o'clock, he'll be so knackered he won't have the energy to fart, Jack reckoned.

When they arrived at work it was all smiles and slaps on the back. 'Thanks for helping us out, really appreciate it eh,' said Ross. 'Time to gear up and go get us some oysters. Jack can show you where the waders are. Tea and coffee over there. Jack? Make us a coffee while I get the barge ready, will ya? Okay, Ryan? I'll shout you a beer at knock off.'

Like an ambitious whirlwind he was out the door and throwing stuff in piles on the barge. They could hear objects hitting the deck, the sound carried from the water up to the shed on a light breeze. Can of petrol, thunk. Coil of rope, thunk. Boat rod (just in case), thunk. Jack made three coffees and put his waders on while they waited for Ross. Ryan squeezed into his. They were so snug Jack could see he had a pot belly. That would soon disappear.

Jack had difficulty maintaining a healthy weight in winter despite a large appetite. He never missed a meal, and kept a pocket stuffed with muesli bars to snack on. Ross preferred to skip breakfast, always ate no more and no less than two sandwiches at lunch, and a single serving of dinner. Jack couldn't understand how he stayed the same size year round. Maybe it was all the beer.

The farm lay in the shallow waters of the bay, a long inlet like a finger pointing to the surrounding hills. Fish came in with the tides to breed, the mangroves at the top of the inlet where the water was brackish making a good fish nursery. There were clumps of mangroves dotted around the shore near the oyster farm too, and Ross made sporadic attempts to pull them out with the tractor. They were protected by the conservation laws, but that didn't hold much water with Ross. He was afraid the mangroves would spread and cause a buildup of silt in the bay, and encouraged his son to stomp on the seedlings when the tide went out.

During low tide the rows of sticks were exposed making rippling lines across the surface of the water.

It was a remote place ideal for an oyster farm. There was little stock on the surrounding land to foul the water which swirled in and out. On this side the land fed sixty sheep and half a dozen cattle; the lifestyle farm of a retired accountant turned shepard called Dave. On the other side there was even less stock, just a tiny hamlet of holiday houses which could only be accessed by water, and a much larger oyster farm, its grey steel shed close to the shore. Jack loved it here. The serenity around him always had a calming effect no matter what his thoughts were. Right now as he helped push the barge into the calm water his thoughts were on speculating how long the current display of matey-ness would last.

Ross was known as a good-time guy with the rugby club members. Someone fun to get on the piss with. A nice guy, a good bloke. He knew lots of dirty jokes, and even more extremely lame ones. While all this was true, it was also true that Ross the Boss was a slave driver with no tolerance for slackness. His livelihood depended on the farm running at peak at all times. He knew to the last dozen what the farm could produce, and aimed to beat it. If machinery broke it went unfixed until the next quarter and he expected his men to carry on regardless. Well, we'll see how long he can keep up the good guy image, Jack thought. In the meantime Jack would tag along for the honeymoon, enjoy the pleasantries while it lasted.

Jack hadn't started here as a mate, and hadn't been fooled by the friendly banter. He saw the underlying aggression in the way Ross treated his gear roughly, and he had a habit of flaring his nostrils which Jack quickly realized was a sign of suppressed annoyance. Ross had figured out by the second week that he was wasting his time befriending Jack, that he didn't mind working hard for money. Jack tolerated the constant demands to work harder and faster, and the frequent temper tantrums when plans went foul because of human error, mechanical failures, or weather conditions. But he drew the line at insults. Ross had once called him a 'dumb prick' for backing over a crate of oysters which Ross had forgotten to move. Jack had been about to apologize. Instead, he froze, gave Ross a hard stare, and drove off without a word. Over the next week Jack let him feel his displeasure with every look, and his words were doled out sparingly. Ross didn't mention the incident though Jack knew he got the message. Since then Ross was mindful to keep his rage generalized, kicking things and swearing at objects as if they were responsible. Ryan would have to define his own boundaries if there was to be a lasting harmony because Ross on a tangent was like a blind bull on heat who couldn't see the fence.

The three men had lowered themselves into the water which came up to the waist. Small whirls spread out from them and puffs of mud rose up from the bottom where their boots landed. 'Bit nippy in the water this morning eh? Just wait till summer. The cool water will be your best friend,' Ross said to Ryan. Jack was holding the other side of the barge.

There was a southerly wind pushing the barge onto the farm structures, and someone had to hold it steady until it was in the right postion.

'My balls have just met my tonsils, mate!' Ryan shouted back. 'I'll have to grow a bit more insulation down there; or a possum skin in my undies might work. What's with pubes, anyway? Not exactly designed for the job of keeping the nuts warm, are they?' Jack chuckled. It was a relief to have another man about. Sometimes it was a bit intense being just the two of them, and Jack wasn't just meaning the workload.

As they went deeper, pulling the barge with them, the water pressed their waders against their legs. The neoprene was cold until you warmed it up, but it kept out the water unless you leaned too far over and it came in at the neck or arms. On the bottom of the waders there were industrial gumboots glued to the legs, and if they got a hole you didn't stand a chance of staying dry. Ryan froze and gasped, and Ross laughed at his expression of shock.

'Sorry about that, mate! I think you got the leaky ones! We'll measure you up for a new pair. Those belonged to the last guy - didn't think you'd fit mine.'

Ross was an average height but thin and wiry. There wasn't a scrap of fat on him and his muscles and tendons were clearly defined. When he moved you could see the concentration of energy in his tensed muscles as they twitched, and he was rarely still. He was blond with fair skin and pale blue eyes with a jaw like a Viking warrior. It wasn't a friendly face unless he smiled, but all the same he wasn't an ugly fella. Ryan was shorter and more solidly built. His muscles seemed to roll under his skin like sacks of water, and his smooth, fluid movements reminded Jack of a seal. His hair was a shaggy mess and his features were rough; a big nose with a bump on its ridge curved down to fleshy lips and crooked teeth, but what you saw looking at him was friendly and approachable. The two were complete opposites.

'Don't worry, you'll warm up once we get stuck in!' shouted Ross encouragingly. Jack was used to Ross shouting. Usually he mumble-shouted, what Jack called 'Yumbling', but he was making an effort for Ryan. Ross had lost the hearing in one ear from repeated damage in scrums and tackles on the rugby field, so if he couldn't hear you he would turn the good ear your way and failing that, just pretend to understand. He often watched your lips when you spoke to him. He wasn't the sort to live comfortably with a disability and did his best to hide it.

'We need all this row loaded up,' Ross said, and he added for Jack's attention, 'you take it from here. I'll leave you guys to it, I've got plenty of stuff to sort out on the harvest rack.' The last bit sounded like 'Youtakit fromere. Iffgot plenny uffuff tsorton tharvestrack'. He waded off and Jack stood a minute deciphering it. There were other meanings behind the words which Jack was aware of too. What he was really saying was: 'I've had quite a heavy weekend of drinking, so I'll be walking around in the mud while I recover thanks to the fresh air, the cool water and the sweating. In the mean time, you get the job done, you sort that guy out, and you make it all look easy and pleasant.'

Jack knew the tide was a big one, and he estimated the barge would go dry within 40 minutes. It didn't leave him much time to get the job done, let alone train someone up and make it feel like a walk in the park. He thought 'Fuck you, Ross' and went on with the work.

First he made sure the spud poles were driven well into the mud to hold the barge steady; with a wind blowing like this the barge would bust a rail if it wasn't. The spud poles were three metre lengths of wood, slotted through holes either side of the barge. Next, Jack adjusted his woolen hat over his ears, and called out, 'Look Ryan, it's easy as. You start loading from your end of the barge, doing exactly the same as I do. Then we pick up Ross and the crates, and go back for a coffee. Piece of piss, mate.' He started whistling merrily, as if he really enjoyed being wet and cold, but mostly to give the new guy some illusion of privacy while he floundered around. From experience he knew men didn't like to be watched if they weren't already confident in their actions. It was hard enough on the ego to feel incompetent without someone gawking at you.

It was always a laugh to watch someone struggle in the mud for the first time, and Ryan's weight was making his boots sink in faster than he could lift them out. He had surrendered his pride and was merely trying to stay upright and keep his legs moving as he came around the boat and climbed over the rail after Jack. Once they were in position between the rails, the lifting began. Jack grinned to himself but didn't laugh, looking away when Ryan stopped for a breather. It was the sort of job that looked dead easy, but required an exact amount of force. Ryan loaded one stick for every five of Jack's, but that wasn't bad for a first go.

It was simple but hard work. Each oyster-laden stick weighed about 20 kgs, but only held about five dozen commercial size oysters. The rest of the weight was made up of smaller oysters, barnacles, seaweed, and water-logged timber. Once there was a decent pile of sticks along the edge of the deck Jack left Ryan to work alone and jumped on board to begin knocking the oysters off the sticks. They fell into crates that could be stacked to one side, and the empty sticks were stacked on the other. Every ten minutes Jack would go and help Ryan get ahead again and move the barge a few feet along the row, keeping it as close to where they worked as possible.

By the time they had finished the job Ryan was sweating profusely and no longer feeling the cold. Coated in mud, he stood on the barge looking disoriented, dribbling slightly. He could be mistaken for a deranged caveman after a fight with wild animals. Not his best look. When Ross asked him to lift a crate his arms shook with fatigue. Jack had to admit the new guy was doing well; he wasn't giving in and wasn't moaning. The sign of a good worker.

They stripped off their waders and hung them up to dry, though at this time of year they would still be damp come tomorrow. That was one good thing about Mondays; the only day you didn't have to climb into cold, damp waders.

As usual Ross made the smoko, and as usual Jack drank the sweet, watery piss that passed as coffee. The only thing in its favour was the heat. Ross had a strange theory that Jack would ruin the budget if he was allowed to do smoko duty, because you could taste Jack's coffee and get a caffeine kick out of it. Ross tried to compensate for economizing on coffee by being generous with the sugar, which was much cheaper. He let Jack take over when there were visitors, or on special occasions like today when he felt magnanimous. He knew Jack would wash the cups first, and no one liked Ross's brew, not even Ross. At home, Nancy, Ross's wife, made him real coffee with little pottles of flavored milk to choose from, like hazelnut or caramel, but Ross's moral code demanded that he shouldn't dish out what he couldn't take. What was good enough for the workers was good enough for the boss. He made an exception for criticisms, and was prone to a good grump if anyone dared offer him one. Being of choleric temperament he had two moods; energetic or shitty. If you got both at once it was best to find yourself busy elsewhere as it was a bit like explosive diarrhea - it covered a wide area. Jack was at the point where he could predict what would trigger Cross Ross, and be well away before it happened. He could relax this morning knowing it wouldn't happen in front of Ryan.

After drinking his last can of caffeinated fizz and eating his final meat pie, Ryan seemed to recover his ruddy complexion. Ross slapped him on the shoulder and said, 'You'll get the hang of it mate!' in a jovial manner. They spent the rest of the morning washing and culling what they'd harvested at the tide.

The washer was in need of repair. The amount of bailing twine holding it together was more than the remaining rivets. It shuddered and vibrated but still did the job. The men stood around a table selecting oysters at random and singling them if they were stuck together, then put them in crates depending on size. They wore gloves to protect their hands from the sharp frill along the edge of the shells, sunnies to protect their eyes, and thick PVC aprons over their clothes. Although the oysters had been washed there was always mud stuck in the crevices between clumps, and it splattered the man who separated them. Ross let Jack demonstrate how to drive the singling knife between the shells and twist it to part them. 'Here you go, Ryan. Your turn,' said Jack handing him the knife.

After successfully singling five oysters Ryan looked up grinning with self satisfaction, until he saw the crates waiting to be done and let his breath out slow. Jack on the other hand had a large pile finished and his apron, face, and hands, were flecked with mud and bits of shell. 'Keep going, it gets easier eventually,' Jack commented. 'Just watch the knife doesn't...do that.'

Ryan had his hand cupped under a clump of oysters and his knife had shot out sideways. He'd cut his glove, but when he took it off his hand was okay, just a scratch. 'You were lucky that time,' said Jack. 'Try holding them on the table and keep your fingers

clear. We don't get new gloves too often round here.'
He spoke the last bit loudly so Ross would hear. A
pair of gloves usually lasted a week, but Ryan's had
been the last pair in the box. Ross had forgotten to
order more so now they were all wearing shredded
gloves, which was only marginally better than
wearing none.

Ross was grading the smaller oysters by size into
baskets to be put back out. Since some grew faster
than others there were always oysters which needed
longer to reach harvest size. He turned his good ear
towards Jack. 'Eh?'

'You order those gloves yet?' Jack shouted. Ross
smiled and nodded, but that didn't mean he'd heard.

'Geez, my fingers might look like crooked
sausages, but I've had them so long I don't know
what I'd do without them,' Ryan laughed heartily.

'How'd they get like that then?' Jack asked. The
fingertips had a withered look about them, like they
belonged to an elderly man who had been left in the
bath too long.

'Ah, well, my parents owned an orchard when I
was a kid and I used to do the spraying on weekends
when I was at uni, if there was nothing to pick. No
one told me I should have gloves on, and I didn't
think about it until after a couple of months my nails
started falling off. For a while I thought they'd never
grow again. The girl I was dating wouldn't go out
with me unless I wore motorcycle gloves
everywhere.' Jack just shook his head in pity.

Before lunch he went through Ryan's cull, and
taught him a bit about grading. 'Boss will tell you to

grade slightly different than me because it's a matter of opinion, mostly. There's the shell size, shape, and weight all playing into it. The ideal oyster is oval with one flat shell and one deeply cupped shell. It should feel heavy in your hand, and roughly this size.' He pulled out a handsome specimen from the pile and opened it. 'Beautiful. See how creamy and plump the fish is?' When he poked the fish with his knife it contracted, the mantle retreating towards the centre. 'That's a sign of good health. Here you go. Lunch.' Ryan accepted the oyster enthusiastically. Having nothing left to eat he wasn't about to say no. 'Ahh, damn that's good. I could eat a few more of those.' Jack passed him the knife.

'Knock yourself out. Boss doesn't mind us having a few.' He left Ryan trying to dig his way through an oyster shell. If he got that open he'd earned it.

Jack went to the shed and flicked the jug on. Smell Hound was waiting there for him, her tongue out and tail thumping the floor. She knew she could beg a few scraps at lunchtime, and maybe a pat on the head.

Ross lived a minute up the road and usually lunched at home where his wife would have some waiting for him, even if she'd gone out. Today he joined them for Ryan's sake, and Jack was sore to see him making the coffees. 'Here you go boys. Get that in ya.' Ross made it sound like a treat when Jack knew it wasn't.

They heard a vehicle pull up outside and Smell wiggled her body as her tail went into overdrive signaling she knew the visitor. Ross's wife came in and beamed smiles all round. 'Hi Ryan! Jack. Here's your lunch Rossy, and the beer you wanted. So how'd your morning go? He hasn't been too hard on you has he Ryan?'

Ross mumbled something in the way of thanks and Jack said, 'Hello.' She didn't show up at the yard often, except to take what she needed for the shop. She was too busy looking after kids, managing the accounts, and filling orders. Good thing too, thought Jack. Nancy's a decent girl, likeable, but always playing for attention - from anyone. Even the dog wasn't safe, not that Smell minded being petted and fussed over. Sheesh, I bet she got all dressed up just to come down here. Fancy boots, lipstick, hair pinned up, and a dress on under a coat that wouldn't keep a flea warm. She had the right build for a farmer's wife, and probably didn't feel the cold. Jack had seen her lift full crates with less fuss than some of the workers they'd had. She was broad all over with big arms and a chest like a nursemaid, but her face was heart-shaped and sweet.

'I'm having a great time,' Ryan answered. 'It's a bit more physical than sitting on the couch watching tele, but it was time I gave that up anyway. Jack here's been showing me the ropes and Ross keeps an eye on me.'

'Too right I do. Don't want you trying to do a runna,' Ross shot back.

'Oh, that's nice, Rossy. Sounds like you guys are having fun,' and she winked at Ryan. 'Better go, kids in the car. Tootleloo!' She left them, wiggling all her fingers as she said goodbye. The men all took a moment to recover their thoughts after the nylon-clad apparition disappeared. It was hard to think of anything not related to women after being confronted with so much of it. 'You got a girl, Ryan?' asked Jack.

'Nah, having a break from chicks. My last girlfriend broke up with me a few months ago. Made a big fuss about me stashing a bit of pot in her kid's bag.' Jack and Ross stopped chewing.

'What the hell man!' Ross spluttered spraying crumbs. 'Were you trying to get it arrested or something?' Ross's face flushed red as it always did when he was excited. Was it possible his blood rushed around his body faster than a normal person's? That could explain why he was so impatient, Jack reasoned.

'Oh, nah, nah, nothing like that,' Ryan shook his head decisively. 'I see what you're thinking, but it was one of those teddy bear things and she never used it. The kid's only three years old. It was hanging up in the wardrobe, and since the house two doors down from mine got raided, I thought it would be a good place to hide my medicine bag until things cooled off. Anyway, the real issue was...she got the wrong end of the stick. Ha ha! Literally! Caught me sneaking into the kid's bedroom to get it out one night - my stash, you know - and, well, I was pretty bloody offended when she said what she did. We had a bit of an argey bargey and she told me to take my pot and fuck off and don't come back. She was too uptight anyway. Who needs it, eh?' Thoughtful chewing resumed all round until Ross broke the silence.

'I heard she was back with her ex.'

'Yep, that's correct, but I think she's still got the hots for me. She rang me a month ago to thank me, of all bloody things. She said, 'You really helped me put things in perspective. I have trust issues with men I don't know well, so I figured I should give it another try with Frankie's dad.' Ryan said this in a whiny nasal voice to show how stupid he thought it was.

'What did you say to that?' Ross was looking amused, like he knew the next bit could only be good.

'Oh, I said no need to thank me, and if she liked I could help her put a few more things in perspective, like the size of her ass when she stopped the diet. Cheap shot, but I felt a bit put-out, and it's only the truth. I wanted to mention it when we were together, but I was afraid she'd go off the deep end.' Jack and Ross laughed, but Jack noticed Ross instinctively checking the doorway.

'And what did she say when you told her she has a big ass?' Ross whispered. Even the man who constantly made sexist comments about his wife in public had never dared to say anything about her weight. Nancy was always generously sized, but a little more so since the kids were born. A woman's figure was dangerous ground to tread. Even sweet Nancy might turn on him for that, or worse, she might refuse to have sex for a week.

'She didn't have anything to say about her big,

fat, wobbly ass, Ross. She bloody hung up on me. Just when I thought we could have a good fight for old times sake. I must have gone a bit far.' Jack was entertained listening to Ryan relate his clumsy way with women. He was honest, not trying to tell it like he was the victim as another man might, but he couldn't follow the man's logic.

'What makes you think she's still got the hots for you then?' Jack asked.

'Well, I came home from the pub on Monday night and went to get the washing off the clothesline. Someone had cut the ass out of my favourite pair of jeans. Who else knows I do my washing on Sunday and bring it in on Monday evening? You see? No fire without a spark,' Ryan winked at Jack.

Geez, this guy's a real optimist alright. It sounded more like a hate crime than lust, but it takes all sorts. 'Hey,' Ross cut into Jack's thoughts, 'what do you call a man who's lucky in love? A bachelor. Ha!' Ross was hugely amused at his own wit, and the other two laughed, Ryan throwing his head back to show a mouthful of molars, Jack less enthusiastically. He'd heard the joke already, it was on the rota, and it got less funny every time. As a bachelor, Jack wasn't convinced he was the lucky one. He wouldn't mind a bit of company of an evening, even if it did mean the occasional argey bargey. Maybe this was what happened to a man on his own past a certain age. At thirty five he hadn't been this bitter about the relationships others took for granted. Ross might moan about his wife but she doted on him. That had to be worth something.

Jack gave Smell a pat and rubbed circles on her head. She'd have to do as company for now. There was no one he'd met recently that he fancied much, and that led to thinking about his recent blunder. Luckily his thoughts were interrupted by a loud and musical fart. He looked up but couldn't say who'd done it. The other two were both grinning. The lunch chairs were quickly vacated and they regrouped outside. 'So I guess we gotta keep culling, eh?' said Ryan looking at the stacks of crates.

'Yeah, every last one of them,' replied Ross. 'Let's get into it boys!' With that he flicked on the classic rock station and all attention was focused on the oyster covered table for the next three hours. The fast beat and scream of electric guitars gave them a good pace to set the work to, and they fell into a rhythm. Select oyster, separate it from others, put it in crate. There wasn't much chance to chat since the work required focus to go at a good pace. The few times Ryan tried to start a conversation he was put off with short answers if anyone heard him over the blasting music. Finally, at a little after 4 p.m. Ross lugged the last crate of oysters to the deck of the ute and the cleanup began. It didn't take long to hose it all down and rake away the muck. What they'd culled today would be put back in the water tomorrow to recover. The oysters loaded on the ute were from the harvest rack, culled the week before and ready for sale.

The air had cooled off as early evening prepared to take over the day, and it settled damply on the men.

'Right boys, my shout. A quick beer to finish the day and you can go home to take a shower - I can smell you from here. You might think about investing in some heavy duty deodorant, mate.' This comment was aimed at Ryan, who sniffed under his arms and pulled a face. 'I think I just singed my nostril hairs,' he said proudly. When it came to his body, Ryan obviously had no shame. He seemed to accept his body and all its functions as perfectly natural. Jack wasn't one to worry much about how he looked, but he didn't get the attraction of burping and farting publicly. He didn't smell much sweeter than the other two by this time of day, deodorant had its limits, but it was a smell Jack associated with a day of honest work, and that was satisfying. The mingled smells of sea mud, rotting shellfish, and stale sweat in exchange for plenty of fresh air and all the exercise you could handle. You got used to the smell.

On an average day they shifted a ton of oysters three or four times. The farm had been a man down for almost two months and Jack could feel the knots in his back from the extra lifting. Still, he wouldn't trade this job for a warm office anywhere in the world. Jack had found out early that some were suited for working indoors and he wasn't one of them. He had once tried working for a big company that exported seafood. They hired him as a sales rep, a position he bluffed his way into. He knew enough about dealing with the processors and suppliers, but what he didn't realize was that the job involved sitting in a cubbyhole making phone calls all day. He asked a colleague at the next desk when they would hit the floor, meet the customers, do some leg work. 'About this time next year if you've proved yourself,' he said.

Jack lasted thirty two hours, all of them boring as cabin bread. He didn't want to end up like his boss who was a fat, depressed man in a suit. When he explained to the boss that he would go mad if he stayed another day the man had sympathized. Since Jack was leaving he didn't mind admitting he fantasized about being a builder; as it was he couldn't afford to stop sales unless his wife went back to work. 'How likely is that?' Jack enquired.

'Ha. Don't ask,' the man said darkly. 'You're single, aren't you?' Jack nodded. 'Then keep it that way until you've found a job you love. Once the babies start coming you're toast.'

Ross handed out cans of lager from a plastic wrapped slab in the fridge. Like the coffee Ross made, its main flavor was sweet.

'So you think you'll stick around, mate?' asked Ross. 'You'll get paid every Thursday, and six weeks of holiday when we stop the harvest in December.' Ryan nodded his head vigorously. Ross knew how to make it sound like a sweet deal.

'I reckon I can handle it. How come we get more holidays than anyone else?'

'Ah, well we don't give sick leave, so you get it as paid leave. If you're sick it's your own problem.'

Jack hadn't yet tested this arrangement to see if Ross was bluffing, but he sure sounded serious. Glad I'm not one of his poker buddies, he mused. I bet he cleans up. Despite being a highly illegal practice

Ross was confident that his workers would rather have guaranteed holidays than sick days they might not use.

'Don't worry mate, suits me. I haven't been crook in years.' Ryan tilted his head back and drained the can of beer.

'That's funny coming from a man who just spent twelve months on ACC.' Ross gave Ryan a playful punch on the arm.

Smell was already waiting in her box on the ute when the men left the shed. She thumped her tail and curled up as they jumped in. Leaving the yard in the long shadow of the hill Jack felt more buoyant than usual; with Ryan around it hadn't been a bad day at all.

Chapter 2

On the way home the men were restful and relaxed. The heat in the truck combined with their damp, smelly clothes to create an atmosphere of warm, fetid fug. Ryan was physically exhausted from struggling to keep pace all day, and didn't try to hide it. He slumped back in his seat resting his chin on his meaty chest, eyes half closed. Without stirring or opening his eyes he began to talk.

'I used to break horses for a living.' He said it as if the question had been asked. Jack was curious of course, but didn't think it was good manners to ask a man he'd just met who looked to be half asleep. He didn't have to worry, Ryan loved to talk if there was a story in it.

'Oh yeah?' Jack prompted.

'Haven't ridden for a year now. Took a fall last winter and broke my arm in two places and fractured my collar bone. Been on ACC, smoking pot out of boredom and thinking what I'd do once the payments ran out. Decided I had enough of being thrown round, and I'm not so young that I can bounce back like I used to. I figured it was a warning. Shit of a year, but it feels great to be working again, even if I am a bit out of shape. I still don't know what I want to do, but Ross said he needed a hand, and A.C.C. say they don't count falling off the career wagon as an accident.'

There was a pause, and Ryan's eyes opened momentarily as he asked, 'What about you, Jack?

How'd you end up at the farm?' Jack wondered how much he should tell him, and decided to keep the story simple without actually lying. Well, maybe bend the truth a bit like he had with everyone else.

'I was up north doing a bit of boat building for this old guy who owns a big oyster lease. He got me to build him a new barge. Anyway, this joker said he'd heard Ross was looking for a farmhand and gave me his number. That's it really. What have you heard?'

Ryan laughed quietly. 'Oh you know, Ross isn't big on compliments. He said you were a good workhorse, but a silent type who kept to himself. I thought you might be one of those moody buggers.'

This was on par with what he'd heard from other sources, and an accurate summation, although he wasn't naturally introverted. Jack had held off the social scene to start with, sure that he wouldn't be here long. When time dragged on he started getting to know the local crowd, but maybe they sensed he was keeping something back. There were pauses in the conversation where he didn't leap in quick enough with an antidote because he was running it through the checkpoint marked Dead Giveaway.

The truth of Jack's arrival was a little more complicated than his explanation revealed. The old guy was Jack's older brother, and he wasn't quite fifty yet. Joshua had been at the annual Oyster Farmer's Conference and heard something was going on that needed checking up on. He didn't say who he'd talked to, just that the concern involved a small farm run by a bloke named Ross Sargent. He asked Jack to go and see what the story was. The bank check Jack received for $5000 to help towards his expenses came from the Oyster Farmer's Association, so Jack figured there were more than a few interested parties. 'Snoop around a bit, see what this guy's up to. Let me know if anything seems odd, and I want to know what sort of character he is.'

Joshua's farm was isolated enough that they had few visitors and no other farmers working close by, so Jack was unknown in the oyster farming circles. Combined with his knowledge of how a farm worked, he made an ideal candidate for the task. Joshua had been vague about what rumors were circulating, and wouldn't say more.

It was common knowledge Ross was always looking for workers so it wasn't difficult for Jack to get the job. Ross didn't have trouble finding people, but for some reason he didn't understand, they never stayed long. Jack knew Ross put it down to individual weakness; he was always talking about past employees who couldn't hack it, weren't man enough. It was obvious that Ross's problem had more to do with his management skills than the work itself, but Jack didn't think it was worth pointing this out. Even if he did it would fall on deaf ears. Ross never reflected on his behavior because he was convinced of his own reasonable nature.

Over the phone Ross said he'd been let down by his most recent employee who had taken a job at the local hardware store and not bothered to tell him he wouldn't be turning up for work again. He was keen to give Jack a trial straight away. Ross didn't mention that he'd come across his previous employee a week later when he'd happened to go into the store to order some timber. The little sod had tried to hide under the counter. Ross was especially pleased to hire Jack because he still wasn't allowed back in the hardware store and the delivery fees they charged were disgusting.

For Jack the hardest part starting the new job had been acting like he knew nothing about the work. You could say Jack was an experienced oyster farmer, having helped his brother out between jobs over the years. Normally he liked to travel a bit, doing any kind of work that involved the sea or boats. He had worked trawlers, passenger ferries, yachts, boat yards, mussel farms, even an oil rig once. His work had taken him all over the world but he always came home. Joshua liked having him around; if only he would stick it out long term they could come to a business arrangement. The young Jack couldn't see the point in staying still too long, but he could hardly call himself young now. The last job he'd taken down south had left him mildly depressed. Jack felt the time for adventure was over and he intended to knuckle down as soon as he came back with the information Joshua wanted. He had expected to be away two or three months but here he was, still with nothing but a character assessment to show for it.

Deceiving people didn't come easily to Jack but whatever was going on seemed to be a big deal to his brother, and it wasn't like he was hurting anyone with his fibs. He liked life to be simple and believed in honesty, but there was almost nothing he wouldn't do for his big brother. Although they were ten years apart in age they had always got along well. Joshua had played Jack's childish games with him when he could have been on another level. Jack, grateful for the attention, tried not to be annoying and behaved like a much older boy, mimicking his brother. When Joshua went off to do things with older boys and his mum said he couldn't go, he waited patiently without resentment for Joshua to come back and tell him all about it. There was an awkward stage when Joshua was eighteen and got his first real girlfriend. There was a lot he wouldn't talk about, like what happened after the kissing part, but they had old amusements to fall back on.

Jack dropped Ryan off at his letterbox and made the oyster deliveries to the shops and restaurants in town who had put in orders. Connie, one of the chefs, had a soft spot for Smell and always saved her a few kitchen scraps in a special bowl which she placed on the ute's tray, waiting until it was licked clean before taking it back. It hadn't taken long for Jack to figure out her interest was really for him, but he didn't mind. It was a nice distraction from his otherwise quiet life.

'You fancy a quick one, Jack?' she asked. Jack raised his eyebrows at her.

'Is that a proposition, or are you offering me a drink?' This had become their standard joke. Connie didn't always have time to stop, but business was slow in winter, especially on a Monday. She had already finished prep for tonight, and was mucking about trying new dishes.

'Your choice, Jack. I've never kept my desires a secret.' Jack was flattered, and he appreciated her honesty. If she hadn't have been married, and to one of Ross's oldest buddies to boot, there was a time early on when he would have said yes. They were of a similar age and temperament, and Connie was a handsome woman. Instead he settled for a drink.

'Wouldn't mind picking your brains Connie, on a woman related topic.' She poured them both a glass of wine and sat down at the small outside table by the back door.

'Let's do a swap. You give me your opinion on a new recipe, and I'll give you mine on whatever it is you're stuck with - although I think I already know.' She patted his hand.

'Oh jeez, you heard then.' Jack hung his head. Word had gotten round alright.

'Right, me first. Close your eyes. Tell me what you taste.' Jack felt something brush his lips and he opened them willingly. Connie was a mean cook.

'Mmm, oysters on toast. My favourite.'

'Actually, it's baked oyster served on toasted baguette ficelle with horse radish sauce,' answered Connie flatly.

'Yeah, like I said. Oysters on toast.' He enjoyed winding her up.

'Very funny, but tell me what you think.'

'Well, ok. It's tangy, creamy, and brings out the sweetness in the oyster. It's very more-ish,' Jack hinted.

'That's more like it. Here you are then, have a few more.' Connie offered him a plate, explaining, 'These are the new winter appetizers. Everyone ordering a seafood dish will get a few while they wait. A good chef knows oysters are a winter indulgence not to be missed. Now enough about me. What on earth were you thinking, going off with that ninny of a woman at Merv's party?'

'Hang on!' Jack said, raising his hands in defense. 'I thought she was a friend of yours.' Connie laughed.

'Oh boy, Jack. This is a small community. If I gave the cold shoulder to everyone I didn't like I'd have no friends at all. That doesn't mean I'd sleep with all of them!' She rolled her eyes at him.

It was common knowledge that Connie had extramarital affairs, and her husband, a business man in the city with his fingers in plenty of pies, kept a mistress in his apartment. Connie was happy with this arrangement as long as her husband continued to handle the business end of the restaurant. Their marriage had become more of a friendship, and used as a reference by local couples who tired of each other and wanted an easy way out. The only person who didn't know about their infidelity was their teenage son. Luckily, the deception was easy to cover as the boy attended a boarding school, and they made sure holidays were spent as a family.

Jack sat scowling at Connie. For someone who liked frequent casual sex she wasn't being very generous in her judgment. Perhaps she was jealous. It could be tricky asking for a woman's opinion because you couldn't be sure what angle she'd take. A man on the other hand was more consistent, but lacked finesse when it came to such delicate matters as this.

'That's a bit unfair,' Jack said. 'I've been here a year without a single lay. I'm a man with manly urges, and I'd had a few beers and felt like letting my guard down. I admit I don't usually go for the Giggling Gerties but Lara's a nice looking lady, and a nice person from what I can tell. Anyway, don't worry, I didn't shag her. It was a disaster if you must know. We went back to the boat, which turned out was the wrong move. Every time she tried to come close Smell started growling. I put Smell outside and she started to howl. She was going to wake up the whole town. I realized it wasn't going to work, and I was just taking advantage of Lara anyway. I told her it might be best if we just called it a night, but if she'd suggested something else I'd have gone along with it, but she just starts blubbing! So I rang for a taxi and waited with her. Then she stops crying and starts saying I preferred the company of a bitch to a real woman. What could I say? In some ways that's true. Now everyone thinks it's on between us. Just wait till the truth comes out. Do you think I should go and apologize?'

Connie shook her head. She shouldn't have been surprised that Jack had shown a conscience, but did he have to be so damn moral all the time? Lara's ego might have suffered but she would be sure to use the episode to generate sympathy for weeks to follow. Her closest friends would make a point of ignoring

Jack if she was about, but that wasn't much punishment.

'I'd say Smell saved you from a complicated situation. Lara *is* nice but she's forever making a fuss about things. Over-emotional type. I can't see you putting up with that for long, so better it never started. You don't need to apologize because you never did her any harm. It would have been worse if you'd slept with her and *then* told her you weren't interested. And don't worry about the gossip, it'll soon be forgotten. Now, it's been lovely Jack, but I've got six tables arriving in half an hour.' Connie heaved herself up. If a quick fling was all he wanted she'd be delighted to give him her time, but Jack was still keeping his distance. She hadn't considered getting Jack drunk and taking advantage of him, she didn't usually have to resort to those kind of tactics when it came to getting men in bed, and thanks to Lara he wouldn't be likely to make the same mistake twice.

Jack guessed Connie was putting his situation into the context of their friendship, and reaffirmed to himself it would never work; he admired her too much, and would be in a real mess when she reminded him it couldn't be anything more than back-door sex. Giving up a friendship in return for heartache was a fools game.

It was dark now and Jack was cold. The lights of the other boat dwellers reflected on the water as he drove along the harbour. He was glad he had someone like Connie to talk things over with, and his head felt settled again. She was probably right, the gossip would disappear when something more interesting happened. 'Coo-ee Jack!' Betty called out as he walked up the plank to his boat. 'If you want a bit of dinner there's some mutton stew on the fire. I couldn't eat it all and I thought I'd keep it warm just in case.'

'Thanks Betty, that'd be lovely. Just let me have a quick wash and get out of these dirty rags,' Jack hollered back.

God it was good to feel the end of the day and some small home comforts. He washed quickly and put on clean jeans and a jersey before stepping outside and whistling for Smell to follow. Smell gave him a mournful look and flopped on the door mat. This was her way of telling him she would rather wait here, and Jack didn't mind this new independence. She was aging faster than him, and as long as he wasn't going far she could bear the separation. Jack had seen her clock the car keys on the table, a sure sign he would be nearby.

Betty's houseboat was neat and tidy and crammed full of knick knacks which made it look homely and inviting compared to Jacks no frills cabin. Betty was almost sixty and had been living here since her husband died fifteen years ago. Her step-children had taken the house off her. They still blamed Betty for their parents divorce and had made it their priority to see her homeless.

Betty had been the younger woman who they referred to as 'the home-wrecker.' It hadn't mattered that she'd loved their father and made him happy for twenty years. She'd admitted to Jack that she let them do it, never put up resistance, because it was true she'd been a home-wrecker. She hadn't thought of the children, she'd been smitten by Donald and thought the rest would fall into place. He was a depressed man who spent all his time on his boat to avoid his wife, and young Betty was a keen sailor. They saw each other at the boat club often, and one day she packed a picnic basket and invited herself on board Donald's boat. She was shocked to find out he was married, but Donald assured her it was a ticking time bomb. He didn't plan on staying married, he was waiting for the youngest child to be of school age so his wife could return to work, and that happy day was in three weeks time. Donald had already been to see his solicitor. Betty thought it might be wise to wait until the dust had settled, but Donald was fed up with waiting for his life to resume. Betty was young and impetuous, her need for love outweighing reason. That was how their love story began.

'I've no regrets, you know,' she'd told Jack. 'Donald was worth every penny. I gave it all up gladly in exchange for those years we had together.'

Donald had left her the boat in his will, but everything else was in his name. There was a little money from the sale of the house which Betty was entitled to, just enough to convert the old tub into a houseboat and cover the funeral costs. In this way she could live quite simply on her small income, and the boat, the bay, the foreshore were full of a young woman's memories of falling in love. Betty felt sure

Donald would be pleased knowing she was there in the place they met. Once the structural work was completed she had painted the whole boat bright yellow with white trim, and flower boxes hung off the railings. Geraniums of all colours flourished despite the salty air. 'I wanted to make a statement, to show those children that stripping me of the life we'd had, the material life, wasn't a cause for sorrow. What we lived was untouchable. I supposed I was a bit deranged with grief because thinking you can change the way people think by painting your home happy colours is daft, but it helped me at the time.'

Betty served Jack some stew and poured the tea, asking how his day had been. 'Alright, Betty. Nothing a pair of clean, dry socks can't fix. You'd be amazed at the amount of pleasure I get from clean socks after a day at work.' He told her about Ryan's first day and made her laugh with his impersonations of Ross.

Jack and Betty had struck up a friendship when he first arrived. She thought it odd that such a pleasant, handsome man should be alone in his prime, but Jack told her something of his difficulties. He didn't spend much time in the sort of places you were likely to meet available females. Most of the ones who lived in the country were married, and the city didn't suit him at all. When someone new showed up in town there were at least half a dozen single men all vying for attention and Jack wasn't one to put himself forward. He wasn't interested in the short term love affairs offered by lonely tourists, but now he was beginning to rethink his guiding principles. Wasn't a little love better than none? He missed sex, but more than that he missed the intimacy that came with sex. And the sex, of course. He tried to think of a way to describe what he wanted in a relationship; deep sex? No, that sounded like porn. Meaningful sex? Nah, too girly. It needed to be about love as well. Love-sex? Yeah, that'll do. He wanted a big dose of love-sex, the kind that just got better and better, and you don't even mind if the person is staring at you while you're doing it because you're both so into it and you're staring back at them thinking - well no, not thinking at all. Delightfully lost.

Jack lifted his spoon to his lips and burnt his tongue. 'Shit that's hot!' Instead of really good love-sex he was getting pleasure from clean socks, and the hottest thing in his life was soup. It had been two years since he'd had a girlfriend, and she only lasted four months before Jack discovered her chronic drug problem. It was no wonder she was such a vivacious, outgoing woman with all those chemicals to help her feel good. It wasn't until he started to see a pattern in the mornings, especially after a busy weekend, that he realized he was dating two different personalities.

Betty drank her tea and watched Jack as he ate. Jack was a good man and she was glad to have his company. He came and fixed her boat when it leaked in the roof during the spring storms as she imagined a son might do for his mother.

Betty had wanted children desperately but Donald hadn't. He admitted it was foolish of him not to have seen this coming. Betty was eighteen years his junior, but they'd met at a time when he was busy dealing with a nasty divorce. Donald's ex-wife had fought him on every issue, even trying to prevent him access to the children. After, he had hoped to make her so happy that she wouldn't feel the need to share their life. Betty said that was precisely why she longed for a child - if they were this happy now wouldn't a child just triple their joy? It was the one time their relationship faltered.

Donald was terrified that she would change after having a baby, like his first wife had. She hadn't always been an uptight, selfish shrew. That had happened gradually after the first child and grew worse with the next two until Donald couldn't remember what he'd liked about her to start with. Although Betty pleaded and argued he wouldn't compromise. She could ask for anything else, but not that. To take her mind off her heartbreak, and smooth over the blip, Betty took Donald at his word. They took a year's leave from work to sail all over the Pacific, and by the time they returned Betty was satisfied, the moment of obsession had passed, but now she thought about it Jack was almost the right age to be her love child, and he'd make such a lovely son.

'I'm worried about Smell,' Jack confessed. 'She's slowed down this winter, and she gets cranky a lot. She had a feed at Connie's and wouldn't leave the boat tonight.'

Betty was drawn back to the present, and Jack saw he'd interrupted a good day dream. Her old face had gone soft at the edges and her eyes had been misty. The look vanished as she spoke. 'Maybe she's like most old people. She needs to rest and take it easy, and be somewhere warm. You could try leaving her with me sometimes. I could do Tuesdays and Thursdays - the rest of the week's busy with bowls, painting, bridge, and the charity shop, not to mention the paperwork this place generates.' Obviously Betty didn't think she was among those who needed rest.

'That's a kind offer Betty, I'll give it some thought.' He knew what Smell would say about being left behind, but maybe it would do her good. The two old girls could keep each other company.

'And next time you want to bring a lady friend home I could doggy-sit,' she added. This was followed by a huge fit of laughing. Jack hung his head, but couldn't help smiling despite his shame. 'No need to be embarrassed Jack. It was the funniest thing I've seen in ages! Poor Lara, she must have been mortified!'

'Yes, she was.'

'I'm guessing you weren't *too* disappointed, or you'd have made alternative arrangements. I had quite a penchant for alternative arrangements as a young thing,' Betty sighed wistfully. 'I'd give the hammock a miss though. Quite dangerous.' Her eyes became round and staring as she drifted back down time's tunnel, a look of consternation bending her face. Jack raised his head sharply and choked on a slurp of stew, coughed into the crook of his elbow, and reminded Betty of his presence. 'Sorry, Jack. I don't seem to be good at censoring what comes out of my mouth nowadays. I just can't be bothered anymore.'

Now it was Jack's turn to laugh, but Betty wasn't the slightest bit embarrassed. Did the world still produce women like Betty? So full of decorum and propriety on the surface, and mischief underneath? Women's emancipation had eroded the need for all that repressive secrecy, and the ladies his age were bold and brassy to one degree or another, Jack mused. You couldn't have it both ways, could you.

'I don't think I'll be seeing Lara again.' Jack resumed eating with more thought to how he chewed. 'I doubt she'll even talk to me. I'm just glad Smell stopped me from making a mistake.'

'Yes, Smell has a fine nose for people. Remember the Peeping Tom we had? That young scoundrel came and asked me how much it cost to moor a boat here, but he was just finding out what boat I lived on. Smell was growling from your deck the whole time he stood at my door.'

'That's right. She must have caught his scent later that night when she went ballistic. I can't sand the claw marks out of the door.'

Betty had been preparing for bed when she'd heard Smell Hound making a terrible noise, barking and growling. A second later there was the thud of feet running along her deck from just outside the bedroom window. Smell's barking had scared off the pervert just as Betty began to undress. She heard Jack shouting and ran outside with a severely rusted garden fork. It wasn't a lethal weapon but it could sure give someone a nasty case of tetanus.

Once Smell was released from the cabin she belted after the running figure. He was found crying and whimpering up the nearest tree where the police collected him from Smell's guard. They chose not to notice the four red marks on a protruding leg, or the rusty fork tucked into the belt of Betty's dressing gown. They knew the man; he had been caught standing on a garden seat peeping through a bathroom window at the rest home last month, and given him a warning. It was lucky the elderly woman in the toilet hadn't had a heart attack. Smell had gone up in local estimation after that, and she didn't lack for pats or treats from those who knew what she'd done.

The next two weeks at work passed with everyone in a jolly mood. It looked like Ryan would stay, and he was quickly learning to master the mud walk and the basic culling. Jack and Ross gave him pointers, but most of his training fell to Jack, who had more patience.

It was all going well until the fork on the tractor broke. They had to catch the afternoon tide if they didn't want a 5am start the next day and they needed the tractor to load up the culled oysters to go back in the water. There was about fifteen metres of sloping beach between where the barge docked and the shed, and the tractor saved them carrying each 20kg crate the whole way. They had just finished loading the crates onto a wooden pallet, and left a second pile stacked along the shed. Jack and Ryan were in the shed pulling on their waders while Ross was taking the first load down. Jack knew something was up when Ross came in the shed a few minutes later. He had the sorry face of a man about to ask a favour for something he didn't want you to know about.

'Hey, do you think you guys could give me a hand?' Ross asked. 'One of the forks has snapped and we won't make the tide if we have to carry them all.' Ah heck, thought Jack. I bet he's tried to load the whole lot in one go. Bloody impatient bastard.

'Oh shit!' Ryan laughed. 'Hey, aren't those the new forks you put on last week?' They were walking towards the tractor as they spoke.

'Ahh, yeah. They must be faulty,' Ross said looking shifty. Jack could see there was only half the crates loaded up, and the second stack of crates was still along the wall. Jack looked at them dubiously. The third tray down was poking out at a funny angle. Ross knew Jack had noticed and avoided his gaze, giving his instructions to no one in particular. 'I'lliftit justoff thegron annootwo grabba cornaeach, annalker down tothe barge. K?'

'Eh?' shouted Ryan over the noise of the tractor engine.

'Eh?' Ross shouted back.

'What do you want us to do?' Jack shouted. Ross was loosing his cool. His face was heating up, but Jack didn't feel like letting him off easy. He could guess what Ross wanted, as incredible as it was.

Ross repeated his instructions, a little louder but no clearer, and pointed at the corner of the pallet making a lifting gesture. All this talk was wasting time. If he didn't like repeating things, why didn't he make an effort to speak properly, Jack wondered. Jack placed Ryan beside him and translated Ross's orders. 'Basically, we're on fork duty.' All signs of mirth vanished from Ryan's face. Maybe he was expecting the sort of boss who said, 'Ah stuff it. I'll call the engineer. Let's take the afternoon off.'

They struggled to hold the load steady as the tractor moved along, the two of them taking the weight on the side where the snapped fork was. Their hands were white with the strain and tendons stood out on their necks. Ryan grunted under his breath taking small side steps and trying not to tangle his feet with Jack's. Ross gave his attention to the steering, and went as fast as he dared.

They went back for the second load in silence. Once it was loaded on the barge Ross gunned the motor over the water, shouting, 'I'll have to try and hammer the old forks back into shape for tomorrow.' He was still cross that they'd lost ten minutes of the tide but his guilt was preventing an all out rage.

Jack had nothing nice to say about the situation, so he said nothing. Privately he thought it would be a miracle if Ross could straighten the old forks enough to carry even an empty pallet without it sliding off. They were so bent they stuck into the ground when the arm of the tractor wasn't raised high, and until last week they had to strap each layer of crates to the tractor's arm as they loaded them. It made for slow work, but this was worse.

On the ride home that day Ryan expressed his

feelings on the way Ross ran his business. It was the first sign that the wool was lifting from his eyes.

'Faulty metal my ass. I *know* we stacked the second load tidy. I bet he tried to put the whole lot on. Why? It only saves a coupla minutes, and I bet those new forks aren't cheap. He's totally fucked em!'

Jack couldn't agree more, but he wasn't quite ready to diss the boss to the new guy. To show solidarity he said, 'Well, don't expect a replacement any time soon. And as for the old ones being resurrected...that's wishful thinking alright.'

'I don't see him offering to prop up the load either.'

'No, but just think, he's the one who has to spend all evening hammering steel. Most men wouldn't even bother, but Ross believes in determination overcoming physics.' He could see this thought cheered Ryan slightly.

The next morning a moody Ross said nothing about the tractor. He didn't need to. In the lean-to where the tractor was kept was a typical Ross attempt to fix something. Tools were scattered over the ground, a can of oil lay on its side, and a broken sledge hammer had been thrown at the old chicken coop; the wire netting making a basket around the hammer's head. Beside the tractor the old forks looked like an angry giant's dinnerware. They were dented and bent at odd angles. Jack and Ryan shared a laugh in the safety of the ute, and the rest of the day were careful not to look at the tractor shed.

Ryan's tact meant he was learning as much about how to handle Ross as he was about the other aspects of the job.

The second thing to go was the steering on the outboard. It was a week after the fork broke, and since then they had been taking the strain of moving heavy loads up and down the beach. This new breakage made work just that touch more difficult. The bolt holding the steering arm had been coming loose for months, and instead of finding a tool to tighten it properly, Ross had been giving it a few turns by hand when he thought to, despite Jack casually mentioning several times that it needed some attention. Consequently, the thread and surrounding anchor points were worn through, and the steering arm finally fell off and hung useless. Now the barge could only be driven if there was one man to move the outboard left or right to steer it, and another man to control the throttle.

'OK, you two'll have to work together down there on throttle and rudder. I'll stand up front and give directions,' Ross told them.

Since it was a large motor, steering it required both hands. They got into position in the only way practical, with Ryan facing backwards holding the engine casing, and Jack on his knees facing forwards. It was a bloody awkward arrangement. Jack was almost between Ryan's knees trying to judge when to give it more or less speed. Ross kept shouting at them, 'Come on, give it some more gas!' but Jack didn't think it was safe. Ryan was relying on the others to guide him left or right and by the time Ross told Jack and Jack told Ryan it was cutting it close.

Half way out they could see the barge of the neighbouring farmer coming in from the harbour mouth. A slim figure in waders, and a podgy one driving the barge in casuals. As the barges got nearer they saw the fatter one, a man known as Shorty, widen his eyes and his eyebrows shoot up into his hairline. He nudged his companion who turned to look. Soon they were both pointing and laughing, slapping their thighs and doubling over. They diverged from their course and drifted closer. 'Oi, you dirty fuckers, put it away!' said the one called Shorty. Ross had gone red in the face and he shouted back, 'Giving you a hard-on eh, Shorty? Hey fella! Don't let him get behind ya today!' He was shouting at the other bloke now. The barge turned away, the two men on her looking back at them and laughing hysterically. All Jack could do in retaliation was raise a finger on his free hand. It wasn't much but it made him feel better. Ross seemed to see the funny side and laughed, 'Well it does look a bit personal, but I guess it can't be helped for now. Better just enjoy yourselves then, eh?' Ryan swore, but only Jack could hear him.

Neither the tractor's forks or the outboard were able to be fixed for the time being. They would just have to 'man up,' as Ross put it. He explained there simply wasn't money in the budget for it. Ryan's new waders had been ordered at a cost of $800, and Ross had spent the rest on a new pump and PVC pipe to take sea water up to the ponds in the shed behind his house. This was his pet project. He'd told Jack when he arrived that he was working on setting up a small scale oyster nursery. It was supposed to be hush hush because he'd made an agreement when he bought the lease off the council that his farm would be run as a stick farm, not a single-seed system like his competitor, Shorty. Jack asked around about this Shorty fella, turning up bits of information here and there. Shorty might look a rough and uncouth man, but he was surprisingly well connected. In the city he'd made a name for himself as a larger than life entrepreneur who made stuff happen. He was entertaining to have around and what he lacked in finesse he made up for with enthusiasm. His family had owned most of the land around here since the 1900's but they had sold a lot of it off over the last generation, freeing up some cash. Shorty had kept the hills overlooking the bay and the old homestead with his oyster shed just above the water, all new and shiny looking.

The homestead had been renovated and turned into luxury accommodation for wealthy holiday makers who wanted a retreat to serenity and the simple life. It was still lit at night by oil lanterns, and water was heated by a wetback on the fire. Jack went to the library and used the computer to look up the web page for it. Although the house was beautiful inside and out, there were no mod cons what so ever. He saw the price per night, with a minimum two night stay being a full weeks wages. It was amazing what some people would pay for primitive living, he thought.

Because of the family's history in the area plenty of people knew something about them. A caretaker called George lived in a small cottage further up the hill and was on hand to see guests had everything they needed, while his wife cleaned the house and made up the beds. George raised pigs and a small amount of livestock, just enough to supply himself and the homestead with meat and eggs. He had refused to make the guest experience more authentic by keeping a house cow. There weren't enough hours in the day to cut firewood, spray weeds, see to the animals, mend fences, and mind the guests as it was. If Shorty wanted a pet cow he could find someone else for the job. Since living in the back of beyond with only a boat to get in and out wasn't high on many people's wish list, Shorty had dropped the issue and mostly left George and his wife alone to manage the land.

Jack had pieced together a rough picture of how Shorty and Ross came to be farming the same waters, from asking around. No one found it strange that he wanted to know, it was natural to be curious about where you worked.

When Shorty's father passed away he left his fortune to the children, with enough set aside to take care of his wife who was in a nursing home. Shorty had invested his inheritance wisely, and then used his capital to set up a single-seed oyster farm, which his uncle, a personal friend of the Minister of Fisheries, helped him secure.

Two years after Shorty's oyster farm was established, Ross requested to lease a derelict stick farm in the bay and turn it into a single seed operation. He didn't have the cash behind him to do it all at once, but he had worked out a way to transition from one system to the other as earnings allowed. When word came back that someone had opposed the application, Ross knew who to blame. The application was held back but finally went ahead because no one came forward with a reasonable enough explanation why two farms couldn't exist so closely. It was granted on the proviso that the old lease remain a stick farm. Shorty must have known there were changes looming in the industry. There would be less processors wanting to buy sticks straight out of the water, and more who wanted the oysters taken off the stick, washed, and graded. This would put the squeeze on stick farmers who would need to double their labour and production to make the same money as they did now.

That had been five years ago, and Shorty had given up hoping Ross would go bankrupt. What he hadn't predicted was the inflation of oyster prices triggered by a widespread shortage. The shortage was the result of a virus, and even now no one could say where or how it entered the waters. Ross wasn't stupid. He knew what the game was, and was determined not be the loser. Right from the start he sold all his produce washed and culled to local restaurants, markets, festivals, online orders, and a retail shop. While processors were paying $1.20 a dozen he was selling at five bucks a dozen. He was an example of what could be achieved if you thought outside the square, and other small farms were starting to catch on. Shorty was spewing. His own setup had cost more than a million dollars, and though the processors loved his clean, uniform product they wouldn't pay more than $2.50 a dozen. His production had increased in the last two years but the lease could only hold so much before they ran out of space.

The series of ponds which Ross called a nursery were inside a large shed which was padlocked from the outside, supposedly in case Shorty ever came snooping. Since Shorty hardly ever came in the bay this was unlikely, and his foreman and other workers had no time to muck about. They must have heard their boss gripe about Ross, but they weren't paid enough to care. Jack had lifted his hand in greeting when they came in the bay his first week on the job, and someone had shouted 'Good day for it, eh?' but Ross had ignored them. Jack only found out much later that they weren't locals, which was a shame. They might have been a good source of information.

The only wildcard was George, who came and went across the land and water when he felt like it. George had been working for Shorty when Ross left, and Ross had always thought the man was a sneak. He was small and wiry with a pinched face and dark eyes. The caretaker came across to see Dave the shepherd every couple of weeks. The two land farmers had become good friends over the last six years, having arrived at their new occupations at roughly the same time. George never came to the yard, but the gravel road up to Dave's place went behind the cottage. There was an orchard of cider apples on the Shawe land, a legacy from the old days, and George turned them into liquid gold. Dave confessed he had a fondness for George's hard cider and had tried inviting Ross up to drink with them, but was always turned down. Ross might have a weakness for drink, but damned if he'd share it with Shorty's right hand man. Once, Ross had had to take George home in his dinghy after he found the two men literally rolling drunk down the hill. It was either that or fish the bugger out in the morning. Jack guessed it was more likely the shed was locked for George's sake, but when he'd tried asking Ross about his setup in there he said nothing. 'As far as you know that shed's full of sheep dip and chook food, got that?' He'd stormed off and been in a nasty mood all day. He told Jack to clean out the sump, a job which took all week and was without a doubt the foulest job on an oyster farm.

The sump was where all the mud and bits of shell and oyster got washed when they did clean up. Every summer when the harvest slowed down the sump had to be emptied to make room for more waste. It was the hole from hell. When it was over Jack had put his clothes through the wash three times before he gave up and burnt them on the beach. The fine silt and the smell of rotten muck wouldn't come out. The flames had been weirdly green and blue.

Jack filed the incident away in his mind as 'suspicious' and tried to keep an eye on how often Ross went to his private shed. It wasn't easy to say, since Ross lunched at home and sometimes came back late, saying he'd had office work to do.

Going back to the situation at hand, Jack could see Ryan was losing his cool. He'd been with them six weeks now and the atmosphere was getting progressively worse. Ryan was starting to feel like a tool. He was a tool, they all were; but unlike Jack he had started the job thinking he was doing his mate Ross a favour in exchange for an income while he made up his mind what to do next in life. He hadn't expected to be worked into the mud and shouted at five days a week.

Ross's best mate persona had worn right off and he was losing patience with Ryan. He had gone easy on Ryan while he settled in, but now he expected results. Jack could see it was a lost cause. Ryan was a strong and methodical worker who had enormous amounts of endurance and stamina, but he was no racehorse. Even Jack, a fast and competent worker found Ross hard to please, and only kept him happy by anticipating what he wanted. The work always got done in time, and Ross needed reminding of that when he got in a flap. Jack counted managing Ross's moods as part of the job. Seeing it like that made it less personal - sort of like cleaning the sump - distasteful but necessary. Ryan did a good job, but what was the use in working your guts out for a man who would always want more? He'd found his groove and stayed in it.

Chapter 3

On the drive to work on Thursday morning of the sixth week Ryan thumped the dash and complained, 'I'm still wearing wet waders, my new gloves are torn up, my arms are covered in cuts, we have to carry pallets that weigh a tonne, make dicks of ourselves driving the boat, and Ross is on our back to pick up the fucking pace every five minutes! How the fuck have you lasted a year?' Jack raised an eyebrow at him.

'Not thinking of chucking it in are you mate? Look on the bright side a minute. We work in paradise, we can eat as many oysters as we like, and we get paid a decent wage. Ross can be a bit of a prick at times, but the work itself isn't bad. A few more weeks and the weather will start warming up and the new gear will arrive.'

Jack didn't want Ryan to leave. The season was in full swing now, the oysters at their best. If Ryan left he'd be hard to replace, and you never knew what kind of good-for-nothing would turn up next. That was one of the difficult things to manage on an oyster operation; when you advertised for workers you got all sorts of low-lifes applying because it was unskilled labour.

He had sat in on an interview with his brother once. The lad who turned up was hardly 20 years old, and he didn't wait to be asked questions, just started off demanding the job. Joshua asked him why he should hire him, and the kid basically said if he wasn't going to be paid to work on the farm he'd be back later to help himself. Joshua had leaned in towards Jack and pretended to whisper, 'Better tell crazy ol' Norman who sleeps out on the pontoon to keep his shotgun loaded for the next few months.' The kid had kicked the chair over and left the room swearing, but there'd been no trouble.

Ross's system of hand-picking from the rugby club was more successful because the men were fit and keen but he had to wait until someone was desperate for work. For most of them it meant taking a pay cut; they were teachers, or plumbers, or builders. Ross didn't have a reputation with that crowd as a wanker to work for because there was a code of honor. You didn't stir shit or spit on a man's back. If you had a problem you went and had it out, which meant there were hardly ever any problems because the guys weren't much into talking about problems, unless you counted complaining about your Mrs. Sometimes fists spoke instead.

Ryan said work felt like intensive rugby training with all the fun taken out. The way Ross shouted stuff to motivate them like, 'Man up, come on team,' and, 'Let's get into it,' as if there was a trophy at the end.

'Your waders should be here next week and we'll get new gear. Look on the bright side, it's Friday tomorrow, and after that no Ross for *two whole days*.' Jack smiled at the thought. It was exceptional in this trade to have whole weekends off, but he could hardly tell Ryan he knew this for a fact; that would be letting on he knew more about it than he should.

Ross made a point of almost never asking Jack to work on a weekend, and went out alone most weekends to pick up what they needed for Monday. If he didn't fetch sticks on Sunday and the farm was dry until noon on Monday, then there would be nothing to cull on Monday morning. For all his faults, Jack conceded, he had good points too. Ross believed he was only entitled to work the men like billy-o if they could rest on the weekend.

Ryan had grown on Jack in the sense that Jack had begun to look forward to work a little more because the company was pleasant. You could ask Ryan anything you liked about horses and he could answer it. He was usually an upbeat kind of person who was happy to do anything you asked, if you asked nicely. If Ross left them to work alone just as much got done but everyone was happy. For some reason that displeased Ross. Ryan confessed that morning on the way to work that at least he appreciated his weekends now. 'So what's he got in that big shed? Do you think he's working on another invention?' Ryan mused. Jack was careful not to sound too interested.

'I wouldn't know, mate. He said it's something he doesn't want his nosey neighbour seeing.' He couldn't be certain but he doubted it was much of a nursery. Jack knew what it would require in terms of labour to maintain a project like that. Even a small nursery needed consistent monitoring, and Ross didn't go over there more than once a week now. Six months ago he was in there at least every other day.

Either it had already failed, or he must spend his evenings in there. It was something that needed more investigation, that was for sure.

'Oh, well that makes sense,' said Ryan relaxing into his seat. Jack braced himself. Nothing put Ryan at ease like a good yarn, so he obviously had something to say.

'You know he started out working for Shorty?' He clocked the look of surprise on Jack's face. 'Yeah I bet he didn't tell you that.' Jack shook his head slowly. 'Fresh out of uni, he was. Degree in marine sciences. Ross knows a lot more about his job than he lets on. Worked for Shorty for two years before they had a bust up. You know why he's called Shorty?'

'Because he's short?' Jack replied.

'No. Short temper. Famous for it, according to Ross.'

'Ha. What was their falling out over?' Ryan shrugged.

'It was technical. Ross developed something that would give Shorty's farm a boost. He told Shorty about it and asked for a cut of the profits, or a partnership, I don't remember. Shorty turned him down and used his idea anyway. When Ross found out he wouldn't get anything he complained that it was his intellectual property. Shorty had a field day on that. He's more of a business man than Ross, so he knew what he was on about. He said it was his property because it was on his farm. Ross was raving about it to everyone, the great swindle of the century. Then he went to see a lawyer. He went a bit dark after that. Turns out Shorty was right. Anything an employee comes up with is the property of whoever he works for. It might not seem fair, but it's true.'

Jack couldn't see how all this fit together with his brother's suspicions that something fishy was going on, but he could feel the threads of the net. Now all he had to do was untangle them and haul it in. He was curious what sort of monster he would catch.

As they came past the boss's house Nancy waved from the kitchen window. They had arrived especially early this morning to catch the tide, and she hadn't left to take the kids to school yet.

'She's a sweet lady, that Nancy,' said Ryan.

'Yep,' Jack nodded.

'Sure knows how to run a business. Got business sense, you know? That's what Ross lacks. He's only good at the production side of things. You know it was her dough got this farm off the ground? She was the one who told Ross to sell straight to the customers.'

'You don't say?' Jack said. 'You're a mine of information, Ryan.'

They pulled up at the yard where Ross was busy loading gear on the barge. A spare tank of petrol, a coil of rope, anchor, and all the waders thrown in a messy heap. They were hardly out of the ute before Ross called, 'Come on you boys, let's get moving!'

'What'd he say?' asked Ryan.

'He said hurry up, storm's coming.'

They jumped from the dock onto the barge. Jack saw a centipede glide out from under the ropes and shuddered. It vanished under a crate of oysters. He'd never seen them so big as the ones here. As fat as a man's finger, and twice as long, some of them. It always paid to check your waders. They liked to hide where it was dark and damp.

They pulled waders on over their clothing, Jack taking the time to shake his vigorously first while Ross tried to start the outboard. Last week they'd been stuck out at the tide for fifteen minutes while Ross tinkered with it. Ryan suggested he get the marine mechanic to look at it but Ross didn't agree. The thing was poked but he didn't want to admit it. The repair man would charge $80 before he even got here just to tell him it was stuffed.

There was a thick fog on the water this morning but the sun was beginning to burn away the cloud cover, showing the promise of imminent blue skies. Maybe Ross hadn't been talking about a storm. 'We've got company this afternoon!' he called over the thrum of the outboard as they got underway. The new outboard adjustments included a screwdriver with its green plastic handle sticking out of the guts. Whether it was there as a handy spot to keep a tool, or because it served a mechanical purpose Jack couldn't tell.

Jack and Ryan were in their customized steering position, one leaning down, the other crouched. Ross outlined the day's plan. 'A few sues are tur... up t ee ow their inventmen's ...king. ...'ve ot t...'

Jack waved his free hand dismissively at Ross, 'We can't hear shit down here!' Ross nodded and stopped his explanation.

Once they had reached the start of row twelve where they would start today, Ross adopted his giving orders stance and returned to his aborted speech.

'As I was saying, a few suits are turning up to see how the farm's looking. They're new investors I'm lining up. We need to put the grow-ons back on the farm and pick up enough for today's orders, plus an extra hundred and fifty sticks for the wine festival this weekend. The extra sticks can be washed and banged, but leave them like that in a bin. Nancy will have her ladies cull them tomorrow 'cos we don't have time. While you're culling the regulars, I'll give a tour of the farm to the gentlemen in suits.'

'How're you going to do that?' said Jack as he pulled his gloves on.

'Eh?' Ross screwed his face up in an effort to hear. He was standing at the other end of the barge with hands on hips like he was addressing a crowd.

'The barge. How will you drive it?' Jack repeated.

'Oh. Have to take them in the dinghy won't I?' Ross shouted back. 'With these men on board we might get a few new toys, so be nice.'

In the mud they worked using wire to hold sacks of grow-ons (oysters off the sticks which were too small to sell) onto rails. A weak sun had finally appeared to warm their backs a little. Jack's boot slid forward over the smooth mud, covered in four feet of water, and disturbed a stingray who was sunbathing in the shallows. It shot off in a whoosh of fright, the silt puffing up at every wing beat. This was a king tide; the water would be lapping the top of the banks when it was full, and recede much further out leaving bare sea bed, not often seen. The big tides required more effort and stamina from the men. The sea dragged at the legs in its haste to obey the moon's pull, making movement against the flow more strenuous than usual. Ross had given them just enough time to do the work required, but it was easy to underestimate. If they weren't careful the barge would go dry, and be left stranded till the next tide.

Once all the sacks were secured the harvest began. Ryan was in the water with Jack loading sticks coated in seaweed, barnacles, and oysters. Each stick was nailed to the rails at each end with thin Brad nails, the kind used in small furniture. With a tug the sticks came free, and a person soon learnt to keep clear of the rusty needles left protruding. Ross was stacking the sticks on the barge, keeping up with what they brought him easily and yelling for them to 'Pick up the pace.'

Ryan was slower in the water than Jack; he had more bulk to move and less height, so the water reached up to his waist. The barge's deck sat a good half a metre above the water and he was stretched to his full height, muscles straining to lift the sticks up there. Jack could see Ross was getting impatient watching him, waiting to grab the baton when it arrived.

'Ryan, get up here and stack the sticks. I need the loading to go faster than that.' They swapped jobs and Ross made a point of outpacing Jack. It wasn't by much, but Ross shouted anyway, 'Come on you guys, faster! I want a hundred percent effort!'

Ryan couldn't stack as fast as Ross and fifteen minutes later the sticks waiting to be stacked were blocking the way for more to come. Ross was making a mess on the deck, throwing sticks on top of the pile and causing some to overshoot or land sideways to the rest. Ryan's progress slowed further as he side-stepped the scattered batons, trying to choose the ones on top.

'Move to the other side,' Ross told him turning to lift a stick.

'What's that about the tide?' Ryan shouted back. Ross didn't hear him. As Ryan leaned down to grab a stick Ross threw another one up. It just missed Ryan's face and connected with his hand instead, slamming it down onto the pile. 'Fuck!' Ryan cursed, clamping his hand between his thighs.

'Are you deaf? I said the other side! Get over there!' bellowed Ross in frustration, jabbing in the direction with his finger. Ryan got the message and moved over, his face crunched in on itself in a mixture of pain and anger.

Jack had been wondering if Ryan suffered from the same hearing difficulties as the boss. Ryan often looked to Jack to explain what Ross said, and at first Jack put it down to the yumbling effect. Lately he'd caught Ryan not responding if he said something quietly, especially when there was white noise in the background like the heater in the truck going. 'Jack! Get that pile shifted would you?' Ross ordered.

Jack stopped adding sticks to the pile and climbed onto the barge. If Ross would just stop throwing them for a minute they might be able to get ahead. It was bad practice anyway; an hour from now there would be a number of casualties - oysters with broken shells, gaping open like a man suffocating, trying to snatch a last breath. Jack dodged the incoming missiles to grab at the nearest sticks, and passed them on to Ryan to stack. In this way they fared better, and to his credit Ryan hadn't let his sore hand stop him doing his best, though Jack saw him wince.

'We're off the farm in ten minutes. Pull your finger out!' When it got tense like this there wasn't any point arguing, and it was probable Ross was enjoying the stress. Going hard-out and feeling the strain was a way to prove your mettle. Ross loaded those oysters like a man in a house fire trying to save his belongings, to show them he could do the work of two. 'Hey Ryan!' Jack called. 'Still got any of those relaxing herbs at home? He's been so nice to us lately I was thinking of making him some biscuits.' Jack was trying to restore the other man's good humor. Ryan didn't look up, a bad sign.

'Not enough to fix that bastard. I could get my hands on some horse tranquilizers though.' Yup, that goose was cooked, Jack grimaced. From mates to open aggression in nine weeks. Ryan had lasted a week longer than the previous record holder, who lost it after eight weeks, and quit a month later. Shawn had refused to hold a post while Ross walloped it into the mud with a sledge hammer, after losing the post rammer. Ross had shouted, 'Just hold the fucking post!'

Shawn had stuck his neck out. 'You think I'm stupid? Who's the dumb ass that lost the post rammer then? It wasn't me. Hey Jack, did you lose the rammer? Nah, wasn't him. It was *you*.' He pointed a finger at Ross. '*You* hold the fucking post.' Jack had stepped in and held the post, not daring to blink as the hammer swept down in a menacing arc toward his hands, clenched onto the sides. If the hammer didn't land square on top there was every chance it would slide off and connect with a part of Jack, but it was better than standing in the mud while the men bickered.

Ross lobbed a final two sticks on deck and followed them aboard. Jack already had the motor running, tilted right up so it didn't scrape the sea floor. They were all sweating and out of breath, Ryan happy to have his back to Ross as he turned the outboard with both hands. The barge was loaded to capacity and sat low in the water. Five more minutes and she would have been stranded. There was hardly room to move, and from his crouched position Jack couldn't see over the oysters, so they had to rely on Ross to guide them back. There was nearly a collision with the dock when Ross shouted, 'Hard right.' Since Ryan was facing the back of the barge his right was Ross's left. The back of the boat swung out, just missing the corner of the concrete dock, and a fair bit of shouting went on before the error was corrected.

There was still the unloading to do, holding up the corner of the pallet and staggering back and forth to the shed. The last weeks had been easy compared to now. The spat had caught especially well the summer before Jack arrived and the farm was choc-a-block. It was only ten o'clock in the morning and it felt like they'd done a full day's work, but Ryan's anger kept him going.

Jack entered the shed to see him taking it out on an empty soft drink can, squeezing it with his uninjured hand then stomping it into the concrete floor. 'Son of a bitch,' Ryan growled. He'd taken off his gloves and Jack could see two fingers were torn and bloody.

'You should put a bit of electrical tape round those fingers. It'll stop the swelling and protect them. We've got a bit of culling to do.' Jack offered him a roll from the kitchen drawer. Ryan took it, the small kindness cracking through the anger and relaxing his face. They stripped off their waders and Jack sat down for smoko, peeling the wrapper off a snack bar. Ryan broke all protocol by going right ahead and making coffee before Ross could come in from parking the tractor, saying in an over bright voice, 'Two spoons of coffee for my mate Jack, two for me, and half a spoon with three sugars for Ross.'

Jack was impressed; Ross came in, saw the coffee was waiting, and drank it without comment. Perhaps he felt a smidgeon of guilt for Ryan's hand, the blue tape round the fingers holding his mug. He was a cool customer alright.

After smoko they tidied the yard. Ross wanted it looking neat before his guests arrived. It was clear Ryan was still pissed off, but Ross was ignoring him except to give brusque orders. Jack was familiar with the underlying message. 'If you're waiting for an apology it's not gonna happen. Do the job properly and next time you won't get hurt.'

A man could accept Ross the way he was or take a hike. There was no bargaining to be had. What Ross couldn't see was that all they wanted from him was a little compassion. If you hurt someone, say sorry. If you stuffed up, take the blame. You wouldn't be any less the boss; you might even earn some respect.

At lunch break Ross must have felt it was time to lighten things up. Having a worker give you dirty looks wasn't going to inspire confidence in the business men who were due to arrive soon. Jack and Ryan found it hard to reciprocate. After ordering them around tersely for the last hour the abrupt change in mood seemed false.

'You got plans this weekend Jack?'

Jack did for once have plans, other than washing the dog and doing his laundry, but he didn't want to share them with Ross. Finishing a ham sandwich he wiped his hands on his trousers and took time to reply. 'Might see a few people, nothing special.' Ryan kept eating. He had learnt by now to reserve some food for lunch, and to make sure he never went hungry he kept a large supply of instant noodles in the kitchen cupboard. He was busy forking them into his mouth, huffing because they were too hot. Ross nodded thoughtfully, as if Jack had said something important. Several minutes passed in silence. Jack picked up a slice of cake. Betty had insisted he take it home after supper last night and he put half of it in his mouth, watching the crumbs fall on Smell.

'Hey, what did the leper say to the prostitute?' Ross smiled at them expectantly. Steady chewing continued, although Jack shook his head. 'Ha! Keep the tip!' At another time the joke might have been funny. In current hostilities it sounded stupid and inappropriate. As peace-keeper Jack felt compelled to force a few chuckles and made his lips curve upwards in what he hoped was a smile. Ryan remained silent.

Jack and Ryan started with the cull as Ross dragged the dinghy down to the water ready for his visitors. No one offered to help and he didn't ask, though it looked difficult. The aluminum made a screeching sound on the rocks uncovered by the tide. He came back for two pairs of old gumboots belonging to departed employees, and gave them a whack to knock the old mud off. He sure was going the extra mile.

From their stations at the culling table Jack and Ryan had a clear view out over the bay. The sun had strengthened and there was a damp shiny-ness to the day that felt both fresh and mellow; the season was suspended, resting between the stillness of winter and bustle of early spring. With Ross out of the way it was peaceful, the radio so quiet they could still hear the seagulls. Jack could feel his shoulders warming up and he stripped off his top jersey. Betty kept him supplied with old woolens from the charity shop where she volunteered. They couldn't be sold due to holes or stains, but were perfect for work. He didn't have to worry if they got covered in muck.

A shiny, dark grey Mercedes came slowly into the yard, old shells crunching under its weight. This must be the visitors. They were late; Ross might not have warned them the gravel road was full of large pot holes. Ten minutes later Ross brought them to inspect the shed, then circled around it and stopped to watch the men culling oysters. Their suit pants were tucked into the borrowed gumboots, looking like a couple of farmers on their way to church. Smell sniffed at their boots and wandered off. The men smelt of peppermints and aftershave, a strong contrast to the organic scents of nature around them. Everyone was introduced and a round of nods passed as greetings, Jack generously adding a 'Gidday.' This wasn't a social call.

Ross lined up a few oyster specimens, explaining about the shell formation typically found in this area, and why they grew so well here. Jack knew this from his chats with Connie that her husband Marty had found the investors for Ross from among his contacts. What Jack couldn't work out was what Ross wanted money for. A new barge maybe, but the farm pulled in enough to pay that off in a few years with a bank loan. Taking on investors, especially two of them, meant he was after more than new equipment. Jack knew he'd be wasting breath to ask Ross straight out. He never disclosed anything until the last moment, and Jack couldn't really blame him if sharing information had burnt him in the past.

The city men listened carefully. This meeting would determine if they invested, and to what extent. Ross was doing a fine job of talking like a man who knew his job, and Jack was impressed. He must have spent half the night with a dictionary, and the other half with an investors almanac.

'This specimen here is *crassostrea gigas*, and has a growth rate of point four two millimetres a month. That's an average, of course. Eighteen months from when they catch until commercial size. Fifteen percent exceed that growth rate.' Ross was serious but upbeat in his delivery, like a keen science teacher. Anyone could see he was passionate about his subject. 'Now over here we have the smaller catch that falls off the harvest sticks. Due to multiple spawn cycles occurring close together over a three month window, we have spat from different periods growing on the same substrate. Most stick farmers throw these away, but that isn't fiscally responsible. With minimum labour output and basic equipment, these juveniles can be retained and on-grown to produce a premium product that requires less processing prior to sale.' The men nodded, they liked the sound of that.

Ryan had stiffened when Ross appeared, and made more mistakes in five minutes culling than he usually would in an hour so Jack was relieved when Ross said they should get out on the water. He would show them how the farm was organized and do a tasting out there. Ross took a shucking knife and left, talking about tides and water quality with more long words than you could shake a stick at.

'And now you've met Ross the manager,' Jack said once the trio had gone. He continued with a fairly good impersonation of Ross's way of speaking to men in suits. 'Chief Cull Operator Jack has an average cull speed of forty two dozen an hour. His assistant with less experience, has an average cull rate of thirty dozen an hour; but they can both exceed current figures if I use the horse whip.' Ryan and Jack both sniggered.

Ryan took a while to relax into his work, but his temper cooled as the effect of the tide work finally hit him. He would be feeling put out by Ross's attitude, and Jack had a suspicion that under the swagger and joking manner Ryan was more sensitive than people guessed. Jack went easy on him, going to fetch the next crate and empty it on the table when the last one was done, and keeping up the conversation.

With half an eye on the boat in the water, Jack checked their progress every so often. After an hour, when the Chief Cull Operator told his assistant it was almost time for lunch, he saw the boat begin to head back. Suddenly, the progress of the dinghy came to a halt half way between the farm and the dock. Maybe they'd spotted a big kingfish or stingray. They came right in here, some of them were huge. If your boot connected with the edge of a ray it would shoot off, like the one Jack had disturbed earlier - a kick in the guts was better than a stomp on the head. We all know what happened to the crocodile man.

Jack nudged Ryan and they both squinted at the water. There was some kind of fuss breaking out. The two farmers off to church weren't looking at the water, they were staring at Ross who appeared to be doing a striptease dance. He wasn't very good at it. Maybe he should have put in a bit more practice. First he jigged on one leg, then the other, wriggling his hips while pulling his waders down about his waist. 'They must be playing hard to get out there,' said Jack coming round to Ryan's side of the table to see better.

'Not very sexy is it? He should slow it down. Looks too robotic.' Ryan analyzed the performance which was nearing a frantic finale. The dinghy was rocking dangerously from side to side and they could see the other men were holding tight to the boat. There was a snatch of shouting carried in on the wind. Ross was bent over with his waders pulled down around knees now, and the rocking motion slowed. Straightening up again Ross stomped his boot on the hull of the boat. This must be the Latin dance routine. They heard the muffled thud of his boots. Jack wondered if he'd make a hole and disappear like Rumple Stiltskin. There was certainly a resemblance. 'Doesn't he look daft? What do you really think's going on?' Ryan said, his eyes not leaving the action.

The commotion on the boat stopped as Ross sat down again and the dinghy started to cruise back in. The visitors jumped out, barely waiting till the boat touched land. Jack saw the gumboots being handed back and a quick handshake before they hurried straight to their car. No one said goodbye to the cullers.

Ross came striding up to the shed with his lips in an upside down smile. It looked like he might cry. Jack noted his face had a sheen of perspiration and he was white about the gills. It flushed with colour when he saw them, but not with embarrassment. Jack had just enough time to warn Ryan, 'Uh oh,' before Ross arrived shouting, 'Which one of you evil bastards put the fucking centipede in my pants?'

Ryan and Jack had been feigning concentration on their work but their heads went up and their eyebrows too.

'Is that what you were doing out there? We thought you might be seducing them into buying a new barge,' Jack said, trying to make Ross see the funny side. The centipede must have been sleeping at the toe of his boot all morning and when it woke to find itself trapped by a hot, hairy leg hit panic mode. If you weren't in such a rush this morning you might have remembered to check your waders, but Jack kept that thought to himself. Ryan began to snigger while trying to hold a straight face, his cheeks puffing out.

'That was a shitty thing to do!' Ross glared at Ryan with narrowed eyes, but it was more than Ryan could manage to hold back his mirth. A loud laugh erupted from his open mouth, and Ross took two strides towards him, his hands tensed. Jack wasn't sure what Ross was about to do, but it didn't look good. Jack stepped between the men as Ryan realized Ross was seriously pissed off and backed away laughing.

'Hey mate, woah there,' Jack put his hands up. 'No one put that thing in your pants. I saw one this morning on the barge, it could have crawled in there by itself. It's not the first time we've been bitten.'

A centipede had run up Jack's body and bitten him under the chin last winter. It had dangled there by its teeth like a Chinaman's beard until Jack had pulled it off. Jack rubbed at his chin remembering the pain.

Ross let his hands fall and pulled himself together. 'I fucking *hate* creepy crawlies. I just made a complete dick of myself in front of my new shareholders. Fuck.' He pulled his waders down and showed them an angry red mark on his thigh beside his left testicle. 'It bit me! Cunt of a thing wouldn't let go. I'm going to lunch.' He revved the engine of his truck and left the yard with a spray of gravel hitting the tin shed. One look from Ryan and both men were bent over the table in hysterics. They rocked with laughter, hardly drawing a breath, and Ryan drooled while Jack shed tears. Either Ryan was letting off steam from this morning, or he'd set Ross up, Jack wasn't sure which.

Ross's fear of crawling, biting things was legendary; wetas, centipedes and spiders in particular. There was a story he liked to recount about how a spider had almost been the death of him. This had happened some five years ago, when he was fixing the old wiring in the cottage before he moved the family in. Dave had given them free rein to do what they liked to the house, as long as he wasn't paying. The rent was dirt cheap so they couldn't expect a better deal. The job of fixing the wiring called for an electrician, but Ross didn't think it was beyond his abilities. It was just one circuit which only worked spasmodically that needed replacing, and wasn't worth the callout fee.

After removing the fuse to what he figured was the right circuit he crawled under the house, taking care not to brush against the flooring above which was thick with cobwebs. He was damp from the rain sheeting down outside, and the old, dry earth stuck to his knees. Next he pulled out the faulty wire from it's socket. So far so good. When he looked up to follow the path of the wire along the beams he saw a big spider directly above him letting itself down on a thread. Not letting go of the frayed wire he jerked sideways to avoid the spider which was now almost upon him, and saw a streak of electricity arc towards him. It was the last thing he recalled before blacking out. Nancy turned up two hours later and couldn't find him. He came to, hearing his name called, and the first thing he did was check there were no spiders on him.

'So, did you do it?' Jack asked.

'What? Put the 'pede in his pants?' Jack nodded. 'Nup. Looks like he pede his own pants,' Ryan said, cracking up again.

The rest of the afternoon they found themselves giggling every time they looked at each other, Ross, or just thought about it. Jack was pleased it had improved Ryan's mood and cemented their friendship, but Ross didn't share the joke. He found jobs to do alone and didn't talk to either of them until after work when his mood sweetened. It was customary to finish half an hour early on a Thursday and sink a few beers in the shed.

'Good tide for fishing. I think I'll go and throw a line in,' Ross said after the second beer. Jack fretted he was about to ask them to go with him, and felt pressured to accept. They were always gone twice as long as promised; Ross would say, 'Just one more cast,' until he ran out of bait or it got dark.

Before Jack could make up an excuse Ryan turned to him and said, 'Do you mind if we head off, Jack? I need to get a few things before town closes.' Ross looked disappointed. He probably thought fishing could restore team morale. Instead, they left him rummaging in the freezer for bait and went to the pub. The taste of beer and fish 'n' chips was more enjoyable in easy company.

=Chapter 4=

Friday they culled all morning, working through yesterday's harvest. The afternoon tide would be another big one. By Tuesday the tides should go back to normal when the moon began to wane. Culling was repetitive work, but Jack didn't mind so much because it gave him time to think without thinking being a job in itself. This was when he often had his best ideas.

Although he'd forgotten the night he was drunk and almost had a woman in his bed, he hadn't forgotten the longing that had led him there. When Nancy arrived to take the bins of un-culled oysters to the shop he caught himself staring at her fleshy bosom and quickly looked away. Arrgh, what's gotten into me? It can't be healthy to go this long without some affection, he decided, but no reasonable opportunities had presented themselves. He would have to take matters into his own hands, so to speak.

When he was in his twenties there'd been plenty of single girls around. He had dated his fair share, and some of them stuck around until they realized Jack wasn't about to settle down. He wouldn't stay in town for the sake of a girl if a job came up somewhere else, and though he didn't mean to, his lovers felt used. If they were having casual sex they soon wanted a relationship. If they were having a relationship they wanted a future. It didn't seem to matter how often he explained his modus operandi, girls lived in hope.

It wasn't until Jack passed thirty he saw the field begin to dwindle. He was still working up and down the country, sometimes away at sea trawling for months. After he returned from one of these jobs he rang up a woman he'd been seeing before he left. They had left things open with no promises either way. Jack had spent many nights on the ship thinking about her, especially lingering over the intimacy they had enjoyed. He wasn't in love with her, but he was firmly in lust. For the first time he wondered if lust could lead to love. Although the woman was pleased to hear from him, she declined an invitation to meet. She was seeing someone else. 'I like you, Jack, but I want to have children before I'm forty, and I just didn't get the feeling you wanted more than sex.'

A while after that he hooked up with an old fling, and decided to have a go at the long term. Joshua gave him work on the farm and the relationship was easy until they began spending more time together. Julie now had a five year old son.

Jack soon learnt two important things; kids were pretty cool when they weren't being little shits, and being the mum's boyfriend was like dating two people. If Jack sat beside Julie or put his arms around her there was a child-shaped lump squirming between them seconds later. He never knew who he'd wake up next to in bed. Then there were the tantrums. It was incredible to hear so much noise coming from such a small person, and all because of something minor, like a toy being lost. Julie was exhausted trying to be mother, father, and girlfriend, while Jack felt like he was getting a raw deal.

It limped on like that till the end of the year, with the bad times outweighing the good until Julie gave up. She admitted it had been a mistake thinking her boy would be okay with a man around, and decided she was better off single. Jack hid his relief.

This last year Jack had experienced moments of acute loneliness, which even Smell's faithful company hadn't been able to diminish. From what he could tell he had never been in love. He had never felt a rush of euphoria thinking about someone, or stepped on the gas just to see them two minutes sooner. With the age had come a refinement in what he liked in a person, and that made it even harder. If a woman passed the test in looks it wasn't enough any more. He had to talk to her and still like her an hour later or his gear wouldn't even twitch.

Betty and the houseboat community were having a party on Saturday night. Jack was supplying the oysters, of course. He resolved to make an effort and try to look at his options in a more liberal way. He would try practicing not being too particular in what he liked. If she was ugly, she might be smart and interesting instead. If she was silly, maybe she would be the nicest person you could meet. He even thought about asking Lara to come along, but then again she had snobbed him last time he said 'Gidday,' so maybe not.

Looking at it from another angle he considered that possibly he wasn't doing enough to make himself attractive to the right sort of woman. He would see if Rex could give him a haircut, that should help. Even some new clothes might be a good idea. Women noticed that sort of thing. It wasn't often you saw a top bird with a scruffy, rough-looking bloke, unless he had a good excuse. Money got attention too, but using it to find a woman was wrong in Jack's mind. He would always have that option if he needed it because of a healthy savings account. Jack saved because he didn't need much, and wasn't sure what to spend money on anyway. He hadn't been clothes shopping since before he came here, but that would have to wait. There wasn't time. Clothes shopping required mental preparation. His current 'good' clothes were an old shirt of Joshua's, one of the nicer jerseys Betty had brought home for him, and his 'going out' jacket, a navy blue suede blazer which had lasted ten years because it was hardly ever taken out of the cupboard. It would have to do.

By most standards Jack was a good looking man, unless you preferred the sort who always looked clean shaven and well presented. One of his girlfriends had tried to remake him into a metropolitan, but it had lasted less than two weeks before Jack's natural untidiness had crept back and taken the shine off her work. He'd agreed to the makeover so she would leave him in peace but he never agreed to maintain it. He refused to put gunk in his hair, didn't own a hair brush or comb, shaved only when he felt like it, and wore his clothes casually. He'd stayed away from city girls after that, he could only disappoint them.

Jack would be thirty eight this year and he was sick of drifting. As soon as he cleared up this business with Ross he could go home and do something about it. He envied Ross in some ways. He might be a sexist shit but he was part of a team, and his own boss; he and Nancy worked on a common goal, planned the future together, shared friends, and the responsibilities of a business, home, and children. Why had it taken him so long to see value in these things? And the sex, of course. Was there an age limit on one night stands? They held so much less appeal for him now. It was only after consuming too much alcohol he'd let Lara squeeze up next to him, and after that his body took charge, hands finding their way beneath the waist of her top and enjoying the smooth warmth of her skin.

At lunch break Jack took pity on Ryan who'd eaten all his food earlier and forgotten to stock up on noodles. Jack offered him half a sandwich, and Smell followed its progress from one hand to the other with interest. Ross had gone to his house earlier than usual, claiming he needed to do some office work, which really meant looking up jokes on google. Jack and Ryan knew this because he would come back in the afternoon with fresh material.

'I'm guessing you're what, 32, 33 this year?' Jack asked Ryan as they ate their halves of the sandwich.

'That's about right, mate,' Ryan nodded.

'Well, don't wait too long to find someone and get settled. You get a bit older and the future starts to look different. It's like you've got this chest full of treasure but you don't know what to spend it on 'cos you've already got everything you need. I'm starting to think life might have more meaning with someone to share the treasure, you know what I mean?'

'Woah! You're not, um, trying to tell me something there, I hope. I mean, the barge thing is a joke right? Should I have said 'No' to that sandwich?' Ryan was looking at Jack warily. Jack just cracked up laughing, burying his face in his hands. Ryan let out a whoop of relief.

'Don't be daft, mate,' Jack shook his head, 'It's just I haven't had a relationship for a while, and I really like women. I like their company, their strange habits, their weird way of seeing things, and their beautiful bodies.'

'Yeah, that's what I thought. I saw you clock an eyeful of Nancy yesterday, eh? You just caught me off guard. I don't usually have meaningful conversations unless I'm drunk. My last girlfriend was always complaining that I wasn't in touch with my *emotions*. She wanted me to talk about my feelings, but all I could come up with was, hungry, thirsty, bored, or horny,' Ryan confessed. 'It takes a special sort of woman to appreciate the advantages of dealing with a simple life form. Me? I'd be wrapped if women were half as simple.'

'Sorry, mate. I didn't mean to give you a fright.'

'I'd offer to set you up with someone, but I'm having a hard time finding one myself just now,' said Ryan. 'And yeah, I have been thinking it's time I got on with life. This job was a step forward, but I can't see myself here in a years time, and maybe kids wouldn't be so bad if I meet the right girl.'

'It only gets harder the longer you wait, I can tell you. I don't have a solution to our girlfriend problems, but I know where we might meet some. Have you got plans on Saturday?' Jack flicked the jug on.

'Well, there's a rugby game down at the sports field that I'll go see, then if I can be bothered I'll do some shopping, tidy the house, and have a few beers.'

'Sounds riveting. How'd you like to come along to a party instead?'

'Oh yeah? What party's this?'

'Houseboat party. We have them every few months. There's the permanent residents but we get new people coming through all the time, so it's a way for everyone to know who's around. It's not your usual scene, but maybe you need to branch out a bit. You might meet someone who isn't the girlfriend, sister, or mother of a rugby player.'

'Alright, you're on,' Ryan punched Jack's shoulder lightly.

These plans weren't mentioned to Ross. He would have scoffed at the idea of spending the night in the company of the wharfies. Jack knew he considered them a bunch of weirdos, mostly because he called them the Weirdo Wharfies. To Ross anyone who lived differently must be a bit strange.

After work Jack delivered a load of oysters to the shop and went to the pub for a meal. It wasn't what you'd call fine dining, but it was usually filling. There was a choice on the menu tonight; steak and eggs, or crumbed fish. Because it was Friday, people from the outlying countryside would crowd into town looking for kicks. Coins were lined up along the edge of the pool table signaling those next in line to play.

Jack chose the steak because he needed a hit of protein after a day of sweat. If Connie knew he was eating here she'd tell him off. The things she could tell you about the cook had put him off eating here for a month, which had been her intention. She hardly charged him when he ate at the restaurant but she'd be busy with the weekend crowd tonight and he hadn't booked a table. He'd make up for it and eat there tomorrow.

Jack greeted the other locals; a few tradies, and retired old men, and had a beer with them while he waited. The men were taking what they thought to be discreet glances at a woman who sat alone. A glass of white wine accompanied her crumbed fish. 'Who's that then?' someone asked. A look went from man to man but no one knew. 'Must be new,' said the same bloke. 'Do you think I'd have a chance?' he asked down the bar. Considering he was about seventy, and had more hair in his ears than on his head it wasn't meant to be a serious question. There were plenty of good humored put-downs and jokes in response, which had been his main aim anyway.

'She's not exactly dressed like a lady, is she?' said Bert. 'In my day ladies all wore skirts or dresses and did their hair up nice, and put lipstick on before leaving the house. Now you can hardly tell if they're blokes or not.' A murmur of assent went up. Warming to his theme Bert added, 'And if you've been to the city lately...well, some of the men are wearing make-up!' A young builder beside Jack rolled his eyes. The old men were always talking like this. They loved a good scandal. 'That Lara, now she knows how to dress nice. What happened with you two, Jack?'

'Nothing happened, Bert. It just wasn't meant to be.'

'I heard her telling someone you were a lost cause. You got problems with the hydraulics? You should ask Ted to tell you about them blue pills. Hey Ted! Tell Oyster Boy here about them little blue pills doc gave you!'

Ted hissed down the bar, 'Ah shut up will ya Bert. The wife will hear about it with you mouthing off.'

'You mean you haven't told her? Well, how did you explain the sudden return of vigor after three years of nothing then?'

'I didn't have to,' Ted mumbled into his pint glass. 'She thinks I was playing away, and now I'm back.' Bert let out a hoot.

Jack tuned out of the banter and let his eyes wander in the direction of the woman eating alone. She was fine boned and lean, but it was hard to say if she was pretty or not because she'd dressed in such an un-lady-like way. She wore an old pair of baggy jeans, workman's boots, a checkered flannel shirt, and a cap. A fringe of brown hair peeked out from under the rim, and she wore no make-up that he could see. If it weren't for the breasts filling the front of the shirt she could be mistaken for a young man. Smart girl, jack thought. If I was a woman alone in a new place it's exactly the look I'd go for. Every man here had taken a look at her in a passing manner; if she came in dressed up the attention wouldn't have stopped at looking, whether she wanted it or not.

Jack watched as she finished her meal and went to pay at the bar. He heard her thank the bartender and say goodnight as she shrugged on a coat. When she passed the men Jack noticed her eyes were a warm brown like melted chocolate. She nodded once and said, 'Gentlemen.' She was smiling as she walked out the door. Sharp too, Jack noted. She knew they'd been talking about her. Someone used to looking out for herself but with a sense of humor. He hoped he'd run into her again.

'Oooo, Oyster Boy, I think she was checking you out.' Someone nudged him in the ribs and a round of hoots and laughs started up. Jack was certain she hadn't looked at him, but he wished she had. It would have been flattering. He wasn't a vain man, but didn't everyone like to feel wanted occasionally? Yes, he thought, glancing down at his torn shorts and shirt covered in dried mud, time I did something about my appearance.

Friday nights he always rang his big brother Joshua, to give him a progress report. Most weeks he had nothing important to say, so he would tell about what was happening to the people he'd come to know here. He made a cuppa and put his feet up. Smell was already curled up on the bed. She was sleeping more lately, not even waiting until Jack retired for the night. 'Hey brother, what's up?' Joshua answered his phone.

'Not much. How's your week been?' They swapped trivial news about their respective lives before Jack got more serious.

'I think something's going to happen, soon. Not much has been going on, but Ross has got some investors in, and I've got a feeling it's building up to something. I also learnt a few things about the other farmer here. You remember a while back I was telling you about a guy named Shorty who runs the other lease?'

'Yeah, I remember.'

'There's no love lost between them. Did you know Ross used to be his employee? It seems they had a big falling out five years ago just before Ross started his farm.'

In fact, Joshua knew all about the long standing animosity between the two farmers, but he hadn't wanted to influence Jack's observations by giving him too much information. If he had noticed the connection then it was relevant. Jack had an excellent nose for trouble.

'Well, I do know the story. Maybe it's time I told you.' Joshua explained at some length the details of how the relationship had gone sour. 'I'm sorry I got you into this mess Jack, especially since I'd rather have you here. I was going to suggest you chuck it in since it's been a year and nothing's happened, but it's up to you. If you've got a feeling about it...stay, if it's what you want.'

'I need to see what's in that shed, then I might know something. If I find nothing I'm out of here.' On the other end of the phone Joshua sighed.

'Okay, but just try not to get yourself in trouble.'

'You know me. I'm careful.'

If Jack had a middle name it wouldn't be Danger, or even Trouble - it would be Self-Preservation - not very James Bond, but it had kept him out of many interesting situations. It was probably even why he was single. Joshua was always the risk taker, and Jack the one to say, 'I don't know if that's such a good idea, Josh,' right before Joshua did it. He had lived through his brother's hair raising experiences, and that was close enough for Jack.

While he lay in the dark, the hammock swaying just a touch, Jack mulled over the possibilities of getting access to Ross's shed. Last year Ross had left him in charge of the farm for three days while he went to a friend's wedding in Southland. Jack had tried then to get access to the shed.

Nancy's car had been in the drive as he drove past on the second morning, which gave him an idea. He came up with a plan, but by the time he was ready for action Nancy had already left for the day. He would need her for the plan to work.

There was no toilet at the yard so when the

workers needed the toilet (they pissed behind the shed) they had to go up to the house for a sit down. Jack always tried to have his morning constitutional on the boat before work, but there were a few occasions when he was running late, or his body was out of sync, and he had to slink into Ross and Nancy's, hoping no one was home. He didn't like to stink out someone else's house, and because he always took off his muddy boots, it meant his socks soaked up the puddle of kiddy wee that was usually waiting somewhere between the door and the toilet.

Hoping to take advantage of Ross being away, he wandered up to the house on the third morning soon after arriving at work and asked to use the toilet. Nancy was packing the kid's lunches in the kitchen and shouted for him to go ahead. He waited a few minutes before he flushed the toilet and washed his hands. Coming into the kitchen he apologized for interrupting her morning, and casually mentioned how he hadn't heard the pump for the nursery running on his way past. Did she think he should check up on it? Nancy supposed he should. A recirculating pond setup had to have a pump running all the time for any sea life to stay alive. If the pump stopped for more than a few hours the water would foul up and everything die off. Oysters produced a lot of waste product.

There was just one flaw with this plan. Nancy didn't have a key. Ross must have taken it with him. 'I know Dave who owns the sheep station has a key 'cos he used to keep the quad bike in there, but he went on holiday last week,' Nancy said. 'Sorry, not much help am I?'

'Don't worry, it could just be a fuse. I'll check the box on my way back and if I can't fix it I'll ring Ross and ask him what he wants me to do.'

As a precaution he had removed a fuse from the box in case Nancy had decided to come and see for herself, so he wandered back to the shed and replaced it in the box. The pump noise started up again and Jack went back to work. It was a failed mission, but at least Ross would be none the wiser. It hadn't been a total waste of time; thanks to Nancy he had a new thread to follow.

He made a point of buying a beer for Dave the shepherd whenever he saw him in the pub, and stay to chat a minute. A man with a spare key might be a useful person to know.

Jack spent Saturday morning washing his weeks worth of dirty clothes at the laundromat and left them there to dry. They would be done by the time Smell had her bath.

Back at the wharf Smell had gone into hiding. She was under a dinghy pulled up on the beach. She knew it was bath day, and this was her customary spot to hide in. Like it or not, that dog was having a bath. She liked to roll in the dead oysters at work and carried her name like a trademark. Jack had to drag her out from under the dingy, but once she was tied to the tap outside the toilet block he hosed her down and she gave up struggling. She stood passively, tail curled under her body and legs shaking.

Town was too far to walk with a heavy load, especially since the day was warm, so Jack put the clean dog on the back of the ute and went back to collect his laundry. Spring was coming in slowly, the daffodils and narcissi first to leave their dark, moist, earthen sanctuary. Nature was against him, spring was such a suggestive time of year. Jack swore at himself, 'Pull yourself together, man.'

The main street was busy with families and couples; the cafe brimming with weekenders. Good weather at this time of year made folks want to leave the city for a taste of that fresh air, drink in the green hills and look at holiday houses they could fantasize about next week at the office.

Next he stopped by Rex's boat and asked if he had time to give his hair a trim. The boat had a hand-painted sign in red and blue saying, 'The Barber Boat - You'll float out the door.' This was a good example of a poetic license being employed. Rex only did three hair styles; short all over, slightly longer on top, or the comb-over cut - very popular with older gentlemen.

Rex was one of the permanently moored houseboat owners. There were seven houseboats here this winter, and space for about ten more in this stretch of the bay. There were also two families with five children between them, and another young couple Jay and Amanda, modern hippy types. Passing their boat in the evenings you could smell oriental incense and marijuana, but during the day they both worked normal jobs.

Beside them was Sonny, a mechanic's apprentice

in his early twenties. The boat he lived on belonged to Betty. She had decided to buy an investment houseboat and rent it out when she gave up her job at the accountancy. Sonny said it suited him to live here because the rent was no more than flatting, and he could walk to work. The auto workshop was attached to a petrol station beside the 4square.

During summer the harbour was overcrowded due to the facilities offered, but in winter they didn't get many visitors. Thanks to the local council, and Betty's nagging until they upgraded the wharf area, it had become an ideal location to moor a houseboat or yacht. There was a large, park-like expanse of grass with native trees planted around it, a kids play area, a gas barbecue, and a toilet block. The shower only had cold water, but in summer no one minded. Most of the boats were self sufficient anyway, and there was enough rainfall in winter to keep their on-board water tanks full. Rubbish was collected by the council from the parking area once a week, so long as it was in the official blue rubbish bags. Residents paid a small rates fee on top of mooring fees for these amenities and agreed to keep the place tidy and respectable.

A new wharf with a long wooden jetty lies at the northern end of the bay, where the yacht club is. In the opposite direction where the land slopes down to grass and sand banks, there are spaces reserved for houseboats thanks to an old policy. Visiting houseboats are charged a higher fee than residents with the extra revenue going to put on these 'meet and greet' parties.

Betty administered all the activity regarding boats coming in or out of the houseboat moorings, kept the books for the houseboat community meetings, and paid the council rates and fees each month. She did receive a small wage from the council, but would have done it for free. The shore was Betty's home and her pet project; she even had a Suggestions and Comments box nailed to her front veranda railings.

One night a year ago Betty told Jack the history of this area, passing him newspaper clippings and old photos from a shoe box as she spoke. There had been a time, many years ago, when not everyone was happy to have the wharfies living here, and despite it having changed significantly since then, it still had that reputation in the town as being full of people who were *different*. Betty herself had once thought it was a disgrace. Back then some not-so-nice types had squatted here permanently; living in wrecks which were covered in salvaged scraps of ply and tin, barely watertight and listing to one side, a description that described the inhabitants as well as the accommodation. Most of them were drunks. They fought amongst themselves and committed minor thefts about town (fruit from trees, loose timber from fences), and major theft from their fellows (cigarettes, booze, a mattress, a radio); but because they didn't pose a threat to anyone directly they were left alone. If you should pass one in daylight there would be no look or word of greeting; they knew where they stood, and a long way off was best for all. There was rubbish everywhere, piles of old building materials left over from patching the boats or huts they lived in, and more general rubbish too.

A population of rats lived in the sandy banks. People with houses along the road complained that the drunks disturbed the peace at night with their fighting. Sometimes they set light to a pile of rubbish and left it burning untended. Once, an empty shack had caught fire, but this was considered a good thing by the neighbourhood, one less eyesore to moan about. Rex had been one of these smelly, unshaven men.

That was how it was when Betty moved onto her houseboat, a grieving widow in her mid forties. Her friends thought she was crazy; first letting her husband's children take everything, and now living in the most unsuitable way in a place full of vagabonds. Betty admitted to no one that she spent every night scared stiff someone would try to set her boat on fire or break the door down.

One afternoon she had come home with her shopping to see a man dressed in a blanket pull out his willy and urinate on her ramp. She shouted at him, and he ran away laughing. That was what riled her most, the laughter. He ran, his blanket flapping like the wings of a bird, down the grass bank to his hovel under the trees. At least that explained the slippery patch on the end of the wooden ramp leading up to her boat. The blanket man must have made it a regular habit to stop by when she was out and take a leak on her doorstep, a sign of displeasure that she should settle on their turf. At that moment Betty decided to do something about the place. She organized a petition, going door to door in the area and asking for support for her proposal. It was an effective strategy because the home owners could see her plans would increase the value of their property. Soon there were enough signatures to make council sit up and do something.

In the meantime she tried to get to know some of the friendlier characters who came and went. She asked if there were other places to live, organizations who would give them shelter, and was directed to the local Mission centre. The Mission office was only open two days a week when facilitators from the larger City Mission made the drive here. It was explained to Betty that everything was provided for the homeless, they knew the people living at the wharf, but many didn't want to be helped. There were restrictions as to what they could do at a halfway house; no smoking inside, no fighting, no drugs or alcohol allowed on the premises, no women in the bedrooms, and everyone was expected to help with the chores. If they received a government benefit some of it was deducted to cover their expenses. For these reasons the Mission facilities were used sporadically; mostly when someone was ill, or out of food and money for the week.

Removing the wrecks they lived in would only shift them on to another part of town. They weren't all bad, and Betty felt some guilt for taking away the only homes they had. As a result of this guilt Betty began to volunteer at the church run op shop, taking a place on the committee so that she could raise the issue of aiding the homeless once she was accepted by the other members. Her idea was to ask council to donate a small plot of land out of the way somewhere so that the drunks could live as they wished without disturbing others. The op shop could gift them some useful items to get set up; there was no shortage of old furniture, clothing, and kitchen paraphernalia. The Mission centre could send people out there to check up on conditions, and perhaps nominate one of the squatters to be responsible for a communal vegetable garden.

Within three months of the petition being submitted, all of the illegal dwellings had a fluorescent orange X marked on their side, signaling what was to be removed. Understandably, there was a growing resentment towards Betty from the evictees, and some spat great gobs of phlegm when she passed or pulled the finger. Those who had been friendly towards her became silent and ignored her. Rex was the only one who was always happy to see Betty. His boat was shabby, neglected for many years, but at least he had papers to say he owned it. He had a right to live here, and unlike his companions he never missed a payment for the boat's mooring. Rex was a lovely man when he was sober, but was often incoherently drunk. His seedy friends would stay on his boat and pour him drinks in exchange for a dirty mattress, until the money or drinks ran out and he had to get rid of them. That was often when fights broke out.

Rex's situation became progressively worse as his old chums realized he wasn't affected by the looming demise of their squats, and especially since he was on friendly terms with the woman responsible.

The clean up was expected to take two weeks, and the night after the first shack was dismantled Rex had a stone smash through his window. Betty woke to find her geraniums had all been ripped from the boxes. The police were called but they couldn't be much help. It was suggested Betty and Rex go and stay elsewhere until things calmed down; a suggestion neither of them heeded. The cops agreed to drive down the wharf road every night, but that was the limit of their assistance.

Rex began creeping onto Betty's deck late at night if the weather was clear, bundling up under a canvas to keep the dew off. He knew without asking that Betty didn't want a stinking drunk in her cabin, but he felt they should stay close in case of trouble. Nothing else happened until the weekend. By this time half the wrecks had been towed or demolished and the remaining ones were abandoned. The silence made Betty and Rex nervous. On the Saturday night Rex awoke from his hideout on Betty's deck to the sound of an explosion, a soft bang followed by a whoosh. Peering over the edge of the boat he saw his own vessel was spitting flames from its windows and the roof. The explosion would have been his small gas bottle which was almost empty.

In the weeks that followed the boat fire Rex stayed at the halfway house, until his insurance paid out and he was able to purchase another boat. Betty moved her houseboat to a private beach not very far along the shore. One day Rex came to find her at the op shop where she was sorting goods out the back.

He explained that his new boat would arrive tomorrow, and he intended to moor it where his previous one had been. He wanted Betty to change her mooring to the one beside his, and bring her boat back. By this time the council had finished the clean up and begun putting in rubbish bins and clearing the long grass so that the look of the place was improved tenfold. Betty agreed to Rex's suggestion, but imposed a condition: Rex wasn't to come to her boat or speak to her if he was pissed. 'You're a bore when you're drunk, and you reek of turps,' she explained.

Since all of Rex's friends had gone, and wouldn't talk to him in any case, he found it so lonely being drunk that he began making an effort to drink less just to have Betty's company. He would wake at ten in the morning, have a wash in the basin, get dressed, and eat some food. Breakfast hadn't been on the menu for a long time, so to begin with his stomach complained if he ate more than a biscuit. His first meal of the day was usually lunch; something to line his stomach before the first drink. After three weeks he could eat two whole pieces of toast, and after that things progressed more easily.

After breakfast he would do any little jobs about the place that needed doing; like washing his clothes in a plastic tub, sweeping the floor, and going to the petrol station to refill his gas bottle. After his jobs were done he was surprised to be feeling hungry again. He ate lunch as before, but instead of going directly to the cupboard and pouring his first drink, he went to see Betty instead. She was always home for lunch and liked to rest for an hour after eating before doing anything else. Betty worked three mornings a week as the personal assistant to an accountant. It was a job she had started as a young married woman, and now the son had taken over his father's firm and kept her on. It wasn't very exciting but it kept the wolf from the door.

Rex would knock gently and wait until she called out, 'Come in.' He always tried to take something with him; a packet of mints, a roadside flower, an old photograph to show her. Betty would tidy away her lunch things and make the tea. The hour would fly past in lively conversation. Rex didn't have a drink until well past 2pm some days. Then one day Betty invited him back for dinner. Rex declined. 'Sorry Betty, I just don't think I'll last that long without a swalla'o something.'

'I understand. What if we eat a bit early then? Say, dinner at five, with a glass of wine to steady the nerves. Just the one glass, mind. I usually have one with dinner.'

'Ah, I'm not sure. Not a drop till five sounds dangerous in my condition. Just thinking about it makes my tongue prickle.'

'Maybe it does, but it's almost two o'clock now. That's only another three hours to wait. How about I make dinner and if you turn up, good, if you don't then we'll forget it.'

'Could we try for half four, and you have a glass waiting for me?'

The first day was the worst, but as weeks passed Rex found it easier than he imagined to wait a little longer, so long as he kept busy. If he sat still more than a minute his hands would shake, so he started with doing extra jobs. His new boat needed some repairs and it pleased him to be caring for his home again. Dinner with Betty became a regular occurrence, and on the days he wasn't invited he turned his attention to digging a small patch of sandy soil along the bank where the grass dropped a foot to meet the sand. In this narrow border he planted lettuce, broccoli, radish, carrots, kale, and spinach. The only things which grew to be harvestable were the carrots and the spinach, and these he made regular plantings of, sharing the produce with Betty. But it wasn't all miracles for Rex, he still got completely legless most nights, and woke dazed and muddled each morning.

Slowly, the story of Rex's past came out. Put up for adoption at birth but never adopted, he'd been passed from one state institute to another. Not even the state wanted him, he said. Education had been meager, and he ran away at fifteen to live rough on the street with an older boy.

An old sailor past his prime, and a great drinker of rum, had found him sleeping under a tarpaulin one morning and taken pity on the kid. In exchange for Rex doing menial jobs for him, Daniel let the boy sleep on his boat. Rex's friends urged him to rob the man, but he figured it was because they envied his warm bed and a swig of the bottle.

Daniel taught Rex how to make boat repairs, sand and repaint the hull, splice rope, and other nautical tasks. Having nothing else to do and with a keen mind, Rex made a good apprentice. He was soon trusted with enough cash to buy the bottle of rum, and they drank it together. Four years later when Daniel died, they were as close as father and son.

That was a dark time. Having finally felt some belonging to a person and a place, he was cut loose again. What saved him was a letter from the solicitor; Rex was the sole inheritor of the houseboat and a fortune no one knew about. It was stipulated that he receive small sums every month to cover his bills and maintain the boat, with insurance being automatically deducted. It had been calculated to last him until his ninetieth birthday. A short letter from Daniel that he was also an orphan, not by circumstance but by choice, and because of this he wished none of his family to benefit from his passing. It was up to Rex what he did with his life, but Daniel hoped he would use the small income to live on while he decided what to make of himself.

Until Betty arrived he had forgotten any ambition, but relaxed in her company he confessed, 'Since you came I feel like there's a reason to get up before half the day is gone, but I'm running out of things to fix. Tell me, what should I do next?' Betty didn't know, but there were people who were trained to help. She went with him to his first AA meeting and his first therapy session.

During his rehabilitation Rex had fallen off the wagon so many times that Betty lost count, and he never completely gave up the drinking. He developed an affinity for fine wines, and only occasionally indulged in anything stronger. There'd been other positive changes though. His therapist had helped him choose a job and he began to train as a barber. It meant he could spend all day chewing the fat, and feel useful at the same time.

Rex's dark days were well in the past when Jack arrived, and he had become a semi respectable man. He wouldn't take customers after lunch on Saturdays. This rule had been self imposed early in his career after he'd given a visiting boatie a very unique hairstyle. He'd only had the one bottle of wine, but drinking less meant it affected him more and he was much drunker than he realized. The incident had very nearly become nasty. The man had been extremely upset, and one of the other residents had come running over to see what the shouting was about. He'd had to restrain the man and talk him off Rex's boat while Rex had a good cry. He prided himself on a good cut and was ashamed to let the profession down.

Luckily for Jack it was only 11am when he called on Rex, and he was almost done with a customer. Jack recognized the boy as belonging to one of the families here, but couldn't recall his name. He didn't often socialize with the couples, not having much in common. 'Just got his first job doing the paper run, haven't ya Squirt?' Rex said, ruffling the boys hair. 'Told him he could pay me with his first check.' He removed the cape from the boy and shook it overboard. Since the weather was benevolent the barbers station was out on the deck today; better for attracting new customers and seeing what was happening along the shore. People would stop to chat and Rex could observe the goings on. It helped keep him up to date on gossip.

'What's it today, Jack?' The barber threw the cape over Jack's shoulders, began misting Jack's hair, and combing it down. Jack sat with his back straight. The spray was pleasingly cold on his neck in the sun's warmth.

'Just the usual thanks. No, wait on. Longer on top I think, but a good inch shorter than this.' Jack pulled a length of hair upwards to demonstrate. He usually had it cut short because it was thick and grew out quickly, but he felt like a change.

'What's been keeping you busy, then?' Rex inquired.

'Not much. I won a $50 bar tab in the handle draw on Thursday. I'd have to say that was the highlight of my week.'

'Now you're talking! I used to dream of winning a bar tab, 'cept I couldn't afford the pub so there wasn't a chance of it happening. And how's the new bloke shaping up? Alright is he?'

'Yep, he's a real worker. Pulls his weight, doesn't mind the mud or the repetitive stuff. I've invited him along tonight. He's hit a slump socially speaking, and I thought a new crowd might extend his horizons a little. All his mates are also Ross's mates, and work's been a bit tense lately.'

'The more the merrier. You coping alright with the tension at work then?'

'I guess. I'm doing what I can to keep the peace

because I like Ryan.'

'What about Shorty? You could always go and ask him for a job if things go pear-shaped.'

'I'd rather not. I don't really agree with his farming practice.'

'Couldn't you set up your own venture?'

'I've given it some thought. There's someone I have in mind to partner up with, but I'm not quite ready to leave yet.'

'Glad to hear it! It's good having you about. I know Betty will be sorry when you go.'

'So, who else's coming tonight?' If anyone knew the unofficial guest list it would be Rex.

'Jay said Amanda's bringing a friend, and the Germans have a local friend who's coming. There's three new boats in, four counting the little one. Have you met any of them yet?'

'No, but I bet you have.' No doubt Rex knew them all by now.

'Well, the Germans are a bit boring if I'm honest, but they certainly know a lot about sailing if that's your thing. The couple from down south are more my cup of tea. They say they're here for a change of scene, but I think they're trying to recapture young love. Just don't go a knockin' if the boats a rockin', if you know what I mean.' Rex was snipping away as he talked.

'And the other two?'

'Ah, a bloke who's here on a sheep shearing contract. He'll be gone in a week, but of course he's been invited along tonight, and the last one, ah yes, that reminds me. Did Betty catch you this morning?

She wants to put that one down beside you.'

'I must have been out. She'll want me to move the dinghy off the beach for a ramp to go there I s'pose.'

'I think Betty wanted to introduce you before the party. She sounded excited about it. The boat motored in two nights ago with a woman at the helm. She's about your age, perhaps a touch younger. Short brown hair, small, attractive. I haven't found out why she's here, but she signed on as permanent. Must be planning to stay a while.' Rex grinned at him in the mirror lasciviously, brushing the hair from Jack's neck.

'Rex, you're an incorrigible match maker, you know that? I still haven't forgotten the Swedish dame you tried to set me up with last summer.'

The woman had been very attractive in a Nordic way, and Jack had been egged on by Rex to ask her out. When he finally did after three weeks of telling himself yes one minute and no the next, she had laughed at him.

'Oh yes, I am alone, but I don't think we can be together. I like, how you say? Other pussy.' Yee Gods, the woman was a woman only kind of woman. That was way too much woman for Jack to handle.

Rex had then tried to tell him it was a cover, she was just testing him, but whatever the story Jack wasn't brave enough to persist. Things either happened or they didn't. If a woman wanted to play games, she could play by herself.

'Errr, we all make mistakes, eh? I still think I was right about her, but I guess we'll never know.'

'Never mind, Rex. I appreciate the effort. I know

you mean well.' Jack stood, handing Rex a twenty. 'See you tonight.' He took two strides and jumped overboard, landing on the sandy mud. He ran his hands over his shortened hair enjoying the feeling of freshness.

Betty wasn't at her boat so he went ahead and moved his dinghy and the gear stashed under it to a new spot beneath some spindly tea trees growing above the shoreline. Smell had taken herself for a walk and came running up as he finished coiling a rope. He reached down and thumped her side affectionately before throwing his head up in disgust and tentatively sniffing his hand. 'That's just bloody great. You stink.' Smell sat on her haunches looking smug. She must have found some fish offal to roll in down by the boat ramp. Recreational fishermen used it on the weekends and dumped their fish guts on the shore for the tide or the seagulls to take away. 'Right, you're coming with me.'

Jack took her to the toilet block and washed her again with plenty of soap. It didn't completely get the stink out, but it was a big improvement. She would have to be shut in the cabin for the rest of the day unless he was keeping a close eye, or she would go straight back to roll in what ever she'd found. Shaking the water from her coat, Smell tried to bolt, but Jack was ready for her. Holding her by the collar he dragged her back to the boat and shut her in. Mission accomplished, he left to get some lunch.

Jack pulled up in front of the restaurant where Connie had saved him a table. She was pleased to see him as always, and placed him in his usual spot close to the service entrance in a small nook. That way if she had a minute to spare she could come and chat without other diners bothering them.

Jack chose a creamy leek and bacon soup with rolls of fresh, crusty bread. When he'd finished wiping the bowl clean with his last hunk of bread Connie bought him a slice of apple pie smothered in vanilla custard, and sat down opposite him.

'You not going to the fancy wine festival then?' she asked. Jack shook his head, his mouth full of pie. 'I loaned my kitchen-hand to Nancy to help out shucking. Did you know about this new lease Ross wants to take up?' Connie knew that Ross kept his workers in the dark about everything, and she still hoped that by being an indispensable source of information she could keep Jack's interest. No man had ever held out against her attentions as long as this. If she didn't win by her looks or her personality, she always got them with her cooking. She hadn't considered that it was because Jack liked her so much that he would never do anything to risk their friendship. Connie had lately begun to wonder if she shouldn't just give up.

'No. First I've heard of it, but that's not surprising. I'm sure I'll be told the minute we start farming it.' Jack scraped the last bits of custard from his bowl and resisted the urge to lick it clean.

'I wonder if he's planning a big change, then. You could be in for a promotion Jack!'

'I hope not. I have enough to do tidying up after Ross as it is, and finding more workers will be a problem. I wouldn't be surprised if Ryan quits before Christmas. He thought Ross was his mate, but at work it's a different story. I guess if I was looking to put a positive spin on it I could say he doesn't go in for favouritism.'

'Yes, he has his own strict moral code. It's a bit warped in my opinion. He walks all over Nancy but he'd never cheat on her. Now, I'm sure you didn't come here to talk about work. Let me ask you something personal. Is it because I can't offer an outright relationship that you keep turning me down?'

Jack let his spoon slide into the empty bowl and sighed, 'I wondered how long before you'd ask. The way I see it you're done with love, and I'm still looking for it. You would have been my ideal woman ten years ago, but I don't think I can do casual anymore. I couldn't be your man on tap. I'd want more than that. Besides, you're just bored because it's been a quiet winter. Soon you'll be turning them away.'

'Humpf. So you're a certified romantic then? Okay, I can live with just being mates. You want seconds on that pudding?' Jack laughed at her straight-up talk. Connie kissed him on the cheek and then left through the swing door to the kitchen. Jack missed her look of disappointment, though he did wonder how she could take the rejection so well.

Jack ate his second helping more slowly, enjoying the buttery sweetness of the apples, and the salty pie crust. Connie's news about Ross expanding the farm would have come straight from Nancy, but he couldn't make head or tails of it. Why would they need another lease? Especially one that took half an hour to reach by barge. Jack knew the currents were stronger round the heads, making for a nutrient-rich oyster diet so they'd grow fast there. Maybe Ross was going into single seed production out of the bay. If he could get the spat up to size in his nursery, then put it on another lease to grow...if that's all he was planning then Jack had spent a year here for nothing. Unless there was something other than juvenile oysters in that shed. The only place Ross could hide stuff was in that damn shed. He would have to bide his time for another chance to get in there and do some snooping. He didn't want to leave not knowing.

When Jack arrived back at the wharf preparations were happening for tonight's festivities. A large canvas tent had been raised on the reserve with trestle tables covered in white sheets for tablecloths. Jessie and Steve were helping to build a bonfire on the beach with their three children running to find driftwood and stockpiling it. Later they would toast marshmallows over the fire and Jay would play the guitar.

It was just mild enough for an outdoor party. The yacht club had finished their morning race and someone was locking up the building. The harbour was tranquil apart from the tiny ripples bringing the tide in. Only half of the deeper moorings were in use, and most of the boats were still lashed down with covers, unused since the summer months.

Two of the newly arrived boats were lying at

anchor close in to the shore behind the row of houseboats. A small catamaran drifted beside a larger single hulled vessel of respectable girth. It was of a similar size to the boats the families with children lived on, and much bigger than Jack's. He noted the name, painted in white capitals over the blue. There was a childish uncertainty about the formation of the letters, MISS TERRY ROSE SKYLARK. It must belong to a family. Perhaps they had named it after everyone in the family? He would have to ask them tonight.

The reserve had been freshly mown making it all look neat and tidy. The contractor for the council had become an honorary member of the wharf community and was always invited to these events. It helped to know the barbecue was gassed up and the toilets clean, and it would be unwise to upset the person who made sure they were.

Jack's boat was at the end of the small beach after Betty's, and as Jack pulled up he could see her standing on the grass talking to someone in a familiar looking cap. Jack observed the two as he walked, and realized it was the woman he'd seen in the pub eating fish and chips - the one who had not looked at him. She wasn't wearing the baggy jeans now, but a pair of tight ones which emphasized her small build and a rather shapely derriere, were tucked into sensible leather boots. A sheepskin vest covered the checkered shirt and pulled her in at the waist, so there was no mistaking it was a woman's body he was looking at this time. At Jack's approach the conversation stopped and Betty waved him closer. 'I was hoping you'd turn up. Rose, this is Jack. Jack, I'd like you to meet your new neighbour, Rose.'

'How'd you do?' Jack said offering his hand. She took it and shook assertively, saying, 'Pleased to meet you.' Her brown eyes sparkled with amusement. Possibly Betty had been telling stories about him, or maybe she'd overheard the conversation in the pub about the 'little blue pills' which he certainly didn't need. Damn, it wasn't really something you could address in a first conversation, was it? 'Um, you know how those guys were saying I should take viagra? I swear I don't need to. If you don't believe me come to my boat and I'll show you my huge stiffy.' No. Definitely not a good icebreaker.

Rose wasn't what you would expect from someone called 'Rose.' Though she was small, she looked solid and strong, not soft or blurred at the edges. If she was a rose it would be one from the florist, half open and crisp, not the blowzy ones from his mum's garden. Betty made a polite, guttural noise in her throat. Jack's eyes shifted from Rose to Betty who winked at him.

Oh, Jack clicked, I was staring. What a pillock! He'd been grinning away like a buffoon, his eyes busy gathering information while his brain went on strike. Take your hand back, she'll think your nuts, man! Trying to look casual and hide his embarrassment he let her hand go and cleared his throat. He must have been gazing at her for at least ten seconds. I am so out of practice, he lamented.

Words deserted him. All Jack's attention was focused on his groin, willing the start of an erection to piss off. 'Hairy men with beards, hairy men with beards,' he repeated in the privacy of his head. There, it was going away. He didn't know why but that one always worked.

In those few seconds of staring inadvertently at Rose, he had seen what he considered was a perfect balance of nature. She couldn't be described as pretty or beautiful; her features were too strong. Her looks were old-fashioned; what used to be called handsome, perhaps of Russian or Jewish heritage. She would look haughty or serious if it weren't for the way the corners of her mouth curved upwards, making it look like she was permanently amused by some thought that had just occurred to her.

Smell had heard Jack's voice and whined to be let out of the boat. He felt the urge to speak before the silence went too long, his mind searching for ways to prolong the meeting. 'Tide's on the way in. Do you need a hand moving your boat? There's a small sand bar as you swing in, I could help guide you if you like.' He had used his proper man's voice, all deep and salty. He could prove he was strong, capable, considerate, and skilled on the water.

The brown eyes stared into his, assessing him as he had done to her a moment ago. 'No, I think I can handle it. Sounds like your dog needs you.' Without waiting longer Rose strode off in that self contained way which men found so unreasonable and confusing. It left Jack feeling guilty for not being needed, which made no sense at all. He looked at

Betty and shrugged his shoulders. She smiled at him. 'Perhaps you came on a bit strong, dear. Not that I'd blame you; she is quite striking, isn't she? Don't worry love, some women don't have a lot of trust when it comes to handsome men who give them the glad-eye. Give her time to get to know you so she can see for herself you're not a cad.'

Shut safely inside his boat Jack slapped his forehead, 'What a dick.' He hadn't been prepared for it, that's all. Rose had surprised him. It was like she had sprung up from nowhere, a mythical creature that didn't exist, and he'd been dazzled and curious. She was like a unicorn; it looked like a horse, moved like a horse, but fundamentally it was something else. There was something refreshingly different about her and he was intrigued. Didn't Rex mention she'd come to stay a while? If he had a second chance at talking to her later he would make an effort to play it cool.

Chapter 5

After shucking twelve dozen oysters and preparing his magic sauce, which was a combination of whatever was in the cupboards at the time (today being apple brandy, a small onion, Tabasco, and lemon grass), Jack tidied the cabin and made up the spare bed in case Ryan needed to crash here. Provided Smell didn't sneak off to roll in rotten fish guts she could sleep on the floor tonight. He took an old work jersey which was nearing the end of its secondhand life and laid it on the floor for her. Music drifted in the open door... *'I want to break free-ee...'* Rex with his record collection was probably half pissed by now. He loved these parties.

Someone outside called his name over the noise. Jack threw Smell a dog biscuit and stuck his head out the door to see Ryan clanking his way over from the parking lot with a plastic bag in each hand. He spotted Jack and grinned, eyebrows lifting twice in greeting. The man was almost part troll, he thought. The huge shoulders worked back and forth as he walked, those long arms with mallet fists; the short legs planted firmly on the ground with each step. He wasn't a handsome man, but his looks were genial and he had buckets of charm, especially when he smiled which was most of the time.

'Hey mate, you made it,' Jack slapped him on the back and stood aside to let him in.

'Here, I brought some supplies along.' Ryan took out two cans of lager and handed one to Jack. 'So this is where you hide out, eh?' He looked around the small compartment. There wasn't much to see. The boat really belonged to Joshua. He bought it after separating from his wife as a place to go and think. It was devoid of all but the basic equipment, the only decoration being curtains with a motif of blue forget-me-nots on a pale pink background, the remnant of a previous owner.

'Nice curtains,' Ryan sniggered. Jack wasn't phased. He no longer noticed them.

'They serve their purpose.' Cracking open beers they clinked cans. Ryan took a long gulp and belched. 'Ah, that's better. I didn't drink with the others at rugby. I saved myself for you. I can see you've been to the hairdresser. You must be hoping to pull tonight. I'll drink to that!' he said, finishing off his can of beer.

Ryan had been to the rugby game and then home to take a shower. He had put on his best clothes from what Jack could tell; a shirt with a collar and black jeans with a black woolen coat. He actually looked quite smart. It was the first time Jack had seen him in anything other than old work clothes; the jeans were almost formal in comparison. Ryan told Jack about the game, and said he was disgusted that Ross had been at rugby instead of helping Nancy run the live oyster bar. 'You should have heard him! 'Yeah, I said Nance, important game this weekend. You'll have to mind the kids and sell the oysters,' bragging how he has it so sweet. Makes me wanna spew!'

The eldest child, an energetic boy of seven had been allowed to go with Ross. Ryan reported that in an hour and a half the boy managed to steal enough of his dad's beer to be sick all down his front. Ross had hosed him off in the changing rooms and been extremely annoyed at having to leave because Nancy hadn't packed spare clothes. The longer he worked on the farm the less he liked his old buddy. He found it so irritating seeing Ross on the weekends that he was thinking of giving up his rugby club membership. 'I haven't played since before my fall last year anyway, so it's more of a social outing for me.'

Ryan retold all this while knocking back a second beer. 'You know, I used to think that it was okay, the way he treats Nancy. I thought it was normal. She wanted kids, he wasn't so keen, and they did a deal; he earns the money, she does everything else, but it's not like that. Nancy works as hard as he does, earns half the money, and still does everything else.'

Trying to get off the topic of work and Ross in particular, Jack said, 'Nancy will be fine, she's used to it, and besides, she's got two other sheilas helping. They'll take turns with the kids or something. Women have a wonderful way of working things out between them. Let's drink up and see if this party's about to start.' Unlike Ryan Jack had reached the stage of 'couldn't give a shit' when it came to the Sargent's marital problems. At that moment there was the sound of a boat scraping the sea floor close by.

Outside, the sun was starting to nestle in behind the hill on the other side of the bay, casting a pink glow over the harbour. The water was high now and appeared darkest green in contrast to the setting sun. The scraping they'd heard was a big houseboat coming in to dock alongside. Its white letters glowed in the evening light. It was the *Miss Terry Rose Skylark.*

The person docking the boat was the woman called Rose, so Jack's theory about the boat's name was way off the mark. He expected her to be the owner of the small catamaran, not the skipper of a large houseboat. Ryan seemed intent on watching the procedure so Jack was obliged to stay with him. After his earlier bungled introduction he wanted to steer clear for a while, but Ryan was his guest.

Rose got the boat in position, as far in to the shore as she could nudge it. She threw a gang plank over the side but didn't bother using it. Swinging herself over the side she sploshed into the waist high water and walked ashore. Ignoring her audience she began to drag a wooden construction back into the water and set about wedging it along one side of the boat. She repeated the process on the other side and once the craft was stable, began hauling on a huge rope attached to the prow. She dragged it up the grass bank, and taking a mallet from her belt she hammered a metal spike as thick as her wrist and two feet long into the soil, the hits ringing out over the water and bouncing back off the hills opposite in the still evening air. Straining against the weight of the boat she took up the slack along the length of rope and wrapped it once around the peg. It was like watching a fairy try to lead a giant by his shoe lace.

Who knows how long it would have taken her to

get the rope tight because at that moment Ryan crossed the grass and simply took the rope from her and began to haul on it. Once it was taunt he swiftly tied a winch knot and stood up, hands on hips.

'I don't like to see a lady struggle with something that I can easily take care of.' Rose smiled at him.

'Thanks. You're pretty handy with a rope.' Ryan smiled back.

'I've had some experience. Rope was one of my main tools when I was breaking horses. I'm Ryan,' he said holding out his hand.

'I'm Rose. So Ryan, you have a boat here?' Jack didn't know if it was better to stay where he was or join in the conversation, so he took his time walking slowly towards them and hung back by a few metres.

'Nah nah. Jack invited me over for the party. I'm surprised he didn't offer to help you.' He half turned to Jack who shrugged and smiled weakly. Ryan continued, 'Anything else I can do to help? I don't want to start enjoying myself and turn around to see you lifting sand bags or something.' Was he flirting? Jack was feeling uncomfortable and wanted to walk off, but was curious to see how Rose would respond to Ryan's charms.

'All I have to do now is take off these wet pants get into some dry ones, and I'll be ready to party.'

Ah no, don't say it, Jack begged silently.

'Removing pants is also something I'm pretty good at,' and Ryan did the thing with the eyebrows.

Jack cringed from his place on the sidelines. Ryan's forward nature was part of his charm. If he ever felt shame Jack couldn't tell. He was a take-it or leave-it sort of person, and most people liked his honesty enough to overlook his uncouth manners.

'Yeah, I take mine off every Sunday afternoon and watch TV in my undies. You could join me sometime if you're not too busy.'

Ryan's smile widened hopefully, and Rose giggled. Jack raised his eyebrows in surprise. This wasn't going at all the way he imagined. He had expected her to be insulted by such a blatant come-on. Instead, she was saying Ryan could come and wait on her boat while she changed if he liked. The invitation wasn't extended to include Jack.

Ryan turned to him, 'Hey mate, you go ahead and I'll catch you up in a minute.'

What could he say? Giving Smell a whistle he made his way over to the gathering on the reserve with his bin full of shucked oysters, feeling suddenly deflated. He should be feeling pleased for Ryan. Wasn't that the reason Jack had invited him? To meet someone who wasn't stuck in a small clic in a small town? He might have changed his mind if he'd met Rose sooner. He couldn't ask Ryan to back off, because he wasn't in a position to pursue her himself, though that was precisely what he wanted to do. She had dismissed him without knowing him, and now she wouldn't want to know him because she would be too busy getting friendly with Ryan. Talk about a spanner in the works!

Walking towards the gathering he tried to remind himself what tonight was about, but his heart wasn't in it anymore. He wanted Rose. It hardly mattered who else turned up tonight because he wasn't interested. He wondered if he wasn't just suffering from a case of an object becoming more desirable when you weren't the only one who wanted it. There was probably a word for that but he couldn't think of it; but it was more than that, whatever it was called. The feeling of urgency about his attraction to Rose could be attributed to Ryan, but the attraction itself had been instant and gripping. Envy for the way his friend had easily struck a connection made him morose.

Jack's senses were on hyper-alert; he could separate the sound of each individual's voice ahead of him, hear water shushing on the sand, feel the faintest touch of warmth from the last glow of sun, see the layers of light and shadow weaving about everything. In that moment, despite his downcast mood he felt like he was alive, conscious of himself and awake to the world. The feeling faded as the music closed in on him, stepping into the tent and out of the mind-warp.

Lanterns were strung up under the tent and the trees close by. Betty had recruited the young mechanic to solder some wire into hoops around old jam jars, and one of the mums had put candles in them. Twilight came quickly and Venus hung above them, the evening star. It might be chilly later, but at least there were no mosquitoes at this time of the year. Under the tent, boat dwellers were sipping mulled wine or beer as more guests arrived in small groups. Rex spotted Jack and hollered out. One of the children yelled for Smell Hound to play a game of fetch, but she was more interested in a small dog who was searching for dropped food under the tables.

Jack put his oysters down and poured a beer from the keg into a mug and went to introduce himself to the people milling around. First off, he met the couple from the South Island who had decided to sell their house and buy a boat. The bloke was a photographer and she was a writer. Their children were either working or at university, and they were finally free to travel. Work could be done from anywhere these days, they explained. If the job was far away it was affordable to fly to locations. 'I just regret not having thought of it five years ago,' said the husband.

They were joined by a man in his forties who wore green woolen trousers and a swanni. Jack noted the look of forbearance that passed between the husband and wife, and wondered what he was in for. 'Hello, name's Norman.' Jack shook his hand.

'Jack. You new here?'

'Yep. I own the catamaran. It gets me from job to job, and I don't have to pay for accommodation. I start shearing round here next week.'

'You got transport?' Jack asked.

'Not yet, but The Lord always provides for those who Tend His Flocks.'

There was a suppressed cough from the photographer who was trying not to laugh. So that was the joke, Jack thought.

'Well, where're you heading? I might be going your way.'

'The Rundell's farm. It's out east from here.'

'Ah, no one goes east, much. It's all forestry blocks. Maybe you can hitch a lift with a pig hunter or something.' Norman's face darkened.

'No. Don't like pig hunters. They're mean to their dogs, starve them so they'll hunt better. I used to hunt before The Lord showed me The Way.'

'What way is that, man?' The photographer asked, his wife prodding him to stop.

'The way of peace, Brother. I see you mock me because God has not Touched you. I was the same once until God decided to humble me.'

'Yeah? How'd he do that?' Jack was mildly curious.

'One day, I decided to cut down a mighty Rimu belonging to my neighbour. It blocked the sunlight to my house, but he refused to trim the branches so I took my chainsaw and cut it down. I waited for him to go away and did it at night so no one would witness my act. The Devil had filled my heart with hatred for that man, and I unleashed my hatred on the tree. As the Rimu came down it twisted, and a branch caught my leg ploughing it into the earth. The man I hated found me unconscious the next day and took me to hospital. I was there many weeks. He visited me and brought me to understand God's message; to harm another is to harm oneself.' Norman plucked the green fabric of his trousers lifting the hem slightly. Above his shoe where his ankle should have been they saw a stick of wood.

'Holy shit!' Jack exclaimed. 'You lost your leg?'

'A small price to pay for enlightenment. I carved

this leg from the branch that took my old leg, so I would never forget. The Rimu and I are one.'

'Man, that's some heavy shit,' the photographer said, no longer looking amused.

'But how can you do your job with one leg?' his wife added.

'No trouble at all. In fact, it helps me. When a sheep bucks to get up I use my wooden leg to pin it down. Works every time.'

'That's amazing.' The photographer was impressed. 'Ah, I could give you a ride to the farm on Monday. Would you mind if I took a few photos while you work?'

'It'd be a pleasure. You see? Like I said - The Lord provides.'

Jack quietly slipped away to replenish his drink. That was a strange start to the night. He needed some light-hearted banter to clear his head, but Betty was headed his way with an older couple who must be the Germans.

Helga and Herman were on their second voyage round the Pacific. Much taken with what they saw as the laid-back way of life, where friends dropped in on each other without prior arrangement, they wanted to lose some of their conservative views. They were trying to reunite with people they had met on the first trip so they had stopped here to see a friend who had also been invited tonight. 'Vee just popped in on her! She vas so surprised and so happy to see us, it was vonderful, yah?'

The friend was a woman in her mid forties who turned out to be the owner of the small dog. She introduced herself as Michelle - "Shelly" to her friends. He could smell the white wine she was drinking on her breath as she said, 'I'm so proud of them. It's not easy breaking the mould, trust me. My mother was a heavy drinker so I'm still working on that.' Shelly tipped back her glass and began to twirl the plastic stem. Jack had to keep the conversation going a few minutes longer for politeness, so he told them about his job. 'Oh, I just *looove* oysters.' Shelly did a weird shimmy of excitement and the Germans laughed.

It was an annoyingly common reaction. Most people liked oysters in Jack's experience. It was a bit like saying you liked chocolate. Shelly stood too close and leaned in towards Jack, telling him all about her latest meal at a seafood restaurant in the city. She used one varnished fingernail to prod him in the shoulder when his gaze wondered.

'I said, have you eaten there yet?'

'No, Michelle, can't say I have.'

'Oh, please call me Shelly. We're friends now, eh Jack?' The tip of her tongue sneaked out from between her bright red lips like a sea snail from its shell. Jack felt simultaneously bored and offended by this person and her bolshy personality. Even her hair was rude; the curly mass stuck out all over her head and Jack had to keep brushing it aside. It felt scratchy against his clean shaven cheeks. Perhaps she took this as encouragement, or so he assumed when he felt a knee rub his inner thigh. Oh crap. He was hemmed in, between two long trestle tables and the tent wall. Helga and Herman blocked his path behind her. Jack desperately considered ducking under the tables to escape. She was obviously drunk, maybe she wouldn't even notice.

He was so distracted plotting an escape that he didn't notice Rose and Ryan arrive at the party. Bugger this, he thought, as Michelle's thigh slid between his. He stepped back and bent down to pat Smell, which left his pursuer looking like a pelican with one leg bent at the knee and raised in the air. On impulse Jack just kept sinking towards the ground, down on his knees now, beside a surprised Smell Hound, until he'd rolled right under the table. Shelly's dog thought it was some kind of new game and wanted to play. 'No! Fuck off, Toto.' Jack pushed it away and crawled along under the length of the table to put some distance between himself and Shelly before popping up at the end where the crowd was thickest. Unfortunately, when Jack lifted the edge of the tablecloth to make his reappearance, he also lifted the hem of a skirt. When he tried to stand up his head was thrust into a stocking-clad bottom. The owner of the bottom screamed. Jack was now fighting furiously with handfuls of fabric, trying to unentangle himself from a hysterical skirt. Bewildered at finding himself trapped he yelled out in panic but his mouth was full of cloth. Suddenly the material was lifted off him by a meaty fist which was attached to a long, hairy arm. Jack grabbed the arm and hauled himself up panting. He stared into Ryan's surprised face. Everyone had turned to look at the disturbance and now they all stared at him. 'What on earth are you doing Jack?' said Betty. The woman readjusting her long skirt was one of the mums, and her husband was glaring at him with menace.

'I'm so sorry Janette,' Jack blurted. 'I think I got tangled trying to stand up.' She gave him a cold look and went to her husband's side. Ryan cracked up laughing and Rose beside him covered her mouth and giggled.

'You know Jack, at work you're a clever guy but socially you're a real mess,' Ryan said still laughing. 'I'm gonna have to keep an eye on you tonight.'

'Yeah, I feel like I'm having a run of bad luck.' Jack glanced at Rose as he said it. 'I need a drink like a fish needs water.'

'Here, have one of these,' Ryan thrust a can in his hand. 'I think we should get you out of here till the shock wears off.'

Jack, Ryan, and Rose went out to the fire which had just been lit. As they passed the Germans he overheard the woman responsible for his troubles telling her friends how she'd narrowly escaped from the arms of a pervert. He shot a look of disgust at the back of her head and its crazy hair. Beside the fire Jack tried to explain to Ryan and Rose how he'd ended up someone's bottom, and they were laughing so much that Jack began to see the funny side too. He went to apologize again to Janette and her husband, before Rex declared in a loud voice that it was time for everyone to eat.

The rest of the evening went without a hitch. The record player was exchanged for a CD player, and taken charge of by the younger people. The kids had their marshmallows and were taken off to bed, and tables were pushed back for dancing in the tent. Jack finished his bowl of sticky date pudding and Jay came to put an arm around him. He had just finished dancing to a song, and was out of breath.

'Hey mate, it's a party. Cheer the fuck up. Come and meet Amanda's friend Jasmin. She's the one in the pink skirt. Her boyfriend dumped her last week and I think she wouldn't say no to a root. It might cheer you both up.'

Jack looked over at the girl he was talking about. She was swaying on her feet and trying to light a cigarette by the wrong end. Jack did not find this an alluring sight. Besides that he was almost old enough to be her father. 'I think I'll pass, Jay. I prefer women to girls, but thanks for the thought.'

'Hey, no prob big nob. Maybe Sonny can help us out. I sure don't want to be stuck with her all night.' Jay walked back to Amanda and shrugged to say he'd tried.

Jack found a seat by the fire. He had less chance of being bothered out here. Ryan and Rose came and joined him on the big log that had been dragged up from the beach. Another song started and Ryan tapped his feet, humming the tune. Rose sat in between them. Her short brown hair stuck out from under her woolen hat, just skimming her shoulders, and her perfume smelt of spring flowers after the rain, sweet and earthy. Jack was doing his best to ignore her, so they sat side by side silently staring at the fire. So far he had stared at her in the pub, stared at her when he was introduced, and humiliated himself under a skirt. She must think he was an idiot. When Ryan turned to talk to Sonny about cars, Jack wasn't expecting it when Rose nudged his leg and said, 'Ryan must be a great workmate. He's so easy to get along with.' Jack had to admit he was. 'So how long have you been working together?'

'About two months.' He didn't want to sit here and talk about Ryan, but at least Rose was talking to him, and that was less awkward than the silence. Jack rested his elbows on his knees and turned his head slightly towards her. He didn't want Rose to think he was too keen, though his pulse sped up with the anticipation of speaking to her.

'So what brings you here, Rose?'

'I don't know really. I was born here but we moved to the city not long after that, and I've always wanted to come back to see what it's like. Dad had to stop farming when he damaged his back, and took a job in stock sales. My brother offered me a job working for his company in the city and I didn't have much else going on, so I said I'd take it. Better the devil you know. I was overseas and it was time to come home.' Their breath made small clouds between them and Jack watched it mingle together then dissipate.

'And your boat? You're obviously quite comfortable handling it on your own. Have you lived on boats much?'

'You could say I grew up on that boat. We spent every holiday on her, taking her different places round the country. My dad was mad about sailing when he was young, but when us kids came along mum said if he wanted to be on the water he had to take us all with him. The Terry Rose was his compromise.'

'He sounds like a great dad. How'd she get the name *Miss Terry Rose Skylark*?' Jack was giving the stars his attention, only making eye contact to put forward his questions. It seemed to be working, she was still talking to him.

'I wanted to call her *Mystery* but my brother said he should get to chose the name because he's the eldest. Mum said she should be named after all of us, that way she would know her masters. Terry my brother, me, and my sister Skylar. The Miss to make mystery, and the K on Skylar's name because that was her nickname. She was always singing, like a little skylark.'

Ryan's grin came round her shoulder, 'Alright, mate?' he asked Jack. Ryan had just given his number to Sonny who was going to keep an eye out for a car which didn't require a special warrant of fitness from Fast Billy. It was well known that if you took a car to Fast Billy for a warrant it would get one in five minutes flat. Fast Billy didn't have time for the finer technicalities of vehicle inspection - he was far too busy. After several years of suspicions the local cops had finally cottoned on to Fast Billy. Although they hadn't managed to catch him doing anything illegal, they had recently begun to make life difficult for his customers.

Ryan had been pulled up this week driving with only one headlight. The policeman had checked his warrant and said it must be one of Fast Billy's and if he didn't get a proper one in the next month they'd make a point of pulling him over on a regular basis and give him a fine for everything they found wrong with the car. Ryan knew there was a lot more wrong with his car than a broken light, and wisely decided to upgrade. Now that he was working again he could get a loan for it.

Ryan picked up on the tail of Jack's conversation with Rose. 'Who's always singing? Hey, this song's awesome.' He grabbed Rose and pulled her to her feet, moving his head with the music before leading her to the dance floor and starting to gyrate.

They were joined by other wharfies, and even Rex, well into his cups, was twirling around, with one hand beating the air above his head. Rose danced amongst the crowd, bumping hips with Amanda and laughing at Ryan's moves. The one-legged shearer had been pulled upright from his chair by Shelly who was doing some very dirty dancing. Norman looked a bit stunned. When she grasped his buttocks, slamming into him with her pelvis, his face went like one of those clown's heads at the circus where you put the balls in the mouth to win a prize. If Norman played it right he could have his balls in Shelly's mouth before midnight. Now that would be an odd couple to have over for tea.

Herman and Helga were performing dance moves last seen in the nineteen fifties to a rap song. It actually looked pretty cool. When the track finished playing they got a round of applause from the crowd. Jack stood up and stretched his stiff legs. The damp of the coastal air and the cold were working their way through his layers of clothes; it was either dance or bed, and he didn't think he had reached the same levels of drunken euphoria as the other participants. Ryan would be alright. Smell had already left to find her bed, and Jack called out a goodnight to whoever was listening. Betty was leaving too, so he walked her to her ramp and kissed her on the cheek. Sensing his mood she patted his hand, 'Don't worry Jack, everything always works out the way it should,' and she walked up the plank before he could answer.

Jack lay in the hammock thinking about Rose. The evening hadn't been a total failure. She had talked to him. If Ryan hadn't interrupted...well, there was no use speculating where it might have led because he was in bed alone and they were out there having a good time.

Jack woke early and let Smell out before putting coffee on to brew in a small pot over the gas burner. The spare bed on the double berth was un-slept in, and he wondered how Ryan had spent the night. After a simple breakfast he went to help tidy up the debris left on the reserve.

The children were trying to resurrect the fire while tired looking parents took down lanterns and stuffed a rubbish sack with food scraps and paper napkins. Everything was damp from dew fall. Jack bundled the tablecloths into a bag for the laundry and folded down the trestle tables. One of the dads, Steve, gave him a hand carrying them over the road where they were stored in a shed belonging to the man who owned the house overlooking the harbour.

'So, who were the couple you were with last night?' the man asked as they walked back. He could only be meaning Ryan and Rose, Jack thought sadly.

'That would be Rose who just arrived, and Ryan my workmate, but I wouldn't say they're a couple. They only met last night.'

'Oh. Well, they did leave together, and they looked kinda close to me. I hope you're mate hasn't pipped you at the post, eh buddy? Don't ya hate that? She's a good looker, is Rose - but don't tell my wife I said that. All it takes is the wrong thing when she's had a bad day, or not enough sleep, or whatever, and I'm eating cold beans for dinner and sleeping on the floor. A lifetime commitment isn't always a comfortable experience but if you're careful then it just gets better and better. The early days are both the best and the worst.' Smug married bastard, Jack thought. It must be easy to talk like that when your future is settled. Ryan the old dog, eh? He didn't have to ask why Rose hadn't picked him. Still, the thought stung a little.

Jack wasn't surprised to see Ryan emerge from the *Skylark* at ten o'clock. He pushed the coffee pot back on the burner and waited.

Ryan wasn't looking too flash this morning, and said he felt like cow shit that's been run over with the tractor. He sat down and gratefully took the mug of coffee. 'Arrgh, why does feeling so good lead to feeling so bad?' Ryan groaned. He was such a sorry sight that Jack forgot his resentment.

'You sorry bugger. Well, at least one of us scored

last night.' Ryan's head rolled back and he perked up a bit.

'No! Who was it? You don't mean that weird thing with all the hair? Or was it the desperate young lady in the pink skirt with all the beads? I don't know which one was worse. Jack, tell me you didn't!' He looked seriously concerned for his friend. It took a moment for Ryan's words to make sense and when they did Jack laughed loudly.

'No you daft bugger, Christ no. I was meaning you. Didn't you just step off the *Skylark*?'

'Ahhh, I see what you mean. Unfortunately I was in no fit state to do the beast with two backs last night. I doubt Rose was either. I could really get used to living on a boat though; there's something so tidy about throwing up over the side. No toilet bowl to clean. The little fish....oh God, not again.' Ryan ran for the door and stuck his head over the rails. There goes the coffee, Jack observed.

'You were saying, mate?' Jack was almost enjoying this. Ryan looked sheepish.

'Can we talk about something else?' he pleaded, looking a bit green.

'How about some breakfast to settle your stomach?'

Half an hour later Ryan was full and feeling much better. The second coffee went down better than the first. 'I think Rose likes you Jack. She was asking plenty questions about you last night.'

'I was under the impression you were more her thing. You two seemed to get on alright last night.'

'Oh, we do! But not like that. There's no spark,

you know how I mean? She's too good looking for a brute like me. She came straight out with it when I was waiting for her to get changed on the boat, but I didn't get a chance to tell you. She's not one to muck a guy about. She said there was no way I had a chance of romancing her, but it would be nice to make a few friends. I suggested friends with perks, you know, just for the hell of it, and she said, no, friends who keep their testicles in their pants or wake up without any. I said that suits me fine, I like my testicles right where they are, and then we came to the party.'

'Ha. So what did she want to know about me then?'

'Just the usual. If you had a girl, how big your donga is...'

'Very funny.' Jack threw a wet dishcloth at Ryan, who used it to wipe the crumbs off the table, then lay back on the seat. 'I asked her if she fancied you and she denied it. I said, 'Why not,' and she said because good looking men are just trouble.'

'Did you put in a good word for me then?'

'No, I told her I wouldn't answer any more questions about you unless she admitted she liked you. Finally, around three in the morning she said *maybe* she did fancy you, but it's supposed to be a secret. She was going 'shhh shhhh shh,' so I fell asleep. *Love is in the air, every where I look around...*' Ryan sang teasingly. Jack laughed as a feeling of hope surged through him. He still had a chance after all.

When Smell barked to signal a stranger and Jack opened the door, he found Rose navigating the gang plank on all fours, still dressed in last nights clothes which looked slept in. He shook his head at the strange sight and asked, 'Do you need a hand?' Rose scowled at him and said, 'Yes. Now would be good, or do I have to beg?'

'Well, you're in the right position for it.' He shook his head laughing at her and stepped forward to help. 'Easy,' he cautioned, as she wobbled upright.

'I think I'm still drunk.' Rose clung to him like a limpet. 'I felt fine until I had to walk up the ramp, and then everything started spinning again. Could we just stop for a minute?' She was looking green about the gills and Jack was concerned she would topple them both off the ramp.

'Come on, I'll put you in the sick bay with Ryan.' He lifted her easily in his arms and felt her small bones pressing into him. He was reminded of holding a baby bird in his hands, fragile and helpless. He put her down carefully on the bench-seat beside Ryan, who was reclining with one arm over his eyes. Ryan peeked out from under his arm and grinned, 'Look at what the cat dragged in!'

All Rose said was, '*Shhhhh.*' Jack stood looking at the pair of them.

'Lucky one of us was being sensible last night, or you'd have no one to look after you. Rose, what you need is strong coffee.'

'I could smell it from the Terry. It was my motivation for getting here.'

While the two party animals lounged about

groaning and drinking all Jack's coffee he used the time to tidy up. His mood had improved, not just because there was a chance Rose liked him. It felt pleasant having people lazing about on the boat, even if the conversation was a little sluggish. Most weeks one of the other residents dropped in to have a yarn, but there wasn't anyone he was close to in the way he felt close to Ryan. Busting your guts together at work every day sped up a friendship, especially if there was a common element of discontent.

Ryan left early in the afternoon, and Jack went to see him off. 'Go for it mate!' Ryan encouraged, but Jack knew what he was doing now. He had a feel for the way he should approach Rose, and it wasn't going to be a rushed affair. That was fortunate because when he got back Rose was stretched out on the bench asleep. He left her a note saying he had gone to the shop, and put it with a packet of pain killers and a glass of water beside her. Smell could stay and keep an eye on things. Just to make sure she understood he knelt down and whispered, 'You stay here. Look after Rose, and be nice to her. I like this one a lot.'

At the 4square Mr Chin greeted Jack with a smile and a small bow. 'Hey Chin, how's business? Don't you ever take the weekend off?' Chin nodded, but Jack knew he didn't.

'Weekend good business. Rich man have weekend, Chin no rich.' He checked the price for dried noodles and said, 'Ah, you like noodle? Noodle good for think. Noodle run way when you wan catch him. Catch noodle, you smart!' He made a motion with his hand like trying to catch something with chop sticks. Jack walked the ten minutes back to the wharf, his thoughts occupied by this latest Wisdom of Noodle. It sounded a bit too deep for noodles. He stopped by his truck to see if his boots would be dry for tomorrow, and was shocked at the amount of rubbish in the cab. His first thought was what if Rose saw it? His second thought was why hadn't he noticed before it got this bad? He didn't know the answer to the second question, but he could do something about the first one.

Jack filled his hands with plastic wrappers, coffee cups, chopsticks, and tin cans which Ryan had thoughtfully crushed. The stuff on the floor was crusted with dry mud. He resisted the urge to cram it behind the seats, and made his way back and forth to the rubbish bin by the picnic table. With the junk gone the floor looked filthy, so he pulled out the mats and shook the worst off, wiped the dash with an oily rag, and decided it was better. By the time he'd stopped to wash the dust off his hands and face it was over an hour since he left, and he was anxious to check how his guest was doing.

When he arrived back Rose was still asleep, but was woken by the rustling packages as Jack put things away. A healthy glow had come back to her skin, making the crease-marks on her face white against pink cheeks. She sat up clutching her head. 'Are you aware you snore?' Jack teased. Rose stretched and yawned like a cat.

'Only when I'm drunk, and that doesn't happen often - for obvious reasons. What time is it?'

'Four o'clock. You slept for two hours. I'm making noodles and stir-fry for dinner if you want to stay.' This was a risky move, but Jack didn't want to be alone. Sunday afternoon with the prospect of work tomorrow and a long week ahead was always the low point in his week. In times like this he wished he could put a movie on and forget the world for a while, but everything on the boat ran on solar power apart from the gas cooker. A television would be luxury.

'Dinner sounds great. I'm starving. Would you mind if I went to freshen up and get my things sorted for the big day tomorrow? What time do we eat?'

'Sure, go ahead. Dinner will be ready in half an hour,' Jack answered casually, and pulled out a wok.

He was a pretty good cook in his own estimation. Simple, tasty food, nothing fancy, but that was Jack all over. If it took more than fifteen minutes to prepare you could forget it.

Rose left moving languidly, still groggy with sleep. Jack flicked on the radio and gave Smell a spontaneous hug. The most interesting woman he had met in years was going to have dinner with him on his boat! Jack couldn't stop grinning as he chopped vegetables and sautéed them in oil. He knew he would have to go carefully with Rose, but things were looking up. She hadn't jumped into bed with Ryan, and didn't want to. Like Betty said, she just needed time to realize he wasn't a player, and tonight he would be a gentleman.

Jack went to no extra effort to present the meal as more than a casual dinner with a friend. There was no cloth on the table, no candles, and definitely no flowers. He switched off the music as he saw her approach, and handed her a fork and a plate of steaming noodles without ceremony. 'Here, dig in.'

Over dinner he asked Rose about the kind of work she'd be doing for her brother come tomorrow. 'Well, that's the funny part,' Rose gave him a sly look. 'My brother has this strange attachment to oysters. He doesn't need to make a living, he's loaded, but he likes to think that growing a luxury food item gives him a certain cachet. He mixes with the wealthy crowd, and coming from a farming family meant he had to work hard at getting in. You need more than money in some circles, especially when you lack in social graces.'

'So your brother is an oyster producer? What are the odds? I thought he was a city man from what you said about the job. Which lease does he own?' Jack had almost let it slip that his brother was an oyster farmer too.

'Oh, he's a city man, he oversees the business from there. His manager does the actual day to day stuff. He exploits the biggest lease round here, but actually, you probably already know who he is. Terry. Terrence Shawe? Commonly known as 'Shorty' to his employees. When I told Ryan last night who my brother is he thought it was hilarious, though I don't get why.' Jack's mouth was hanging open, his fork full of noodles suspended in mid air.

He lowered it to his plate slowly.

'Did he tell you who we work for?' Jack's gaze was direct. He watched her carefully as she chewed and swallowed before answering. Since he'd started looking for clues on something amiss in the bay where the oysters were farmed, a red signal went off in his mind every time anything relative was mentioned. Right now his mind was on hyperdrive. At several thoughts a second he ran through any possible scenarios that might put Rose in the thick or thin of it, but nothing seemed plausible. If Shorty was playing his own game with Ross, then Rose turning up here wasn't much advantage. Shorty mustn't be much of a business man if he thought Jack would know any of Ross's plans. It had to be pure coincidence. To be sure, he would tell her how little he knew of Ross's objectives. If she pulled anchor he'd know there was more to it. Rose put her fork down, her plate was empty.

'No, he just laughed. I never got around to asking. Why?' There was nothing in her expression except happiness and slight puzzlement.

'Ryan and I work for a mate of his. Does the name Ross Sargent ring a bell?' This time her face registered understanding. So she knows the background then, Jack surmised.

'Ah. I see. That could be awkward. Well, what should we do? Does this mean we can't be friends?'

Jack suddenly felt like his simple life was taking another complicated turn. He knew Ross wouldn't like it if his workers were friends with Shorty's sister. The same probably went for Shorty. It could also make Ross more wary, and Jack needed to keep his trust for the moment, but, to be reasonable about it, life here wasn't exactly offering him much until now, so why should he let Ross ruin his chance of getting to know Rose?

'Stuff that. I don't know about you, but it's no bother to me. My loyalty is to my paycheck, not my boss. He's an alright sort, but working for him isn't a walk in the park. Half the time he's like a bulldog on acid.'

'That must be why they used to get along so well; Terry's like a rhinoceros on meth. I only agreed to take the job because he offered me stupid amounts of money, plus he begged. Look, I can't really un-meet you and Ryan, and his past is not my problem anyway. It's simple, we'll just have to talk about things that don't involve the company secrets of our employers. Can you handle that?'

'Hmm, let me see...not talking about work...yes, I can definitely handle that. As for secrets, that's easy, because Ross doesn't tell me anything except what he wants me to do that day. I can guess a few days ahead, but that's it.'

'Hang on. Didn't you say Ryan was a mate of your boss?'

'Kind of. They used to be tight, but since Ryan took the job it's gone sour. I'm fairly sure Ryan's loyalties are so eroded from the recent abuse that he won't say anything.'

'It's a deal. You tell Ryan and it's settled. Anything else would just be silly.' Rose stuck her hand out for a handshake. Jack was in such a rush to take it that he knocked over his glass of water, flooding the table. 'Oops!' Rose lowered her hand, cupping it along the edge of the table to collect the water that ran off. Jack grabbed a tea towel and wiped up the spillage, trying not to act like it was a big deal. What the hell is wrong with me? He cursed to himself. Be cool, be cool, don't be a dick.

'Thanks for dinner, Jack. It was delicious, but I should get some rest soon. I've got some stuff to get ready for tomorrow,' Rose stood up, 'and it sort of looks like I've pissed myself.' They both looked at her wet crotch, and Jack just couldn't help a small chuckle. 'Geez, I'm sorry. I didn't know it got you.'

'Never-mind. Night, Jack.'

'Maybe we can do it again sometime?'

'What? Wet my knickers? Oh no, that sounds *so* wrong. Teach me for trying to be a smart-ass. Um, so anyway, good night!' Jack watched Rose go up the plank to *Skylark* holding the front of her skirt bunched in her fist. It looked very much like she was smiling. 'What'd ya reckon Smell? Not a perfect score, but I think we passed.' But I nearly blew it, he added. I think she knows why I knocked the water over. Still too keen. I've got to work on my self-control. Yes. That packet of hazelnut chocolate I was saving for desert? Not having any. That'll teach me a lesson. No chocolate for me tonight.

He almost relented because it was too cruel, but self control had to start somewhere. Jack cleaned the kitchen and got his work clothes ready. Lastly, he brushed his teeth, but the feeling of virtue was diminished from not having eaten any chocolate first.

Chapter 6

On Monday Rose took a bus to the city where Terry had an office. He had offered her a car as part of the job, and she would collect it after work. The commute to the city was about an hour in light traffic, which meant an early departure. Rose didn't mind the distance; she was tired of the noise and dirt of city living. She would need to go clothes shopping soon; Rose hadn't brought much home with her on the plane, and what she had was too casual for office wear. Her old work wardrobe had cost thousands of pounds and she'd given every single piece to the charity shop. Anything that reminded her of the past five years was culled from her life.

At the same time that morning Jack and Ryan were heading half the distance in the opposite direction. They went over the events of the weekend; Ryan teasing Jack about Rose after hearing about dinner for two on his boat, and Jack protesting they were just friends. Ryan said it was the best party in ages. He still wasn't feeling one hundred percent despite a good night's rest. They agreed not to mention their new mate to the boss. Ryan said, 'If he keeps on being a prick I might just ask Shorty what his plans are this weekend.'

Ross was looking exceptionally chirpy this morning despite the grey clouds closing over the bay. 'How's your weekend?' he asked them, stirring coffee into dirty mugs. He signaled it was ready, and Jack almost choked on his first sip. The coffee was regular strength. Ross must be out of his mind with joy. The last time he'd slipped up like this was when Nancy took the kids off for a week of skiing, leaving him a freezer full of meals and a quiet house.

'I've got some good news,' he told them.

'You're going to have another kid?' Ryan asked.

Ross sprayed coffee over the concrete floor and swore, 'Fuck no. Why would that be good news? It wasn't good news last time. Look what you made me do with my coffee! But thank you for reminding me to make an appointment with Doctor Snip.' He shivered, shaking off the thought. 'The good news is we're expanding the operation. Our shareholders have agreed to the purchase of a new lease. From now on we'll only be using the old lease to put out bundles and catch spat. Next spring we'll undo the bundles and lay sticks out on the new lease when they're nine months old. Because it's up near the Heads the oysters will grow faster than in the bay, and won't have to compete for food with the other farm. The catch is as good as ever, but growth rate's down from two years ago. This way we can double our production. With no sticks being laid out in the bay, we can fit twice as many bundles on the farm. Everything we harvest will be from the Heads. It means we'll need another employee and a bigger barge.'

If he expected a round of applause from his workers they let him down; neither cared what happened next, though his improvement in temper prompted them to make grunts of approval and general good cheer.

Out on the water it was calm enough. A drizzle had started as they went out, but it wasn't windy and patches of blue sky hung about behind the hills. Despite the clement conditions and Ross's good humor, Jack felt uneasy. Some of the plans made good sense to Jack, but one thing bothered him. Why didn't Ross want any harvest oysters in the bay next season? There was no time to speculate now, he pushed away his thoughts and pitched in, already working up a sweat. A storm was forecast to hit tonight and they needed to bring in enough to keep them busy over the next two days in case it was too rough to go out.

When Jack and his companion followed the gravel road to work the next morning it was still blowing a gale. Last night Jack had been particularly grateful for the hammock. At a certain point in the road the vegetation was sparse enough to see the shore and a snatch of the bay. Ryan pointed out a couple of sticks which had come loose and stranded on the beach. 'Looks like someone will have to borrow the quad bike from Dave and go gathering. There's bound to be more.'

An unusual amount of sticks came loose every storm; Jack blamed Ross for not taking more care fixing the nails in properly, but Ross blamed the quality of the nails. He had purchased a huge bulk lot online from someone doing parallel imports from China, and he'd been chuffed with the price. He was beginning to think he'd been ripped off.

Ross left to Dave's and the men culled steadily,

working indoors out of the wind and sporadic rain that pelted the tin roof drowning out the radio.

Over the next week Ross pushed them to work faster. Space had to be cleared for more materials to arrive at the yard, and they needed to move last year's bundles out to the new lease and keep up the harvest cycle on the old lease. Ryan got his waders and everyone got new gumboots to wear with their aprons at the culling table. Broken equipment was gradually replaced but other things were broken again in senseless haste. Nothing on the farm lasted long. Jack didn't know anyone else who was so enthusiastic about fixing a broken machine by whacking it all over with a hammer. Ryan and Jack cursed Ross quietly as the champion of 'she'll be right' industry. For someone so outwardly careless he was annoyingly cagey in all other matters. Since there was nothing more Jack could discover for the meantime it was fortunate that he had a new distraction in life called Rose.

Rose had been welcomed into the small community of house-boaters, and Jack increased her circle of friends, introducing her to Connie at the restaurant and the regulars at the pub. Connie graciously accepted Rose, and the two immediately decided they liked the other. 'You know, if you ever gave up the kitchen you'd make a damn good journalist, Connie.'

'What? Me at my age? I don't think I've got enough stuffing left for that game. I may talk tough, but if I'm honest I think I'm heading for fluffy slippers and daytime tele after this. I've a proposition for you now, Rose. I'm sure you're a busy woman, but if you're interested in looking over the new online menu for me, see if anything needs tweaking, I'd be happy to offer you some free meals.'

'Sure, I'd love to. Call it a favour between friends.'

Jack was amazed at how easily they chatted. He had been afraid that there would be an undercurrent of mistrust between the two. It appeared that he had underestimated Connie's ability to move on from a lost cause.

The local pub Jack frequented was a different story. When Lara happened to turn up early for karaoke one night she wasn't at all pleased to see him with a woman. The look she gave Rose was enough to curdle milk, and to top it off she said to the room at large, 'Don't waste your time, honey. He only likes bitches.' This got a mixed reaction; there were a few who chuckled at the pun, several who looked wary, and a chorus of, 'Oi Lara, let the man alone.'

Rose asked Jack what was the problem with the loud, blond woman, and Jack felt it best to explain the full story of their uneventful night. 'You're full of surprises, Jack,' was all Rose had to say. Jack was pleased that she hadn't laughed at him for giving in to his dog. What had seemed like a disaster a few months ago now worked to his advantage; it proved he wasn't only a red blooded male who let lust rule his head.

There were plenty of suggestive looks and jokes being cracked about 'the love birds,' by the regulars at the bar but that was to be expected.

'Pipe down you old romantics. Rose and I are just friends. I'm helping her settle in. You might still have a chance if you behave,' Jack slapped one of them on the back.

'Or maybe I'm just not into men,' Rose smirked at them. This caused all sorts of lewd remarks and gwaufs

'S'alright with me if I can watch!' replied someone enthusiastically - but jokes aside, they were both aware that the more they saw each other the more they wanted to see each other again. Rose was friendly but wary, and Jack kept his distance though he'd ruled out any espionage since she never asked about his work. The rush of adrenalin and endorphins which flooded his body when Rose was near him were a high like any other drug, and he told himself to be careful. She might not want what he wanted, it wouldn't pay to get too carried away, and if she did, then easy does it. He wanted to know more about her, what made her tick, her past; but she never talked about past relationships or personal circumstances. She was proud of being self reliant; but he wondered why she needed to be. A woman like Rose attracted men to her without meaning to, so why was she single? He turned to the only person he knew that gossiped more than a fishwife.

If you weren't in need of a trim, you could always pop in on Rex after five or six o'clock with a bottle of something for a chat. Rex didn't see it as part of his duty to filter information, in fact, a small dose of gossip was part of the service. A barber didn't sign a confidentiality contract, and if you didn't know his reputation to start with you soon found out. He believed that if he'd heard it then it was already out there. To be fair, Rex always warned first time customers that what was said in the chair wouldn't stay in the chair, unless it was explicitly requested.

Jack poured him a glass of merlot, Rex's favourite, and asked him what he knew about Rose. It was three weeks since the *Skylark* had been moored next to Jack, and the time had come to decide where the friendship was heading. There was only so much chocolate he was willing to deny himself.

'Well, let's see. Betty said she's a real sweetie, but nobody's fool. Amanda goes to her yoga class at the hall and thinks she's very grounded. Merv said he remembers her Dad.; when he got sick they moved away to be near the mother's family, and put the farm up for lease. They sold some other land to help them make a new life in the city, and it was worth a fair bit by then. Rose would have been an infant. Dave the shepherd said Shorty, her brother, owns a very tidy parcel of land beside the oyster farm. Who else? Ah yes, Sonny did the tyres on her car and said he was surprised at her amount of car knowledge. She explained about picking up a few things from her last boyfriend. He was a race car champion in England. She didn't have anything good to say about him. Oh, and she's a Virgo. Birthday: 3rd September.

'Rex, you are a marvel. How'd you get her birth date?'

'Took a peek at her file. Had a feeling you might visit me. Age can be a man's friend, Jack.' Rex rested a hand on Jack's shoulder and spoke quietly, 'I like to think I'm a better man now than I was before, but it also makes you less flexible. I love Betty, but I couldn't change any more for her than she could for me. We met young enough, but by the time we realized we had those sort of feelings for each other we were too set in our ways,' Rex shrugged. 'Betty helped me to come to terms with my past, but it still haunts me. That's why I drink; to give me a break. Mostly I'm not aware of my thoughts, I just get these moods when some part of me is hurting, and then I need to drink. Less than before, but still... So when I see a lovely young couple like you and Rose I can't help thinking - you've got all you need to make a good future together. It's obvious you're a good match, and if I can help to bring you together then I will. Betty feels the same. Passing on a bit of information is nothing. You still have the hard work to do, but I've no doubt you're up to the challenge.'

Rose was passionate about her job, and was often a presence at her brother's side in the city. She took care of events where his oysters were presented, and worked on new logos and packaging, as well as the website. She had shown Jack the work in progress on her laptop and he'd been impressed with her skills. After only a month on the job Rose had a lot to show for it. Jack thought it was a good moment to ask some questions. 'So how come you're back here working for your brother?'

'Because things didn't work out for me overseas and life is too short to hold grudges.'

'So who have you forgiven lately?'

'Well, it's certainly not the slime ball I thought I'd be married to a year ago, if that crossed your mind. I'm sure the story is common knowledge by now.' Jack nodded confirming it was. 'So I went to Switzerland, stayed six months with a friend in the Alps, then Terry rang and said he needed me, and I decided to forgive him.'

'Go on.'

'Really? Okay, it's a bit embarrassing even if it was ages ago. I had this boyfriend, we met at uni. He was top of the class studying politics. We decided to take a year out, do some traveling. So, tickets booked, we go round to Terry's for dinner. Terry starts banging on about how he wants to run for city mayor but can't find a good strategist to help him win. I went to bed and left them talking. At breakfast Terry says he hopes I can get a refund on the tickets because he's just hired my boyfriend as his campaign manager. Three months later I flew out alone.'

Jack whistled through his teeth.

'Yep, my brother stole my boyfriend.'

'Remind me to thank him sometime.' Rose punched him lightly on the shoulder.

'When you're young that sort of betrayal really galls - but you're right, he did me a favour.'

'So, how does the story end? Did Terry run for mayor?'

'That's the stupid bit. Three months later he pulled the plug on the whole idea and bought an oyster farm. Jason rang me to say he was sorry, and could he join me. He could catch the next flight. I told him my new boyfriend wouldn't like that much and hung up. I was bluffing, but it sure felt good.'

'And the man who did the dirty on you? Am I allowed to ask?'

'It's a long, boring story. Are you sure you want to know the sordid details?'

'Sure, I've got no place else to be.' Jack was confident that Rose liked him, but he remained in limbo, waiting for her to give him a signal of some sort to say she wanted more from him. Until that happened he made sure he behaved the same way he did with any other mate.

'Ok. So I had a great job working for a big company in London. After three years I was promoted to assistant manager, so my wages were good. I dated a few men, but nothing serious. I wanted to establish myself in a new country before getting too involved with anyone. You know how it is? Otherwise you end up with all his friends and none of your own, and if it all goes wrong then you have to start again with zero.' Jack was in a relaxed mood so he forgave her for not cutting to the heart of the story, and settled into his chair. When a woman said it was a long story, they meant it.

'Go on.'

'So, then we landed this big contract with a motor sports company. Since I was senior management I got to pitch to the client, and they liked my ideas.

That's when I met their rising star, Marcus Riddel. He was a bit older than me, but I liked the idea of a man with maturity. Honestly, some of the men my age were still playing video games.'

'Handsome, was he?' Jack said this without any angst. The women in his past who had tried to use jealously as a tool of entrapment were disappointed. He had felt jealousy, but it lacked the force to turn him against himself; because that's all it amounts to, self destruction.

'Yes. Quite. That was why the company who sponsored him wanted his face on their product. He was also a smooth talker too, good at flattering people, finding their strengths and pretending to overlook the flaws. Anyway, I fell for him. We had a lot of fun when he wasn't away competing, and sometimes I went with him. I saw most of Europe on these trips, one thing I don't regret, but it began to bug me that he was always short of cash when it was time to pay the hotel bill or dinner at a gastronomic restaurant.'

'Why was he short of money? Don't those racing car drivers get paid tons?'

'Yes. They are very well paid, but when I brought it up he told me that big money was new to him, and he was struggling to manage it sensibly. He would do outrageous things, like buy me diamond earrings, or send a hundred red roses to my office. Marc said he'd grown up poor and now he was making up for it. I believed everything he said. He moved into my apartment after two years, and never paid a single bill. I didn't care; I was in love. It was only money and I earned enough. It seemed churlish to begrudge him. He knew I grew up in a wealthy family, and played on my social guilt. I had a great bunch of mates, and they started asking questions. Hadn't Marc had enough time to adjust to his new life? Shouldn't he have someone managing his finances? How long was I prepared to let it go on with him living off me? Did I think about kids or marriage? It wasn't just my girlfriends who were asking, so I started really thinking about it.'

'Did you have it out with him?'

'Not straight away. I knew something needed to be done, but I was afraid of losing him. Women are always told that pushing for commitment is risky. Besides, I thought if it didn't come from him then it wouldn't *mean* anything. I dropped a few hints, but he already knew how I felt and he ignored me.'

'So how did it end?' Jack couldn't believe a man could be stupid enough to let Rose get away when she was offering up her future.

'It ended because I finally got fed up. I proposed to him, and said it was make or break time. He agreed to marry me, but wanted to get his finances straightened out etc etc, meaning not straight away. But I wanted to start planning it, sort of surprise him. Not make bookings or anything, just do the ground work. So, I took our identity documents to the registry office and asked for a marriage license. They told me he was already listed as married.'

'That must have been a bad moment.'

'The worst. I don't know how I would have got home if a friend hadn't come to pick me up. Anyway,

I confronted Marc when he came home and the truth came out. He separated from his wife after he met me, and was filing for divorce. They have two kids. He was paying the mortgage on the family home and supporting them financially. He was also spending time living there when he said he was away racing if I couldn't come. A lot of stuff started to make sense. The trips where I wanted to join him that were suddenly canceled, that sort of thing. So I packed two suitcases and sold everything else to my replacement at work who was moving from Devon. I spent six months at a friend's chalet in the Swiss Alps. In the village they have a special health spa. I spent most of my time at the spa trying to work through all my anger and grief. Then I got Terry's call, and felt like it was time to come home.'

Jack wasn't sure how to respond. What he wanted to do was hold her and tell her how sorry he was that she'd suffered, but if he did, he might not be able to help himself from stepping over the boundaries of friendship. He tried to frame a question - So, how are you placed emotionally towards men now? - but it was too obvious. Time would tell.

'I'm sorry for your troubles, Rose. I can't imagine how hard it was for you to leave everything you'd built up. Do you miss it?'

'Parts of it. Friends, mostly. Travel. I miss being able to jump on a plane and go to Greece, or Rome, or France for the weekend. But realistically, if things had of worked out as I thought I'd be knee deep in nappies and nipple cream; travel wouldn't have been on the cards.'

'I know it's not much to offer, but I'm glad you came back.' The minute it was out he regretted it. Not only was it corny, it gave him away.

'Ah, shucks.' Rose blushed slightly, a sudden bloom on her cheeks which faded a moment later.

Jack looked forward to the end of each day when he might see a little red Peugeot in the parking lot, and lights on inside the cabin beside his. Sometimes Rose would stay in the city if meetings ran late, and on those occasions Jack would fret that some big, swanky hot-shot would charm her away. There was nothing about her or her past that concerned him anymore, and Jack waited for the right moment to make his feelings known. He hoped he wouldn't be making a fool of himself, because he couldn't remember being this infatuated with a woman for a very long time.

'Come on bro, when are you gonna give that Rose a go?' Ryan prodded him as he drove the truck to work. Jack shook his head.

'It's not always about a quick poke, mate. She's special.' He changed the subject. Ryan didn't do deep, and all Jack's feelings were complex at the moment. Finally he knew what it was to fall in love. He chewed his bottom lip and thought what a great word 'smitten' was. He wasn't tempted to share this thought with Ryan who'd be sure to tell Rose and stuff up the ground work Jack was putting in.

'What you need is a girlfriend so you can stop worrying about my lack of one. What do you think this new bloke will be like? You know him?'

'No idea. He answered the ad in the paper, and he's not from the club, but neither are you, and you're alright.'

'That's mighty kind of you, Ryan. Do you know the first question Ross asked me when I turned up?'

'Let me guess...do you play rugby?' Jack laughed.

'You got it. If I'd said 'Yes' it would have been a shorter interview. I had to play up my seamanship skills and tell him about all the hard yakka I'd done on fishing trawlers.'

'Yep, I can believe it.'

There was a young Maori guy sitting in the shed drinking a coffee when they arrived. He was darker than Ryan whose great grandmother had been Maori. Ryan kept a golden tan even in winter, but his hair was a light sandy colour like Jack's and his eyes bright blue. He had wide, full lips and a big nose which was broken and reset crookedly, but that was common amongst rugby players.

The younger man was dark skinned and dark eyed; finely carved features neatly spaced over strong bones, and cheeks that bunched up and dimpled when he smiled. He looked like mischief. Girls liked that look, they thought it was cute. The question was, could Mr Cute work? Jack didn't want to go out with him, he wanted a man who made life easier for the rest of them, who didn't come with a bag of attitude - Ross was monopolizing it all.

The man jumped up and pumped their hands

quickly. 'Gidday yous fellas, I'm Tyrone.'

'Gidday,' they said in unison. He was wearing what Jack called 'trendy' clothes, and several rings on his fingers. He had one ear pierced and long hair tied back. He didn't look like the sort who did labour. Ah heck, Jack thought, I hope he's only on trial.

'Tyrone, this is Jack and Ryan, your new workmates.' Ross gave the introductions. The men sipped appreciatively at their coffees, which were made properly in honor of the new guy.

'So you been in these parts long?' Ryan asked.

'Nah nah, just moved here from Coromandel. All my family's from there, my whakapapa. Met my missus at this choice as party at this fullas place? About three months ago? And she arksd me to come live with her up here. I was like 'only if you cook me eggs for breakfast every day,' ha ha ha I love eggs eh. I bin here three weeks an there's no work, eh, so when I saw the ad, I was like choicceee!'

As he talked his head bobbed and jerked about like a boxer doing warm up. He had fine, handsome features and he smiled a lot.

'So you had eggs this morning?' Ross asked.

'Nup. She said I'll get eggs when I got a job to pay for them. So guess what? I'm having eggs tomorrow. Hey yous should come round, have some kai. My missus can cook mean eggs.'

'What sort of work you done?' Jack asked him.

'Ooor, you know, mostly just farm stuff? Scrubbing, fencing...and on the mussel barge, too.'

Ross finished his coffee and checked the clock.

'Time to work, boys! You might need some of these big guns today.' He pushed up his sleeves and flexed his biceps, giving them a kiss.

If Ross had a motto it would be 'Pussys go home.' Jack contemplated having a t-shirt made for him, but that would be encouraging his masochist streak, which Jack didn't even joke about. No one had ever said to Ross, 'Yeah! Let's work our guts out!' not even to take the piss. He'd think you meant it.

Ross took Ryan and the new guy out to the harvest, and left Jack making up bundles. For the next two hours Jack used the nail gun to bundle the sticks together. The bundles were made of twenty four sticks with bits of wood between to separate each one. This was what the baby oysters would land on and attach themselves to. When the spat reached a size between two and six millimetres the bundles were undone and laid out one by one on the rails. They would be roughly five months old by then. This gave them room to grow, preventing a hiding place for predators like Flat Worm, and increasing the water flow carrying nutrients.

Like most farm work making bundles was tiring, repetitive, and required all of Jack's attention. Let your mind wander too far from the job and you'd be wondering how come there was a nail sticking out of your foot. Wasn't it funny how you came to appreciate small reprieves in life? It wasn't exactly what you'd call 'fun,' but it sure beat doing any job with Ross on your case.

He observed the men as they came walking back from the tide a few hours later. The way they walked said so much about them. Ross walked fast and steady, head up, scanning the yard. Ryan clumped his feet and went slowly, eyes down, daydreaming; and Tyrone concentrated in lifting one foot at a time and propelling it forward, his torso leaning towards the ground as what was left of his energy fought off gravity.

Tyrone was wearing Ryan's old friends, the spare, leaky waders, and he looked shattered. Gone were the quirky mannerisms and joking camaraderie, the tide had whittled him down to basic functioning. Yes, this work took some adjusting to. No doubt he would collapse into bed at six o'clock tonight in a tidal wave of exhaustion.

By the end of smoko the three original crew were stunned to see Tyrone perk up and start with the wise cracks again. He swaggered off for a leak and Ross grinned, 'You Maori buggers sure know how to bounce back.' Jack saw Ryan's shoulders stiffen and watched for any sudden movement. He didn't like confrontations even if the boss had it coming to him. It wouldn't be nice being caught between two tough nuts, but he would be. Jack was the peace keeper. As the only person who could keep a cool head around Ross he saw it as part of his job to diffuse whatever he couldn't prevent.

Ryan didn't identify much with his Maori ancestry because neither of his parents had much to say about it. It was a non issue in their home. A large portrait hung in the lounge of their ancestor, a beautiful but severe looking woman. There were always cousins and relatives staying, Maori and

Pakeha, but no one sang waiata or talked about iwi. The family considered themselves as an average kiwi family of mixed descent; as much Irish or Welsh as anything else. They once went to the tangi of a great aunt and had been awed by the amount of formality and the intricate customs belonging to their tribe. Ryan's father had never met half of the family that came forward to hongi with them, and hadn't been on the marae since his mother's death many years before.

On the long drive home when his parents thought the children were asleep, Ryan heard his father say, 'I used to feel angry and ashamed being part Maori because I didn't understand what it meant. Mum never spoke about the old people or the old ways, and I thought it was from shame, but I was wrong. I think she wanted to protect us, to raise us as good Christians, not Maori or Pakeha. She liked church because God said we are all equal on earth and she believed that. I'm proud of my heritage, but I don't want to carry it on my back. Do you understand, honey?'

At school Ryan's parents had let him choose what cultural studies he would do, and he had joined the kapahaka group for a short time before giving it up for rugby. He didn't feel serious enough about it compared with the other boys and he was only tolerated for his good humor. He wasn't cut out to be a warrior. That didn't mean he tolerated racism, especially from someone who treated him like hired machinery instead of a mate. There were plenty of men who would rather walk out on a job than listen to that sort of talk, but Ryan let it go. In the shed at work Jack managed to catch Ryan's eye and raised his eyebrows in question - 'you okay?' Ryan nodded and went outside.

Beneath Ryan's laid back nature Jack suspected that slow to fire, when he did lose control he'd be very hard to stop. He hoped it never came to blows between Ross and Ryan; it would be messy. One was fast and ruthless, the other slower but powerful. If Ryan landed one you wouldn't know what day it was.

Driving home Ryan told Jack that he'd missed something funny out at the tide. 'We were pulling sticks off the rails, right? And Ross and I pulled at the same time. Whole bloody rail collapsed, mate! You should have seen the look on his face. So we had to pull the rest off under water, him carrying on about how it must'a been that guy last year who patched up the farm crooked.'

'He didn't blame the nails then?'

'No. Reckons those ones were standard supply, and then he checks the whole row and it's all loose. Nails coming loose from the posts. Must have been that storm.'

It wasn't unusual for an old farm to drop the occasional rail, but generally it was in good repair. Every year when the harvest tailed off they would spend some time patching up anything broken or weak. Posts were left to rot into the mud and a new one added alongside, because trying to dig them out was a big ask; once the mud got hold of them it held on tighter than Tyrone off to take a crap. The penguin walk, they called it.

Daylight was slowly stretching out, so it was light when Jack came home in the evenings. Kowhai trees were dripping with gold, their flowers bringing the native birds down to the shore for nectar. More often than not Jack took Smell for a walk along the coast and sometimes Rose would join them, picking bunches of wild freesia for her table. One evening she paused and turned to face him. 'I probably shouldn't tell you this, since you work for the competition, but the real reason Terry hired me is to help launch his new restaurant. I can tell you now since it will soon be common knowledge. I'm preparing a piece for the press this week.'

'What's it called, this new place?'

'Tide to Table. It's a seafood restaurant in the city.'

'That's pretty funny. I am already aware that your brother has a sense of humor.' He told her the story about the broken outboard, and Shorty's delight at witnessing them in compromised positions.

Jack wished he could say his real reason for coming here. He argued with himself that there wasn't really anything to support his case, he'd look like a failure. If there ever was evidence Joshua would have to be the first to know. Instead he offered, 'Well, Ross just took on a new lease out of the bay. Seems like our bosses are both expanding. Has Sh- Terry heard?'

'Yup. Someone he knows at council rang him while we were in a meeting. I heard an earful about that. Terry was quite pissed off. He was hoping to see Ross go under, and here he is expanding. Everyone thinks they fell out over this production technique Ross developed, but there was a personal issue as well. There was a woman involved. He was especially hurt by some of the things Ross said when he left, but all he'll tell me is he was called a 'fat cunt who couldn't keep a goldfish.' Terry doesn't like to be called fat either. He *is* a bit roundish, he's always been that shape. Then Ross moved into the bay. I think that was quite provocative, don't you? Why choose a lease in the same bay as a person you have an issue with? Terry used to worry that Ross would try underhand tactics to muck up the farm, but nothing happened. This new lease has him worried all over again, though I don't know why.' She glanced at him inquiringly.

'I can't answer that for you. I can never guess what Ross will do next. He never mentions the past or Terry, which is strange. I'd expect him to slag Terry off every chance he gets. I know he's preoccupied by it. I've seen him stop and stare out at the water grinding his teeth. He does that when he's pissed about things, the grinding. He just stares at the farms and grinds his teeth, but I don't know what he's thinking, except I doubt he's forgiven Terry. If I was your brother I'd be keeping an eye on him. He's unpredictable and clever.'

'What are you saying? Do you think Ross is waiting for a chance to ruin Terry? Should we be counting the oysters or something?'

'Yes. No. I don't know...Terry's right not to be

complacent about him, that's all.'

'Jack? Would you tell me if you thought there was something fishy going on?' This time Jack didn't hesitate to answer. 'Yes, I would.' Rose smiled.

'Good. That's enough shop talk. Last one back to the boat cooks dinner!' Smell Hound loved this game, and even though she was old she could still outrun her clumsy humans. Jack could tell she liked Rose. She didn't bark when Rose came to call on them.

Betty and Jack had been invited to Rose's boat for dinner, so whether she won or lost the race, Rose was cooking anyway. Terry had given her a bag of his oysters and two dozen scallops which she couldn't eat all on her own.

Rose had adopted Jack's method of cooking most dinners in a wok. Now she threw the scallops in and drenched them in whisky before setting them on fire by tilting the wok into the gas flames. Next she added three bunches of Chinese cabbage and left it to simmer. Once the greens were blanched she added a crack of pepper, a hunk of blue cheese, and cream.

Betty arrived with white wine which she put on the table. Rose had covered the formica table top with a cloth and added a candle and the freesias she had gathered along the banks. The flowers and candle were both making do with old jam jars as holders, but the effect was pretty. 'Oh, doesn't this look lovely! But Rose dear, are you sure I'm not intruding? I mean I'm very flattered you invited me, but well, I don't want to be a third wheel or anything...'

'No! No, Betty. Um, actually, I would rather you were here. I like Jack, a lot. He's great but...it's starting to feel a bit awkward. I keep waiting for something more to happen, and it's been weeks now and nothing. I know I was a bit standoffish to start with, but we get along so well and I thought...I am getting to the point where I'm wondering if he's even interested! Maybe I got the wrong idea.' Rose sighed and sat down.

Betty had seen this coming. The amount of time Jack and Rose spent together had to mean there was a mutual attraction, and there was much speculation amongst the residents about why nothing had developed from it yet. Betty thought it would have been Rose, taking her time deciding, so she was flummoxed to hear this confession.

'Oh, I think there's no doubt he wants you. I've never seen Jack in the whole time he's been here pay so much attention to anyone as he does to you. He looks happier too, but have you considered that Jack might be a bit intimidated by you? Don't misunderstand me Rose, it's just that you're such an independent wee thing, and you don't sit around waiting for things to happen, you just get on with it.'

'You think I've scared him off?'

'Not quite. More like he's waiting for you to get on with it. He thinks you'd let him know if you wanted more. We all know you had a terrible time with the last man, the driver. He might be unsure if you're ready. It's all very well flirting, but he might need something more direct. Have you mentioned your feelings at all? I think you would make him a very happy man if you did.'

'Hmmm, I suppose you're right. You remember the first time we met? I haven't caught him looking at me the way he did then, and now I wish he would. He's always so guarded. I'm completely over Marc, but I didn't want Jack to think I was being pushy or desperate, so I waited.'

They heard footsteps outside and a gentle knock on the door. Jack removed his boots and greeted them both warmly. He pulled a package from behind his back and passed it to Rose, whose mouth dropped open at the unexpected gift. 'Happy birthday!' Betty and Jack shouted together. Betty also took a present from her bag and placed it on the table.

'How did you know? I didn't tell a soul!' exclaimed Rose.

'Well, dear, you know the form you had to fill out when you came here?' Betty said with a cheeky grin.

Rose unwrapped her presents. From Betty a colourful silk scarf, and from Jack a hand blown glass vase with swirls of yellow, cream, and pale violet; the colours of the wild flowers she liked to pick. Rose thanked them both kindly, and poured the wine. Jack shucked the oysters for starters, but didn't eat any himself.

Betty began the dinner raising her glass in a toast, 'To Rose, the loveliest flower of all.'

As they ate Jack let his gaze wonder. This was the first time he had been on the Terry for long enough to really look around. It was homely without being overdone; he took in the details - old family photos, some bright cushions on the seats, and fresh grass mats on the floor. The smell of flowers and seafood. Jack looked closer at the black and white snapshots of the young family. Rose was gangly as a youth before she filled out. The sister and mother were strikingly similar in looks, and taller than Rose. The father was a short, stocky man, and little Terry was so fat his eyes were almost hidden behind pillows of skin. He had his father's short build and stocky frame and was the only person holding food in three of the five photos.

After they had finished eating Jack cleared away the plates and washed up at the small sink. Betty yawned and said she needed an early night, and when Jack and Rose protested she pretended not to hear. That was the beauty of old age, you could be as obstinate as you liked and no one could stop you. As she left she gave Rose a meaningful look, which Rose had no trouble understanding.

Jack and Rose sat down to finish the bottle of wine. They were both drinking more than usual, using Rose's birthday as an excuse, but really there was a bad case of nerves going round. There was a moment when neither of them said anything and then both of them tried to talk at once. The candle flame made the deep brown of Roses's eyes shine, and suddenly Jack knew what to do. Talk was all they had done for the past two months, about everything in life except their feelings for each other.

Jack's body craved physical contact. He wondered if it was possible to go mad with desire. Spending all his days outside tuned him to the greater rhythms of nature; the strong light of spring was stimulating vigorous growth on the land and in the water. He felt like a tree whose sap begins to rise after a winter sleep, and Rose was the light that called him. His body moved with its own intentions and this time he let it. Thought was a pitiful thing, suddenly weak compared to his body's wisdom. His heart thumped in his chest as he leaned over the table, seized Rose's face in both hands and kissed her mouth, shaking in an effort to be gentle. Rose drew back and came around the table to meet him. Jack's eyes were locked on hers, uncertain until she smiled. This time it was Rose who reached up to cup Jack's face and pull his head down to kiss him. It was like a bomb going off. They pulled at clothing on themselves and each other, struggling to remove it without releasing hold of the other person, lips locked like magnets. Rose didn't imagine that quiet, careful Jack could be so full of passion.

Half an hour later they stopped and let go, Rose stepping over the strewn clothes to make a cup of tea while Jack tidied himself up. He looked at the disorderly mess and laughed, 'Look what you made me do. This isn't my style at all.' Rose carried a tea tray back to the bed. 'No? Then maybe it's time you found a new style, because I definitely liked it.'

'So, was there something you wanted to say earlier?' Jack asked cheekily.

'Not anymore. Just what took you so long?'

'Oh man. Alright, you've got one minute to grill me before it's my turn. I wanted you to trust me first.'

'Good answer, but why tonight?'

'I was waiting for the right moment, and today is your birthday, and...ah, I might have overheard the last part of your conversation with Betty.'

'Ah. So do you think I'm pushy or desperate?'

'Sadly, no. You couldn't have held out this long if you were. Time's up!'

'That was never one minute!' But it was too late. Jack was already pulling her back down to him. 'What about your turn?' Rose resisted momentarily.

'This is my turn,' Jack replied, 'and you're wasting precious seconds.'

'Well, buddy, you'll be pleased to know things are happening with Rose.' Jack and Ryan were culling oysters while Ross and Tyrone were out at the tide.

'Finally. I don't know how you lived with the tension.'

'Easy. Slam it in the drawer a couple of times, works a treat.'

'Oh fuck that,' Ryan laughed. 'I'd rather sleep on the kick-stand.'

'You know, I wonder if I shouldn't introduce you to Connie. You know who she is right?'

'Yeah, she's not bad looking, but nah. I'm saving me-self now I've seen true love's work - and she reminds me of my auntie; it would just be too weird.'

'And there's me thinking you didn't have morals.'

Ryan picked up an oyster with a sea squirt attached and fired it at Jack who leaned back, the spray hitting his apron.

A new barge had arrived last week on the deck of a truck, brand spanking new and equipped with all the latest hydraulics. No one except Ross had been allowed to steer it yet. Most of the bundles were made up and ready to go on the farm come summer, which was creeping up fast. It was t-shirt weather but not quite singlet season, and some days there was still a nip in the air. They had been laying out last years catch on the Heads lease for the last two weeks, and despite Tyrone's propensity to tire after a big job, he always bounced back quickly. He didn't pay much attention to detail so he needed monitoring, which fell to Jack, but no one could shut him up. He was even immune to Ross shouting at him.

'Did you see that mean movie last night about the guy who goes to prison and it was that other guy what done it? Awe. That part where that guard comes in an like, wastes him, eh. He's like, all bleeding an shit, and then he does that move eh. Weeyoopah!'

'Hey, Karate Kid, put a sock in it,' someone would suggest.

'Oh, you didn't see it? Okay, what about this then; if you could choose to be a black belt of any martial art, what one would you pick?'

'I'd pick 'Soo Kin Yu,' Ryan answered.

'What? Did you just make that up? I haven't heard of it. Sounds stink.'

'Oh, sorry, the full name is 'I Can Shut Up, Soo Kin Yu.' I'm not surprised you don't know it.'

'Uuuww! Big man makes a wise crack. Well, if it was me I'd be....' and on and on he went until Jack turned the music up soo loud they couldn't hear him. Tyrone didn't care, he would get so caught up working on his dance moves that he'd put harvest oysters in with the grow-ons and put grow-ons in the rubbish pile. Jack would check over his work, and tell him to stop messing around but it never lasted long.

The unexpected thing was the relationship between Ross and Tyrone. They bonded over bad jokes. When Ross told his jokes Tyrone would crack a fit like he'd never heard anything so funny. Soon Ross was running through the back catalogue; 'Hey Ty, what's a blond's favourite ice cream?'

'Ah, dunno.'

'Hope he pokes me.' Cue hysterical laughter. If Ross yelled at Tyrone he would cock a leg and fart, saying, 'Yes! Boss!' like he was in some Monty Python army. Since the boss figured nothing had any effect, he gave up trying. If they fell behind schedule Ryan and Jack got the blame.

'I can't believe that little shit gets away with it just because he's too young to have heard those jokes,' Ryan complained. There was plenty of analysis between Jack and Ryan on the drive home each day, and they found it easier to face work having agreed that Tyrone was a tit, and Ross a loose unit. At least, they had that small comfort until Tyrone stuffed that up too.

'Hey mate, how's it going? All set for work?' It was six o'clock in the morning and Jack was on his second coffee.

'Yeah, Ross, all good.'

'Hey ah, I was wondering if you could give Tyrone a lift to work.'

'Sure. What's up? Car trouble?' Tyrone didn't have Jack's number so he would have called Ross.

'Ahh, yeah, it might be for a while. He got his license taken off him by the cops last night.'

'Ah heck. Drunk?'

'Yeah. He says they pulled him over because he's a Maori, but he was probably speeding or something. So is that alright?'

'Sure, no problem.' Jack hung up. Great. Just what he needed, a gas-bag in the ute twice a day. Not only did they have to spend all day listening to him, now they'd have to listen to him all the way there and all the way back, every day. This was a shit arrangement, but he couldn't really refuse. They couldn't do without a fourth man with the new lease to stock.

Jack collected Ryan first and then found his way to Tyrone's house. It was all the way over the other side of town so he'd be leaving for work fifteen minutes earlier every day. Ryan wasn't too happy either. He was comfortable with their morning routine, bitching about the boss and trying to guess the plan for the day ahead. They couldn't carry on like that with the youngest member of the team with them; it would undermine Ross and they did have some work ethics.

'Cheers for the ride, bro,' Tyrone said jumping into the cab. 'I wasn't meant to be our sober driver last night, 'cos I was pissed, eh! But my mate didn't come to get us, and I didn't wanna be stuck all night at this other fullas place,' or so the story went. 'The cops pulled me up and I was like 'Oh, yes officer?' Tyrone demonstrated his innocent face. 'And he was like 'show me your license,' so I pulled out my wallet and this tinny falls out, and I'm like 'farrk!' 'cos my mate must have put it there, eh, but the pig didn't see it and he goes, 'blow into this,' and...'

Jack and Ryan stared straight ahead, trying to tune out the bullshit. The road to work seemed much longer than usual. The radio didn't get reception out here and the tape player was broken, so they were forced to listen. Jack visualized stuffing his unwashed work socks into Tyrone's mouth, and felt a bit better.

Ross announced at smoko he had a meeting in town that afternoon, and was leaving Jack in charge. Jack supposed that now he had people with money invested, these meetings would be a regular occurrence every few months. The men concerned would want to see what their money was doing.

'Think you can handle it?' Ross asked.

'No problem, boss,' Jack said with confidence. They needed to take the new barge out to the Heads, the old one being too small and unreliable on the open water. Jack took Ross's place at the controls since he was the only one ticketed to handle a vessel out of the bay. Everyone worked hard, including Tyrone, and they finished sooner than Ross had calculated. It was amazing what a little encouragement could do for morale. Afternoon smoko was early, with Jack instructing Tyrone on proper coffee making procedure. 'Wash the cups properly, rinse them, likewise the dirty teaspoon, now *two* teaspoons of coffee per cup, sugar and milk for those who want it, and give it a stir. Now you add the hot water.'

'Ohh, Ross told me you like it weak. He showed me how to make everyone's coffee last week, remember?'

'I bet. Maybe I feel like something stronger today, and so does my mate Ryan. Hey, Ryan, you see Ross here?'

'Nah, he's gone.'

'See? We won't tell on ya.'

'Just make the coffee would ya? I'm parching over here,' Ryan shouted across the room.

'Hey, since we finished all the work do we get to knock off early?' Tyrone piped up. 'Or we could go for a fish! Get us a big snapper for tea.'

'Just because I take liberties with the instant coffee doesn't mean I slack off. I don't think Ross would like to come back to a messy yard and us out having fun, would he? We'll clean this place up.' Tyrone sighed and got the milk from the fridge, opening and shutting the door quickly to keep in the smell. It had worsened lately. Jack wouldn't be surprised if the smell had tainted the milk. It was long overdue a clean and he knew exactly the man for the job.

After the break Jack sent Tyrone into the kitchen to wash the dirty dishes and clean out the fridge. Some of the food in there had melted into a brown sludge. It had been here longer than Jack. Once Tyrone was out of sight Jack pulled Ryan aside.

'I need to use the toilet, can you make a start on the yard and keep Tyrone busy while I'm gone?'

Last week he'd had beers with Dave and told him about the pump cutting out while Ross was away. Without asking, Dave pulled a key off its ring and slid it along the bar to Jack saying, 'You might as well have this one, in case it happens again. I don't have a use for it.' As easy as that the break Jack was waiting for had happened.

Jack ran to the house and skirted around the side. Nancy should be picking up her kids from town about now, but he poked his head around the corner and checked her car wasn't in the drive just to be sure. This must be how it felt to be a thief, he thought. He could feel his heart beat speed up as he thought of what he was about to do next. He hoped Ross didn't come back early because his presence in the shed would be very difficult to explain.

The key was hard to turn in the rusty padlock and he wasted precious seconds flicking it this way and that before it clicked open. He stepped into the dimly lit shed, his eyes quickly noting the layers of undisturbed dust coating everything. A shell crunched underfoot as he went a few steps in, waiting for his eyes to recover from the glare outside. He had about three minutes to finish looking before time would be up. It would be just like Tyrone to tell Ross all about him going for an extra long shit while they did all the work.

He began to make out a black rectangle in the ground that must be the pond. Following its edges he could see it was divided down the middle and lined with plastic. Leaning over showed it to be empty, apart from a few dozen dead oyster shells glowing white at the bottom. The pump was still running, moving water between the pools, but to what purpose? If there was nothing alive in there then it was just a waste of power. He looked around again. Nothing else related to oysters. Lined up along one wall were half a dozen blue plastic drums, the sort farmers bought sheep drench and weed killer in. Some long lengths of PVC pipe lay on the dirt beside the drums, and a pair of old rubber gloves sat on top of the last barrel. Stepping closer he could see the lid of the last barrel was free from dust. Maybe Ross hadn't been joking about sheep dip being all there was in the shed, but the picture didn't add up. The only person here who used farm chemicals had just handed him his key. That could only mean the drums were old empties, so why did the last drum look like a recent addition? The fine dirt of the shed floor in front of it was indented with half circles so it had been shifted not long ago. Jack would have to sit down and think it through later. Time was up. He went out again taking care not to brush against anything on his way.

Ryan handed him the broom as he came around the corner to the yard and hosed down the concrete pad while Jack swept the debris from under the sorting table. Tyrone hadn't missed him at all. They could hear him through the kitchen window swearing at the gunk in the fridge. 'Ohhh, this is sick! Why do I get all the gross jobs? Fuck this! This is even worse than my cousin's fridge. Man, at least if Ross was here I'd be rumbling sticks or something, not this shit. Urghk, I'm gonna throw up!' Ryan stuck his nose in the window and shouted, 'Come on kitchen bitch, I want that fridge to sparkle.' He looked at Jack and giggled.

So far rumbling sticks was Tyrone's favourite job. The rumbler was a square wooden box on an axis with a motor to make it spin. It could be almost any shape or size or material so long as it held sticks, and spun round. A bit like the washer, but without any water. After the oysters were harvested, the sticks were left to dry out. Before they could be re-used they needed cleaning and that's what the rumbler did. Depending on the size of your rumbler you could throw in fifty sticks at a time. They went round and round sending up clouds of fine silt and small pieces of oyster and barnacle shell until eventually they were clean. It was an easy, if boring job. All that was required was to feed in sticks and take them out again.

Ross had come back before knock off time, just as they were tidying away the tools. He criticized their work. 'Who left the hose out? I nearly tripped over the bloody thing. Make sure it's rolled up before you go, Jack.'

Mostly he was disgruntled because they'd done everything in record time, and everyone was in a good mood. Tyrone had recovered from cleaning the kitchen because Jack let him drive the tractor back into the shed, something Ross hadn't let him do yet. Jack knew what Ross thought. Because they were having fun, joking and shouting insults at each other, it had to mean they'd been slacking off, didn't it? If your nose was to the grindstone you couldn't be happy.

Finally, when he could find nothing else bad to say he went to the fridge to find a beer, and complained that someone had chucked out his cheese and onion sandwich.

'Was that the thing with the green and blue furry stuff growing on it?' Tyrone asked. 'It smelt like

Ryan's armpit, man. Jack told me to clean the fridge so I chucked it out.'

'Nothing wrong with a bit of mold, it just needed a few minutes in the microwave.'

Tyrone made a rude face behind Ross's back and mimed putting a finger down his throat and puking, which made Ryan laugh. Ross turned around to see what the joke was and saw him gagging. Tyrone stopped abruptly, his face frozen mid vomit, and Ross scowled at him before stomping off home. Even when they got it right, they got it wrong.

Ryan and Jack had taken to stopping somewhere between work and home for a drink once the kid had been dropped off. This evening it was on Jack's boat. They both felt the need to off-load the day, and Jack knew it kept Ryan even tempered throughout the week.

Smell heard them arrive and came bouncing up, squirming with pleasure to see her master. Jack had taken Betty up on her offer to dog-sit when he realized Smell was struggling to jump onto the tray of the ute in the mornings. Her back legs lacked the strength, and Jack saw she was getting old fast.

'I prefer your place to mine,' Ryan said, 'the beer's much nicer.'

'Cheers, mate.' This covered the compliment and the salutation in one go. Jack liked to be economical with words. After several minutes of tranquil appreciation for the end of the day, Jack decided to probe Ryan on what he might know about Ross's activities. 'I haven't heard Ross talk about that nursery project for a while. You?'

'Nah, not since about six months ago before I started, but then we don't really hang out anymore. What does he need a nursery for anyway? I think he told me, but I tend to zone out when he gets technical.'

'Beats me. He said he was running some trials. Usually that means selecting some young spat and seeing which types do better. Maybe it didn't work out.' The thing Jack couldn't mention was the pump that was still running for no apparent reason. Whatever Ross was up to it wasn't growing spat.

There was a knock at the door, and Rose came in holding a bottle of cider. Behind her stood a woman Jack didn't recognize. 'Okay if I bring a friend?' she asked Jack.

'Sure. Come in and have a seat.'

Rose smiled at Ryan, 'Nice to see you, Ryan.'

'Likewise, Rose,' Ryan said, lifting his beer and tilting it at her.

'Guys, this is Lucy. Lucy and I work together. She does all our publicity shots.'

Lucy was younger than Rose by about two years, roughly the same age as Ryan, but looked much younger. Maybe it was because she didn't wear much make-up. Jack thought she was kind of plain looking, but with an open, friendly face. What made her stand out in the small room was her long blond hair. Now there was a woman who knew what her best feature was and made the most of it. Lucy always wore her hair loose, except when she was taking photos, and it gave her a glamour and polish that her features didn't.

They shuffled around to let everyone have a seat and Jack elbowed Ryan to close his mouth. Ryan, to his own horror, found he was blushing and took a gulp of beer to calm his nerves, almost choking on it instead. He coughed in a spasmodic way, feeling more embarrassed by the attention he was drawing to himself. Once his cough was under control, he sank back into his seat trying to be unobtrusive.

Jack grabbed two glasses for the cider and said, 'So, you're a photographer, Lucy?'

'Yup, freelance.'

'For those of you who don't know what that means, it means she's damn good. You can't making a living freelance unless you're good.' Rose chinked her glass with Lucy's.

'What brings you to our little neck of the woods?' Jack handed Ryan another beer, but Ryan's eyes didn't meet his; they were fixed on Lucy.

'Tomorrow we're shooting on the water, so Rose said I could stay at hers and save myself the rush-hour drive in the morning. I live on the other side of the city from here.'

'Yep, tomorrow I finally get to see what you do all day,' Rose looked at Jack. 'I told Terry I wanted to know more about the growing of oysters to give me some background on what we sell. It's a good chance to get some photos done for the website, and Terry wants new business cards for Tide to Table. Like I really need the extra work.'

Jack couldn't believe the women had been here five minutes and not a word from Ryan. Usually he was all over a conversation like a dog on a bone.

'So you're coming to spy on us tomorrow. Nice.' Jack nodded knowingly, and the women giggled at him.

'Love a man in a skin-tight uniform, don't we Lucy?' Rose made her eyebrows waggle. 'First, we're going to the yard to see grading and packing, then in the afternoon we're out on the barge to see the harvest -but don't worry, Terry won't be with us. He only helps out if he has to. He hasn't done a full week's work on the farm in three years.'

This was getting weird. The conversation had a big, Ryan shaped hole in it. Jack gave his leg a gentle nudge under the table. Ryan pulled his legs up under his chair. No help from him then. 'Your boss might not be there but ours will. We don't want to let on to Ross that we know you. Does Lucy know the situation?'

'Yes, she's all clued up.' Rose frowned at Jack and tilted her head slightly in Ryan's direction. She'd never seen him lost for words either. Jack replied in kind with his eyes flicking to Lucy and then a double jump of eyebrows. It was code for 'her, he likes'. Rose smiled with a cunning gleam in her eyes as she grasped his meaning. 'So you guys got dinner plans?' Jack and Ryan shook their heads. 'Good. Let's show this city slicker what she's missing out on living in the metropolis. Dinner on the *Skylark* at seven.' The women finished their drinks and left, calling out 'Don't be late!'

When they had gone Jack cracked up laughing at Ryan, 'Oh man, you got it *bad*.' Ryan let his breath out in a rush.

'That is one hot chick, bro,' he whispered, still looking stunned. He looked at Jack imploringly, like a scared kid. 'What should I do?'

'Well, you could try moving your mouth and making sounds come out. You know, talking? Women love that stuff. Start with some easy words like 'hello' and work your way up to whole sentences.'

'Ha ha. Very funny. I wanted to say something, but everything sounded so dumb in my head, and I want her to like me. She's so...sophisticated. Why would she look at me anyway?'

'Because you're a top bloke, that's why, and once you've had a shower and you don't stink and you've put on clothes that aren't covered in muck, you'll look a million bucks.'

'Thanks mate.' His big grin came back tentatively at first like it needed a run up, and then there it was, *zing*, back in it's place. 'What should I wear?' His smile wobbled and fell over.

'Hell, I don't know. Something clean and comfortable. It's dinner on a boat, not a first date. A real gentleman would bring a small gift for the hostess, so pick up a bottle of wine or some flowers on your way.'

'Wine it is then.' Ryan shot out the door before Jack could give him flack about being a macho, rugby playing Neanderthal. Alcohol, even wine, was acceptable, but flowers was really pushing the limit. This was as ingrained in Ryan as good manners were in Jack. There was nothing of the new age sensitive man about him. In Ryan's mind buying flowers said you'd lost your dignity, submitted to being pussy-whipped, or done something which required a big, groveling apology. The only person who had ever had flowers from Ryan was his mum; once when he ran over the cat, and once when he'd forgotten her birthday. On both occasions he'd picked them from her garden, not because he was stingy, but as part of the punishment. If giving flowers was soft, picking them yourself was like castration.

Either Ryan had lost his former confidence with women, or the stories he told about pulling all the horsey chicks was exaggerated, Jack thought, before a third thought occurred to him. Maybe Lucy was that rare thing: a hormone triggering, neuron-flaring, match to Ryan's fire.

Jack showered and changed and sent his brother a text. *Going out tonight, ring you this weekend, J.*

He was hoping Joshua might have an insight on the Ross situation. He knew Joshua hadn't told him the full story, and maybe it would help to know more details, like who was so worried about Ross, and what they thought he would do. There was only one thing Jack could think of that could grow in those ponds and not be visible to the naked eye, and he very much doubted Ross would go that far. That was serious indeed. What if Terry was behind the rumors? He could be trying to set Ross up, get him closed down or take him to court for foul practice. Even if nothing could be proved it would drain Ross's resources. He wasn't about to land Ross in shit if he was the victim here.

Dinner with Lucy and Rose was fun. Ryan was a little stiff at first but Lucy was a great storyteller, and soon had him loosening up. She had seen plenty of strange and hilarious things in her job, and used her whole body to exaggerate postures and facial expressions when telling a story, so her audience felt right there with her. They shared an excellent meal and two bottles of wine before Ryan said he had something else to share. They smoked a joint outside watching the moon rise over the sea, and turned sleepily to bed. 'I see why you love it here,' Lucy said. 'Maybe I should move to the country. My parents are driving me nuts! I had to move back in with them last year when I took the plunge to go freelance. Turned out I didn't need to, but it's taken me a while to feel confident enough to live on what I make. I used to have these sudden panic attacks where I'd think I'll wake up tomorrow and the phone won't ring.'

'I'd go crazy living at home,' Ryan admitted. 'My mum's alright, but my dad's such a square. Every time I see him he tries to talk me into getting 'a real job.' He thought horses was bad enough. Mum says he won't even come to the phone since she told him I'm working as a labourer on an oyster farm.'

Rose stood up and stretched. 'I think we'll leave you chatterboxes to it. You take my bed Lucy, Jack will be a gentleman and let me share his, and Ryan can have the bunk bed in here.' Ryan was too tired and relaxed to complain, and how could he pass up the chance to spend a whole night on the same boat as Lucy?

The next morning they were all up at sunrise. Rose went to have breakfast with Lucy and Ryan went to the 4square to buy bacon and eggs to fry up for himself and Jack. 'Morning!' Ryan came in the door and greeted Jack, full of smiles. It was six fifteen am. Jack was less awake, the coffee still brewing.

'Morning. What you got there?'

'Grabbed us some tucker for brekkie. Bacon and eggs ok? Damn, forgot the bread.'

'No sweat, in the cupboard over there. You mind real coffee? I don't have instant.'

'Anything goes for me. Hey, that guy at the shop's a funny one, eh? He opened the door and says, 'Good morning. You first customer, you win lucky magnet.' Here, see?' he tossed it to Jack who caught it. The fridge magnet was a red plastic letter L.

'L for I love Lucy, eh?'

'Let's just stick to L for I *lust* Lucy for now.'

'Whatever, I know that look. You'll be buying her flowers before you know it.' He handed the letter back to Ryan. 'You keep it, it's yours. I've got a few.' He pointed to the door of his tiny fridge. The multi coloured plastic letters on the front spelt out CHUYENDOI.

'Doesn't mean anything. Why don't you rearrange them?'

'That's the order I got them in. I looked it up. It means 'transformation' in Vietnamese. Chuyen doi. You just met Mr Chin. I'm still not sure if that's his first name or his last name. He's a wise man, if you can make sense of what he's saying.'

Ryan put his lucky letter in his pocket, and they

189

headed out the door. Lucy and Rose had changed out of office attire and into jeans and jerseys for their day on the farm. They waved the men off from the deck of their boat. A day of fine weather was opening up, but there was still a chill in the air this early. Once they were on their way Jack asked Ryan, 'So, you and Lucy eh? How did it go?'

'I was a perfect gentleman. I said goodnight and went to sleep. Right after we had full-on sex.' His grin went from one ear all the way to the other. His eyes were alive with the wondrous glow of good fortune when least expected, and Jack knew he wasn't joking. He'd suspected something had happened, the way Ryan had been skipping around all morning, but not that.

'Yeah? You're a fast mover, you sly old dog.'

'It wasn't *me*. She made the first move. I can't remember that ever happening to me before. God, she's lovely.'

'Congratulations, mate. I hope you can see her again.'

'I will, sooner than you think. She's agreed to stay at my place tonight.' He giggled, high on the buzz of love. 'I'll have to get some shopping on the way home. What do you feed a classy lady, Jack?'

'I don't think it's your cooking skills she's after, you daft bugger. Why don't you take her out for tea? I can ring Connie and see if there's a table free if you like. It's Friday so you'll have to make up your mind now, before it's all booked out.' Ryan liked this idea, and when they stopped to collect Tyrone, Jack rang and booked the table.

Ryan's mood wasn't dimmed by the annoying blather that emanated from their passenger, and he couldn't stop smiling. Jack would have a word with Rose about her friend. He knew Ryan looked like Mr Tough-guy but he was sensitive underneath. Rose would know what Lucy's game was, and warn her to be gentle. When it came to the crunch men were as sensitive as women, they just didn't go on and on about it.

Ross gave them the plan for the day with a nasty look at Ryan. There was nothing he disliked more than someone who was enjoying life, because he wanted total focus on the job. You weren't allowed a life until it was time to knock off for the day. If you came to work miserable it went unnoticed. If you came to work in high spirits, you'd end up miserable. Ross would take it personally if you didn't. Tyrone's obtusity left him immune and Ross might as well piss in the wind where he was concerned.

'The old lease needs to be tidied up before we put more bundles in the water after Christmas. There's some rotten posts need replacing, broken rails, and all the rails need a good clean. Get out the big guns, boys, I want a hundred and ten percent out there today.'

Before the tide was at its lowest point they left with the old barge, loaded with posts and tools. The farm would be dry in an hour and they would leave the barge on the mud, using instead a small punt to drag supplies between the rows. By now everyone had mastered the mud walk making it look easy to the uninitiated. Jack had tried to explain it once, but it was one of those things a man had to largely figure out by feel, a subtle shift and balance game. The trick was to lift the foot and slide it over the surface while you pulled the other foot out, so when you had to pull the first foot out again it hadn't had time to sink in much. It was essential to keep your weight spread between the two feet, and never attempt to lift a foot out without first lifting the heel to break the suction. It was a slow, fluid movement which forced even the clumsiest person to move with grace. A kind of ballet for men in gumboots. Jack liked to pretend he was a cosmonaut walking on the moon, his focus on his breathing. Breathe in, slide and plant heel, breathe out, lift heel and slide, breathe in, slide and plant heel...his concentration was broken by Ross. 'Jack, you take Tyrone, yumble, yumble, broken rails and get scraping what's left. Ryan, yumble, posts with me. Let's go boys, go!'

Jack braced himself for several hours of not listening to Tyrone. It didn't make any difference if the conversation was completely one sided, Tyrone would ask and answer the questions for you. He handed Tyrone a small axe and trudged ahead hoping to outpace him. From behind, the endless litany of meaningless words dragged at his ears. 'I mean, this chick was like gnnnrh eh. Like, fat as titties, and this tight little ass and....' Jack tuned his ears to the sounds in the background. The screeching of gulls and the sucking sound his boots made as he walked to the start of a row. Step, slide, step, slide, step... Tyrone was still talking away, oblivious to Jack's silence '...bet you can't do that eh? Yeah I know you wouldn't anyway, but if you were me you'd be like woooh yeah!' Step, slide, and stop.

'How can your mouth be making so much noise and you're still able to breathe?' Jack asked him. 'No, don't answer that, just pick up the broken rail and snap it off the post. Good. Now do it to all the broken ones down the row till I say stop.'

Jack walked to the other end of the row and began working his way back towards Tyrone. Ross hadn't said he had to work *beside* him. He could hear bits of rap song punctuated by snapping timber as the young man attacked the rotten timber with his own style of Kung Fu. By the time he reached Jack in the centre of the first row he was silent, hands hanging limply by his sides, sweat running down his jaw. Jack had hardly broken wind because he could pace himself, save his energy for the duration. Using the tomahawk he demonstrated how to chip away at the rails, scraping off the over-catch, barnacles, and fouling, so the new bundles could be nailed on before the next spawn. Ross was shouting at Ryan about something but Jack didn't have time to investigate. Ross would want this row finished by lunchtime and there was still the new rails to put up and the rubbish to be taken away.

Four hours later they were all sweaty, mud spattered, and stomach-growling hungry. The tide was lapping its way back in and the barge was just afloat. They made their way towards it pulling the punt full of debris. Ryan's face was covered in mud and he had lost his easy demeanor and smiles of the morning, Ross having his usual affect. They knocked off for lunch, Ross going home to his sandwiches.

Jack and Ryan dragged the plastic chairs outside and sat on them in the cool shade on the south side of the shed. Shorty's barge would be coming in with the tide soon. Ryan turned to Jack and said, 'Want to swap jobs after lunch? That maniac almost took my fingers off with the post rammer.' Jack shook his head.

'No, I'd rather listen to Ty than hold posts for Ross.' He could recall the experience from last season and didn't care to repeat it. Even with the proper tool it wasn't safe. Ross could put posts in faster than anyone else because he used the rammer upside down, dangerous but more effective. This meant there was no lip to stop the metal rammer from slipping off the post. You had to be quick getting your hands out of the way if it came down on a bad angle. Even a brave man would flinch. If you escaped harm you would suffer verbal abuse instead. 'Keep that bloody post still, would ya?' or, 'I was miles away from your hands! Harden up, man!'

Mud sometimes came flying up from the bottom of the post, and evidently Ryan had taken a face full of it this morning. He would be washing mud out of his ears and nostrils for a week.

Tyrone pulled his chair up beside them. He was so hungry not a word came out of his bulging cheeks for five minutes straight, but it couldn't last. 'Check it out, here comes those other fullas from the other farm.' Shorty's barge came past with two crew on board. They would be on their way to pick up their visitors from the yard. It was too far for the men to spot anyone on the other shore across. Fifteen minutes later the barge came back again, this time with four on board. Tyrone finished stuffing his bakery bun into his mouth and pointed. 'Hey, that's not a fulla! That's a chick, I can tell, and she's got a friend too. Sweet. You can have the little one, Ryan, and I'll take the blonde. Yeah! Bring them hotties over here!' Jack and Ryan cringed. 'Shut up, Tyrone,' they chorused. The day was calm enough for noise to carry across the water, and the breeze would blow his words right out to the barge. For a second he was quiet. 'Nah, yous are just jealous 'cos I'm young and hot and you're old, and I saw them first.' Ryan made a lunge for him, swiping out with his cap. Tyrone easily ducked it, laughing.

'Go an make us some coffee you little smart-ass,' said Ryan. They saw Rose and Lucy looking their way and grinned. For twenty seconds neither of them moved, drinking in the scene; their women on a barge cruising past. The feeling of a delicious secret.

Back on the water Jack could see Ryan was having trouble concentrating on the job. He kept sneaking glances at the other barge as it worked its way slowly down the rows of baskets. The rammer came down hard and slid towards him as he jerked his head back. Off balance, he wobbled, making circles in the air with his arms before falling on his ass. His legs were stuck in the mud up to his shins from standing in one spot so long, and now he struggled to free them, his chin just above the water. Ross leaned down and pulled him free. 'What the heck's up with you today? You're clumsy as fuck. Go and scrape those rails with Ty and send Jack over.' Ross tried to stomp away to the barge, the mud and water churning around him, but making little forward progress. He looked like a kid having a tantrum, taking out his frustration on the water. You couldn't fight water or mud, it fought back with passive resistance.

'Sorry Jack, he thinks he's punishing me by sending me over here. You're next.' Ryan took Jack's tomahawk and began chipping oysters and barnacles off the rails.

Jack reloaded the punt with posts while Ross threw things around the barge searching for the nails. Ross in a bad mood was like working with a trapped possum; don't get too close. Jack saw Lucy's camera lens trained on them and made frantic throat-slitting gestures, but Ross had spotted her too. 'What the fuck are *you* looking at?' he shouted, the wind whisking the sound towards shore. She lowered the camera, smiled, and raised it again oblivious to his anger. To make things clear, Ross lifted the middle finger of his right hand and kept it extended until the camera was lowered again. 'Shorty's got some nerve sending women out to spy on us. I hope she got a good photo of my salute.'

Jack held a new post at the end of the last row while Ross gave it a good bash. First Ryan slacking off, then being spied on, had wound him up nice and tight. If the post believed in reincarnation, then it must be contemplating some serious past sins about now. Twice Jack had to whip his hands out of the way as the rammer skidded towards his fingers, and twice Ross gave him a hard look, his lips pressed into a white line of annoyance. He knew well Jack's tolerance for personal insults, and all those unspoken words collected at the corners of his mouth as white spit.

Jack thought now was not the time to mention that most of the empty rails he mended or replaced were abnormally loose even by Ross's standards. The rails sagged on the posts, not just the older ones but the timber that had been added last year or the year before too. Maybe some disgruntled worker in the past had jimmied them loose, and it would be a good idea to check the other rows as well, the rows loaded with oysters. If they had another storm then the bay would be afloat with sticks, and maybe it was connected to the incident Ryan related where the rail came loose at harvest. Hopefully none of this will be my concern come next year, thought Jack, and the worry was jolted from his mind by another thud from the upside down finger crusher.

Water began to come up over the top rails, and work had to stop. You couldn't ram posts or scrape rails when they were underwater; not even Ross was that hard. Jack was still in one piece with all his fingers so you could call it a good day. Another week consigned to the alluvial mud that snuck home with them. Ryan said his wash tub, an old concrete double basin was mounded up with it, and a privet seedling had taken off in a corner.

Chapter 8

Lucy had remained in the village with Ryan the whole weekend, so Jack and Rose spent most of Saturday and half of Sunday with them. Ryan was showing Lucy the pleasures of the countryside, and she was having a fantastic time. They made sure to stay clear of any public places where they might be spotted by Ross, and when they went shopping the men went one way and the women another. Lucy hadn't been offended by Ross giving her the finger. She told them instead about the time she was asked to attend a birth and photograph it. When push came to...well, more pushing, the woman had screamed at Lucy every insult she could think of 'And she was showing me much more than her finger,' she added. When they had a moment alone Rose reassured Jack there was no need to worry for Ryan's welfare; Lucy thought he was a total hunk, and the nicest macho she had ever met - and that included the All Blacks.

It wasn't until Sunday night that jack found himself alone to ring Joshua. 'I got a look in his shed,' he said once pleasantries were exchanged, 'and there was nothing. A few ponds with oyster shells, and some barrels, but here's the strange part...the pump's running day and night. What do you make of it?'

'Look, here's the deal. There's concern within the industry that Ross is willing to pay a high price to take down Terry Shawe. No one cares about their feud, but if it's an oyster virus he's cooking up then we could all be wiped out. I can't see how he could contain it. He's got the motive and the knowledge base to do it. No one is willing to speak openly about it, least of all confront him in case they're wrong or it just makes Ross more careful, but from what you've described he could have a virus in the ponds and food to keep it alive in the barrels. The carrier could be much smaller than an oyster.'

'Shit. I was afraid of that, but an outbreak doesn't make sense if he's building up his business. It would wipe him out too. There's something else I wanted to ask. I need to rule out Terry as the motivation for all the heat on Ross. If it's just malicious rumor to stir up trouble, or worse, part of a plan to set him up, then I don't want to help it along. I don't like working for him, but he's not a bad guy. So where does Terry fit in the picture?'

'Well, as you know he tried to put a spanner in the works for Ross earlier on, but Ross is small-fry to him. Terry doesn't hang out with ruffians like us. Heck, he doesn't even come to the conference, sends his manager along. It was decided he wouldn't be told in case it inflamed the situation, so we can assume he doesn't know. As for the rumors, that's easy; Ross told one of the guys Shorty would be sorry he'd crossed him. Two in the morning, pissed as a fart.'

A fair amount of all night drinking was done over the three day annual meet, and all sorts of interesting things came out. Sometimes fists were involved and this was considered healthy. It cleared the air.

Perhaps if Shorty had turned up in the last years Ross could have expressed his feelings and had done with it, but perhaps that was also why Shorty never went. He was a stocky bloke but city life had turned him soft. A boardroom tiger was no threat to the sort of men who worked their own farms every day; words only went so far.

'Doesn't look good for Ross then. Going back to the threat of a virus, there was a smell in there, like cabbage, kind of sulfurous. Does that mean anything to you?'

'You farted? Was your dog in the shed? God, she's got a powerful ass!'

'Yeah, you can joke, but seriously?'

'I've got someone I can ask. I'll let you know, okay? If you get a chance to go back in, a sample of that water would tell us something, or whatever's in the barrels. Put it on the courier right away - and thanks Jack, it means a lot to me. Some of the small farms are only just making a recovery from the last virus and we still don't know where *that* came from. Another one now would finish them.'

'One other thing. The new lease out of the bay. We've been shifting stock out there, adults and juveniles, anything that will be harvestable next season. That would mean he could use some sort of contaminant in the bay and not be affected by it himself, so either we're barking up the wrong tree or he has a containment plan.'

'Not necessarily. You see, we learnt something about the way a virus works last time. The few farms out in the open water suffered almost no damage.

Once the water gets above 17 degrees anything in the bay will be toast, while anything out of the bay will sail through it. The currents will take it out into open sea where it'll concentrate in the next bay, and so on until every bay is hit. I think it's time to worry.'

The next week the farm renovations continued between harvests. It was perfect weather for farm building, warm but not scorching. Being in the water all day was exhausting, but at least they didn't have to cull. Nancy sent two of her shop ladies to the farm to help out. They were both in their fifties, a hard life evident in hands and face but steady workers who got a laugh from parrying light insults with everyone. They were expert at using humor to carry them through the day of monotonous labour, and Ross didn't complain because they weren't strictly his charges. Nancy came by to check on them at lunch break and Jack was impressed by her management skills. Before any talk of work they had a good 'ol natter, then Nancy would check where the work was at and give directions if needed. If only she could give Ross a few pointers they could all share the love - but they weren't old ladies, they were the men; big and tough and rough and ready for thrashing out a day of hard labour, not nattering away by the shed.

Louise was fond of Ryan and tried to chat him up. He obviously didn't feel the same way because he'd ask Jack to bring his coffee outside to avoid her. When she saw him she'd jump on him with loud-mouthed playfulness; 'Oi handsome, bet you like a

201

good massage after a day out there. You come home with me and Lou will take care of you.' He gave it back right enough, 'Geez Lou, tempting, but I reckon you'd break my heart. I'm not just a hunk of muscle you know.' Round the corner he'd shiver, and come knock-off be waiting in the ute. 'Come on, Jack. Get me the fuck outta here. How come she leaves you alone, eh?'

'Ah, I may have insulted her once, accidentally.' At the time, and for a while after, Jack had felt like a bit of a scumbag but now he was seeing the advantages. She didn't even smile at him, which was a good thing; her teeth were crooked and stained.

'Did you? Good call. I'd rather have sex with a cheese grater. If Lucy comes over tonight she can eroticise me.'

'You mean exorcise you?'

'Yeah, yeah, but with sex.' Ryan was in love. He didn't say it, but Jack could tell. Lucy this and Lucy that. They were on the phone every night, and she was planning to spend the weekend at his place again. Ryan had to help her on Saturday at a wedding, carrying her gear around in return for as much free booze as he liked once they were done. Jack was kind of glad. He and Rose might get some time alone and not have to watch the other two making moon-eyes at each other. Hearing about it all week was enough.

On Thursday Tyrone got a nasty cut in his finger from catching a ring on the edge of a crate as he went to load it on the ute. Jack had fixed him up with a bit of tape, but Ross had been unsympathetic.

'I told you those rings would be a danger to you when you started, but you didn't listen. Now you know better. Give them to your girlfriend.'

Tyrone had removed every last one right there in front of them. 'I'm over that shit anyway,' he said, stuffing them in his pocket. He realized it could have been a lot more serious and he was shaken up. Ryan even gave him his last can of energy drink as a gesture of sympathy.

By Friday Jack was desperate to see Rose. She had been more busy than usual this last week, and though she had crawled into his bed at midnight on Tuesday and Wednesday, he hadn't seen much of her since. He cooked dinner and was pleased when her red car pulled into the parking lot early in the evening. She came straight to his boat, and Smell jumped up and down arthritically until Rose patted her.

'Just in time for dinner,' Jack said serving her a plate of pasta while she kicked off her heels.

'You're a wonderful man. I'm starving.' They ate and went straight to bed. Jack got up a while later and made them a cup of tea and brought it back to the bedroom.

'Tomorrow I'm whisking you away, but I'll need your help. It involves a boat,' Rose said looking smug.

'I'm all ears.'

'I need a break, so I've pinched the keys to the old homestead. I thought we could go there tomorrow and spend a night looking round the place. Go for a walk, read a book. Smell can come too. What do you think?'

'Sounds like a fine plan to me. Will it just be us?'

'Oh yes. Don't tell me, Ryan's been driving you nuts with his endless talk of Lucy.'

'You can say that again. How's Lucy doing?'

'Don't know. I stopped answering her calls yesterday.'

'Ah. True romance, eh.'

'Terry said a while ago I can stay at the homestead any time there's no one booked in, and I checked the website today. It's all ours. Don't worry, he's out of town, so we won't get any visitors. The caretakers will be around, but if we don't announce ourselves they might not even notice us. They can't see the house from where they are.'

'Want me to load the dinghy on the ute in the morning then?'

'Yes please.' Rose finished her tea and fell asleep minutes later. Jack was looking forward to tomorrow. The first time away was always a good test for a couple and he felt sure they'd pass it with flying colours.

Aside from the dinghy they took the gas cooker and enough food for two days. There was a barbecue there but if you wanted to boil the kettle or cook a meal you had to light the Agar. Jack lifted Smell into her box on the back and they were good to go.

The ute passed the turn-off to Jack's work, and went another kilometre down the gravel road. Rose pointed out a clearing of grassy verge up ahead, and Jack turned off the road. It looked like no one had been here for a long time, apart from the council mower. After bumping along an old track for half a minute they stopped in front of a wooden fence with a stile for climbing over. A sign said Pioneer's Cemetery.

Rose spent a few minutes picking wild flowers; dog daisies, buttercups, and some flowering grass. 'Right, now I'd like to introduce you to some family,' she said, climbing over the stile. Smell was sniffing eagerly at the damp grass, picking up the scent of wild animals, and Jack whistled for her to follow.

Some two dozen headstones poked up through the long grass inside the fenced area. They were worn away by the elements and covered in lichen, the carving barely legible. Rose placed her flowers in front of a more recent stone, its edges still sharp. 'My grandfather. The last to be buried in the old plot.'

What had begun as a fine day was beginning to turn overcast, and rain had been forecasted for the afternoon. 'We'd better get over the water before the weather turns, Rose.' Leaving the ute where it was they loaded the dinghy with the oars and everything else, and carried it one at each end, past the cemetery along a dirt path to the edge of the water. They were at the very end of the bay where a small stream fed into the estuary and the mangroves were at their thickest. Smell and Rose got in the boat while Jack pushed it out to deeper water before leaping in.

It was a short distance from there to the little strip of sand where they pulled the dinghy ashore. Jack stowed it under a strand of manuka trees up the bank, and Rose found the start of the track to the homestead. It went along the bank and up the hill behind the oyster shed, and they followed it with their gear until it forked.

'That direction will take you further along the bay. It comes back down to the oyster yard, and then up to the caretaker's cottage over the crest of the hill. We go this way. The only place this leads is to the house.'

Jack looked back the way they'd come and marveled at how different the bay looked from this angle. Out to his left across the water he could see the reddish brown roof of Ross and Nancy's place, and further along the dull grey of the old oyster shed.

The walk warmed them up, so when they came up to the porch of the old homestead they took off a jersey each and plonked themselves down. Smell Hound lay panting at their feet; she was getting unfit staying at home all day. 'What do you think?' Rose patted the wooden deck with her hand. The boards were old, their curled edges worn to a shine. The paint work was fresh and crisp on the door and window frames. A climbing rose was growing up the veranda posts, neatly pruned for summer blooms.

'It's a real old beauty. It's a bit like my family's place up north. Same style of building, but this has been done up.'

At home, Joshua and Jack made sure the old building was in good repair and water tight, a bit of paint here 'n' there when they had time, but neither of them had thought to do more. The only major investment they'd made was a new roof, but that was nearly ten years ago. 'Come on, let's take a look inside. I haven't been in here for years, since it was a ramshackle ruin. At one stage the farmer was keeping hay in the lounge. When he left, Ross found some wild goats had made themselves at home and eaten the curtains and the hearth rug.'

She unlocked and opened the front door, casting a weak rectangle of sun on dark, polished wood. 'Wow!' Rose looked around. Every surface gleamed with furniture polish. The walls were tastefully painted or papered, and the furniture carefully chosen to suit the age of the house. 'You can bet Terry had nothing to do with this. He must have paid a designer. This place looks like something from a magazine.'

The only thing which gave it away as a holiday house and not a family residence, was the lack of sumptuous detail you would expect to match the interior. The candlesticks, the pots and pans, the towels, plates, and all other details were new and from Ikea. Just because only wealthy people holidayed here didn't mean precious knick knacks wouldn't walk out the door. If you asked Terry he'd tell you the rich were the worst for petty theft; their mentality was if they wanted something they could have it. Surely you wouldn't have left it there for anyone to help themselves if you valued it? Jack would have been quick to disagree; an opportunist would be an opportunist whatever his means.

'Terry told me all the old family treasure is in the attic, or what the others didn't want. I'm supposed to take a look. He wants to sell most of it, because none of us really know what to do with the rest. Shall we explore?'

They left Smell sleeping on the new lounge rug and spent an hour looking through boxes in the attic. It was mostly silverware and crystal glassware, old paintings, needlework, and a camphor chest holding an ancient wedding dress. Rose set aside a canvas painted with oils from a stack against a wall. Her great grandmother had painted it, according to the date and signature. It was looking out over the bay, the water reflecting the sky, and the hills opposite completely bare, well cropped by cattle. A patch of ruffled water and some black lines marked out the old oyster lease as it had been then, and the roof of the cottage Ross lived in looked freshly painted. Jack looked out the tiny attic window to compare the painting with reality. Now the land was less intensively farmed the trees were growing back hiding the clean lines and contours of the hills. The roof of Nancy and Ross's place was hidden behind a row of macrocarpas, planted along the shore as a windbreak.

'Maybe Lucy could use this old wedding gown for photo shoots or something. I don't think anyone will ever use it again.' Rose sneezed, and wrapped it back in the layers of black tissue paper that stopped it from turning yellow with age.

Rose had packed a basket with sandwiches and a thermos of coffee for lunch. They took it and followed a sheep track behind the house up to an indentation in the hillside where she spread out a picnic blanket. The day was warm despite the cloud cover, and Jack guessed there would be thunder before the rain came. He couldn't remember when he had felt so content. Just to be with Rose made his worries insignificant.

The tide began to go out, exposing the farms a little. Terry's farm looked very different from Ross's. Instead of having rails covered in bundles or sticks, he had rows of posts and batons with a wire stretched along them, like a fence. Baskets of oysters were clipped onto the wire, and were now floating just below the surface of the sea. If Jack had thought to bring some binoculars with them he might make out the boxes Ross had designed to hold the tiny spat. There was no need to set eyes on them but it would satisfy his curiosity. Was it one of those ideas so simple that a man might roll his eyes and say, 'of course,' or was it hi tech and complicated, the work of a genius? The whole subject was a tabu at the yard.

After lunch they went back down and took a nap together. The master bed was a fourposter with muslin drapes, and extremely comfortable compared with what they had on the boats. It was tempting to wallow under the feather duvet all afternoon, but Smell would need to go out soon. 'I'll make a start on dinner if you like,' Jack offered rousing himself. Rose was getting up too, but didn't bother putting her pants back on. 'On second thoughts, Smell can wait.' Jack tackled Rose back onto the bed and made her squeal. Suddenly, Jack could picture the two of them, living in a house like this, being as happy as they were now *every day*. It shocked him.

He had never seen a snapshot of the future with a woman before, and rather than be frightened or feel the dull years stretch ahead like he used to imagine he would feel, he felt thrilled. It was then that Jack knew he loved Rose. Not just 'in love' with her, but a love that radiated right through his body like a physical sensation of warmth, as real as the fine-boned arms around his back.

Jack woke early the next morning. He often had this problem on the weekends. It was his internal alarm set for work which he had difficulty switching off. He pulled back the curtain an inch. It wasn't dawn yet, but the sky was turning from black to inky blue and the moon was half behind the hills. Jack dressed quietly not to wake Rose, and found his way through the dark, quiet house with the candle they had used to light the way to bed last night. He let Smell outside for the toilet, and put water on to boil for coffee.

The kitchen pantry was well stocked with every essential, and to his relief there was ground coffee and a plunger. Jack went to the door and whistled gently for Smell. First light made streaks over the horizon, and Jack paused on the threshold. A noise caught his attention. Smell had heard it too; her ears pricked up and she lifted her nose to the wind. There it was again, the noise of something dragging over the mud, a sucking, scraping sound.

The tide was low but had been on it's way in for more than an hour. The middle of the bay would have water but the shore would be dry for several metres. Jack remembered the water on the cooker and went back inside. By the time he went out again with a black coffee in his hand the dawn had begun to spread across the sky, snuffing out the stars as it went. He could make out the shapes of objects in the distance, and colours slowly appeared, dim and muted. There was something moving down on the mud, a rectangle darker than the rest. He waited, watching it reach the waterline and head further out. It crossed the top end of Shorty's lines, navigating around them, and continued towards the other farm. A smaller shape separated itself from the larger one, growing out of the middle of the rectangle, and Jack realized it was a person, and the larger object a small punt. The shape sat down again and the outlines merged once more, making slow progress away from Jack.

Setting aside his coffee Jack dashed inside and found the binoculars where Rose had said they would be, focusing them first on the water and then on the shape where it floated. The binoculars added definition to the person who was kneeling on the punt, and the movement of arms showed the figure to be using a pole to maneuver the craft rather than rowing. His first thought was of Ross, finally catching him up to no good, or so it could be assumed. Why else would he be on Shorty's farm at this hour? But as he watched he knew it wasn't his boss. Ross was taller and generally of larger build. Jack glanced at the horizon wishing the haze of candy-floss cloud would shift so he could see better. He counted the rows from the nearest marker post and stopped at row four as the punt turned, heading down the row and pausing at the second post. For a moment the figure was upright again but the purpose of this stop was unclear. It wasn't until the fourth post of the fourth row that two things helped Jack to guess what he was seeing; firstly, the cloud had drifted to the left of the horizon, and secondly, Jack recalled the sagging rails he'd seen some weeks ago. At each post along the row there was a pause where the figure rose up slightly for a few seconds before moving on.

Ten minutes later the coffee had gone cold but Jack swallowed it anyway. The punt reached the second to last post and finally there was enough light to see the crow bar as it worked back and forth between the post and the rail, confirming what he'd already guessed. Jack swore under his breath, 'Son of a bitch.'

Reaching the end of the row the punt turned towards the homestead as the sky turned from Prussian to royal blue. The figure poled quickly now, striking left, right, left, right, standing but with knees bent making directly for Terry's yard via the end of the farm. The last glimpse Jack had through the binoculars was of a man in gumboots and a black hat pulling the punt the last ten metres where the water was yet to rise. He stumbled in the mud and his knees left two indents like a plaster cast of a woman's breasts. The man was clearer, closer, but that wasn't the only reason to think it was a man; no woman could pull a punt so fast, even one desperately racing against the sun.

Smell raised her nose to the wind as Jack heard the sound that had first got his attention; the noise of something being dragged over the mud as sunrise made its presence official, a shout of gold rising up, the wisps of cloud like a girl's pink tutu.

Jack went inside and shut the door. He reheated the coffee and poured a second cup, sitting at the table with his head in his hands. He had a feeling there was something off about those loose rails and now he knew why. Whoever it was out there had been gradually sabotaging the structures, taking care not to leave tracks in the mud that would be seen the next day. The pole meant there was no splash from oars, because if the wind blew west on a calm morning the sound would carry to Ross's doorstep. The farm rows one to four, Jack knew, were full of sticks laid out three months ago, and normally that meant they would sit there another six months or more, enough time for the rust to weaken the nails and a storm to thrash them off. What they didn't know was the reorganization Ross was doing, or they wouldn't have bothered. All those rows would be moved out to the new lease early next year and would be secure enough till then. It had to be Shorty behind this. Since Ross suspected nothing it must have been going on since the beginning; if the problem had always existed he probably thought it was part of what happened on a stick farm, having no previous experience to suggest otherwise.

All sympathy Jack might have had was erased in the last twenty minutes. That was about as low down and sneaky as he had ever heard, and Shorty didn't even stand to gain from it. It was just plain petty and mean. Every storm they lost a bunch of sticks, and then there was the time spent looking for them up and down the bay, hoping the oysters hadn't been battered on the rocks. Jack guessed it cost the farm a few thousand a year. What to do next? He definitely couldn't tell Ross. He'd go bananas if he knew Jack was spending his weekends with Shorty's sister in Shorty's house.

All he wanted to do right now was ring Joshua. He pulled his phone from his pocket; two bars of reception, just enough. But what if Rose woke up? Now wasn't the time for confessions. If she heard him talking he'd be obliged to explain and there was no way of telling how she'd react. He wasn't even sure who the man was, but someone in Shorty's pay no doubt. It was six thirty in the morning, three quarters of an hour since he woke up. He slid the phone back in his pocket and padded back into the kitchen. He would make breakfast and take it to Rose in bed.

Cleaning up the kitchen later that morning, Jack looked out the window to see a border collie trotting up the path towards the house. Following at a steady walk was a man who fit the image of number one suspect perfectly, from his mud-slick gumboots to his black woolen beanie. His trousers he must have changed because his dark blue tracksuit pants were clean. Smell began to bark, and Rose who was bundling the sheets from the bed into the laundry basket came to see why.

'That must be the caretaker,' she said, taking a

look out the window. Jack stepped away from the window as the man came closer. The man's dog heard Smell and stopped to bark twice, the noise echoing off the hill and surrounding them. 'Rose, it might be best if he doesn't know I'm here. He's mates with the man Ross leases the yard from, and word could get back to Ross.'

'Has he seen you before?' Jack shook his head.

'Well then, you'll be fine. We just won't say who you are and he'll think I've brought you over from the city.' Jack looked dubiously at his old sweater and worn in jeans, but it was too late to retrieve his boots from the veranda, very countrified looking boots they were too. He would have to leave this one to Rose. There was a knock on the door, and she opened it smiling. 'Hi. You must be the caretaker. George, right? Terry said I might see you around.' Smell stood just behind Rose and growled softly.

'Gidday. Yeah, that's me. I look after the place. I didn't know there was anyone here this weekend. There weren't any bookings. My wife checks that, and lets me know.' His eyes were shifty, looking from Jack to Rose and then at Smell, accusing them of tricking him somehow. 'You know we have a policy about dogs here. She won't touch the sheep will she?'

'No. She won't. Sorry, I didn't introduce myself. I'm Rose, Terry's sister. He said I could come here when it's empty. You can ring him and check if you like. This is a friend of mine.' She indicated Jack. 'We're off soon, but we'll leave it tidy. The bed will need changing before the next guests arrive, but I've stripped it for you.' Jack watched as his manner changed from suspicion to deferential, to leery, taking in Rose's uncombed hair and bra-less chest beneath her t-shirt. She crossed her arms, tucking her hands under her armpits and blocking his view. He looked up, 'Right. I'll leave you to it then. Sorry to have disturbed you both. Ah, if you ring ahead next time I can bring some stuff down. Meat, eggs...what did you say the dog's called?'

'I didn't, but don't worry, we'll keep her indoors until we go. Have a nice day!' Rose practically closed the door on him.

'Urrgh. Did you see the way he was looking me up and down?' she hissed a second later. 'What a knicker licker.'

'Let's get out of here. I'm not so sure it was wise of me to come,' Jack said curtly. He was feeling out of sorts. For a second he'd wanted to punch the silly grin off George's face, an overreaction he quickly suppressed. He couldn't afford to be noticed, and last time he'd checked, looking a woman up and down wasn't a crime, and decking the caretaker was sure to raise questions. Maybe jealously was something that developed side by side with love.

On Sunday night Jack rang his brother. Rose was having an early night, she had another hectic week ahead, and Jack was glad of the time alone to get his head straight on a few things. From her perspective the weekend had been a great escape, and romantically speaking it was. Jack tried to hold that foremost in his thoughts, but keeping a secret from

Rose felt uncomfortable, and now he needed some outsider advice.

'I've got interesting news, but not from where you'd expect,' he said to Joshua. 'You know I said I've been seeing a woman called Rose?'

'Yeah, I remember. What's it got to do with her?'

'The thing is, she's Shorty's sister.'

'You're kidding! I'm surprised to hear that. Not like you to take risks, Jack. Doesn't that complicate things a little?'

'Yes and no. We don't flaunt ourselves around. I'm sure word will get out eventually, but I don't think I'll be here that long. Not many people know who Rose is, and Terry doesn't know me, so there's no problem unless someone goes and makes one. Anyway, we went out to her old family home for the weekend. It looks out over Shorty and Ross's farms in the bay. You'll never guess what I saw.'

'A naked woman?'

'Boy, you're good at this game. Wouldn't have been much of a weekend if I didn't, but I'll save those details for private contemplation if you don't mind. I saw Shorty's caretaker out on Ross's lease. Just before dawn he went out and had a tinker with the rails. I'd guess it's been happening a while, and it sure explains why the sticks come off after a storm.'

'So who's this caretaker, then, and what do you mean exactly by tinker?'

'He had a crowbar, using it to loosen the rails from the posts. The little Brad nails holding the sticks in place get disrupted when the rails move and rust to nothing by harvest time. The guy is some old perv Shorty keeps to oversee the property, general dog's-body sort of thing.'

'What a cheeky bastard! This guy got an issue with Ross, or you think Shorty put him up to it?'

'I'd say he did. I can have a yarn to Dave, he's drinking buddies with the caretaker, see if I can dig any dirt, but my money's on Shorty, and anyway, so far as I know Ross hasn't put a foot wrong all year. In any other circumstance I'd be helping Ross intimidate him today, right now. You should see the little creep! Makes my foot itch. You want to do something, like tip Ross off long distance?'

'Hold on. I'm not sure we should tell him yet. I know how you must feel; hell, if it was me I'd have his guts for garters, but you don't wanna go inflaming Ross without knowing the full picture. Keep it under your hat and we'll see if it's connected, it's gotta be connected. Rule out that caretaker fella while you're waiting, and you might find there's more to the story.'

As usual Joshua managed to calm Jack down. Joshua wasn't any less a fighter for the underdog than Jack but he had more experience in waiting out a situation. Unlike Jack he didn't dwell on problems unless they were unavoidable and immediate. Petty vandalism, unless it happened on his own farm, could be ignored for the time being.

'What about Rose? Does she know anything?'

'Nope. I've been agonizing over telling her.'

'If there's one thing I know about women, Jack, they don't like to find out things after. If you're serious about this girl, then come clean. Unless you think she'll squeal.'

'I'll give it some more thought.' But not tonight, Jack added to himself. He needed a break from thinking it over, everything was grating on his nerves. Of course he would have to explain to Rose, and soon. He was rapidly approaching the point where he lost his famous cool and walked out on the whole mess. He'd probably even slam the door, but not on Rose. He was hoping to carry her over the threshold.

On Monday Jack dropped Ryan and Tyrone home and took a shower, changed his dirty clothes, and headed to the pub. It was darts night and Dave never missed it. Jack would try to catch him before the game got serious. When he had paid for his beer Jack sat down on a bar stool and waited. Half his pint was gone when Dave came up beside him, his hair still wet from his own ablutions.

'Evening, Jack. You joining us for darts?' He handed over a crisp note and took the stool beside Jack.

'Hey, Dave. No, just didn't feel like staying in this evening, something gloomy about Mondays.' Jack was impatient to bring the conversation round to George, but he didn't have a clue how. He had as long as it took Dave to down a beer before the darts began and that would be that, but Jack's luck was in. 'How's the sheep? Did I see you got a new ram?'

'Yeah, well not so much got one, he's borrowed. George loaned him to me. He had it tied up in the bottom of his dinghy to bring it over, and it was pretty upset by the time it arrived. Had to leave it in the barn for a few days to calm down.'

'I bet. Can't say I know George, but he sounds like a hard case. Makes cider doesn't he?'

'Yeah, he's a funny bloke.' Dave screwed his face up a bit, showing he meant funny as in strange. 'Good cider, but he always wants something in return, you know? I thought twice about asking for the ram, but wool prices haven't been good this year, and I need to breed out the bit of Suffolk in the line.'

'Where's he from, this George?'

'Oh, way down south. Used to work a big station, but reckons his wife had enough. I think he was a naughty boy, let his hands wander. Says he came here to save his marriage. His wife doesn't mind him coming to me because I'm a bachelor, but she goes everywhere else with him. See? That's why I'm single.' Dave did a double eyebrow lift at someone. The barman was placing spare darts on the counter.

'I'm not sure Ross likes him much. Suppose it's because he's Shorty's man,' Jack probed.

'Yeah, I got the feeling there's some history between them, but buggered if I know what. Can't be anything major because they tolerate each other. Won't take a drink together though.' Someone was warming up, the thwack of darts hitting the board caught Dave's attention and he knocked back his beer. 'Sure you won't join the fun?' he asked.

'No, mate. Smell will be waiting for dinner. Give us a yell if you need a hand roping that ram.' Jack grabbed his keys off the counter and left a minute later. A weak evening sun was on its last legs and a fine shower of drizzling rain misted his hair. The window wipers screeched on the glass as he drove home, the dust from the road to work smearing the windscreen. Just like the picture in front of me, Jack thought, as clear as poo juice.

The atmosphere at work didn't exactly improve, but Ross's moods leveled out a bit making him more predictable; less of trying to guess what he expected and being yelled at if they didn't perform. Early summer was mostly patching up the farms and laying out sticks and bundles as well as the usual harvesting. All day in shorts and singlets meant they were tanned and fit before summer really began. Ross was the only exception, being fair skinned. No matter how much sun screen he put on he always had a red nose and cheeks, the skin constantly peeling.

By December everyone was needing a break from work and each other. This was normal in most jobs Jack had done where men spent hundreds of hours concentrating in isolation alongside each other. By the end you always knew the others well, even if sometimes you wished you didn't.

Harvest would be finishing for the year in two weeks. The oysters were turning milky, fat and bulging with semen or eggs. They developed a creamy, metallic taste which some people enjoyed and others found sickly. By late December they would be spent, their spawn sent out to sea to swim about until the currents swept them into sheltered nooks where they could settle and attach to something. The breeding oyster's flesh would be skinny and watery, like a woman who spends a year breastfeeding, giving all the nutrients to her child. There wasn't much pleasure in eating them, though some people would eat them at any time. The spawn would be repeated several times over the hottest months, and harvest wouldn't begin again until sometime late April when the oysters were reconditioned. Most stick farms would shut completely over this time, or cut back to a skeleton crew.

Shorty's single seed farm was significantly better off; there was no down season. His spat was purchased from a hatchery at one millimetre in size, the only farm to do so thanks to Ross's technique. How this was done only a few knew, and to make sure that they couldn't steal the idea Shorty had put a copyright on the design. Ross's design. When the tiny seeds were bigger they would be transferred to sacks made from very fine mesh. The sacks were clipped onto wires, with high densities of oysters in them. All he had to do after that was replace the mesh sacks with baskets when they were big enough, decreasing the density of oysters per basket as they grew.

At one time Joshua had shown an interest in converting his farm to single seed, and he and Jack had gone through the preliminary research to learn more about what the hatcheries provided at a high cost that nature couldn't give them for free. Not only was the spat costly, the new set up it required was somewhere in the millions.

Hatcheries would produce two types of spat for sale; diploids and triploids. Wild spat - the diploids - only have two strains of chromosomes, and triploids have three. To produce an oyster with three strains of chromosomes you need to first create one with four strains of chromosomes, a tetraploid, then breed it with the old standard two. The usual method involves a toxic chemical bath to create a tetraploid, though other methods were also used in conjunction with a vortex. Needless to say, there was nothing natural about it though it couldn't be called genetic modification because no foreign tissues were inserted. It was more of a genetic manipulation. In some countries there had been outrage that people were eating these shellfish unaware of its altered nature, mostly by farmers who weren't convinced by the science. They argued that the customer should be allowed to choose a natural product, but the laws for labeling worked against them. To call an oyster 'natural' or 'organic' required traceability to the parent, an impossibility for wild spat. Other less prejudiced farmers jumped on the chance to grow and sell all year round; since a triploid didn't reproduce, its energy was spent solely on growth, reaching maturity months ahead of the wild oyster. It was known as the Four Seasons Oyster.

Joshua had decided he didn't like the idea of interfering with what the sea produced for the sake of money. He was just one person who would live and die within a hundred years, and the sea with its unknown number of living creatures all dependent on each other had existed before him, would exist after him. If he wanted more money all he had to do was grow more oysters, not all that fancy stuff.

Shorty didn't give a shit. He was firmly on the side of new technologies and fast fortunes. In a small country like this it looked good being a front-runner for new methods, and gave him a certain cachet in the business crowd.

There was huge demand for his oysters over the Christmas and New Year holidays when everyone else shut down, and his new restaurant would serve a premium product fifty two weeks of the year, as long as the virus didn't strike again. Once you told the public they could have what they wanted all the time, they soon expected it. He was proud as punch to be one of the first growers using the new seed, and sent an automated email to the hatchery every month asking if they had found a way to breed his logo into the shell yet. 'All I want is a black T, for fuck sake,' he complained to Rose. They were doing that sort of leading edge stuff in America so why not here? Rose told Jack she was beginning to think it had been a mistake coming home to work for Terry. He was far more megalomanic than before, and she couldn't see any improvements at all on a personal level. If he wasn't family she would despise him, but he *was* a great boss.

'Isn't it funny? You work for Ross who's popular with his mates, do a favour for anyone, good all round guy, but a prick to work with. I work for a dodgy, greedy, ethically challenged fathead who's a great boss. Speaking of which I'm going to be extra busy this month with the restaurant opening on the twentieth,' she said, stretching on the bed.

'All the more reason not to get up, then.'

Of all the days in the week this had become Jack's favourite. Sunday morning in bed with Rose, and Monday not yet looming. During the week they shared after work drinks or a meal, sometimes spending the night together, sometimes not. Sunday was their chance to laze about. Yesterday they had helped Lucy move her belongings from her parents garage into Ryan's one bedroom bach. Ryan's bed was replaced with Lucy's modest queen size one, and his collection of porn magazines was burnt in the back yard incinerator. He'd taken them out the back and lit them himself, confiding to Jack that he didn't get time to read them anymore.

Ryan had bought the bach three years ago as an investment and had seldom used it apart from the odd weekend. Back then he was living in a loft apartment over the barn on the horse stud where he worked, and the accommodation was free. It suited him perfectly to roll out of bed and into the stables, sometimes in the clothes he slept in. The barn also made a good base for entertaining young women who came to ride the horses. They were the daughters of wealthy people and not used to slumming it, so Ryan spent all his spare income on a big screen TV, surround sound system, a super king size bed, and consumables like champagne he didn't drink himself. Once his nest was nicely feathered his success rate went from getting them in the door, to getting them in bed. Not one of the women had ever suggested it become a relationship; Ryan was definitely from the wrong side of town, which made the trysts all the more exciting, and that suited him fine. Those posh girls could really let their hair down with him.

After his accident he returned from hospital to find all his belongings packed into banana boxes ready to be collected. His employer, a man who was fond of him but more fond of money, said he needed the barn for his new trainer. Ryan moved into his bach permanently. It needed a lot of work, but his recovery was slow and he couldn't carry out the renovations. He had no money, and his shoulder was buggered. Ross and the other rugby fellas had helped move his furniture. The large TV dominated the bach's lounge, and the extra large bed filled the bedroom almost wall to door. The door wouldn't close, and to get in and out of bed there was a narrow space a foot wide down one side, not even room for a bedside table.

In eighteen months of living there Ryan had stopped noticing the peeling brown and cream wallpaper and sparkly lino with its holes worn through, and that was the best to be said for the decor. The bathroom door stuck half way and the mould was so advanced it grew in black, slimy lumps. Outside, pale blue paint was peeling off the weatherboards in long strips and the yard was knee deep in weeds. In its favour was a fantastic view out over the sea to the west, and to the east partially inhabited hills with a lush canopy of trees. It would make quite a cosy love-nest when done up.

When he'd asked Lucy to live with him she had

agreed, but only if renovations began immediately. Ryan went to the bank to ask for a loan, thinking they would turn him down, and was surprised when they offered him twice what he needed. In three years the value had gone up as the hefty city real estate prices made commuting more attractive. Lucy was spending most nights there anyway since a moldy bathroom and bad decor was better than reliving her teenage years at home.

Ryan had declared that today, since Lucy was an official inhabitant of the blue bach, she would have to participate in the Sunday rituals. This was a strict regime. A late morning fry-up for breakfast, and a movie marathon on the couch in your undies for the rest of the day. In recognition of her new resident status, movies would be alternated; one of her choice, one of his. Participants were not allowed off the couch except for the toilet or bringing more refreshments. He would be drinking a six pack of beer, but Lucy could choose something else if she preferred. Also, if she knew how to make popcorn he would be very grateful. Lucy was obliging in every way, but drew the line at musical farting. If Ryan needed to share his talent he could ring a friend from the toilet, and she most certainly would not pull his finger. Again. Not even if smelling farts prevented cancer, or wrinkles.

Since neither Rose or Jack had a TV on their boats, they went out to see a matinee film instead. After, they stopped by Connie's restaurant for an early dinner. Connie hid them in the nook by the service door as usual and took their orders. 'So lovebirds, what can I get you today?' She wasn't in the least bit jealous of Rose, but she was certainly happy for Jack. There was nothing more criminal in her view than a good man going to waste; if she couldn't have him someone else should. Besides, her current dalliance was working out very nicely. He was a seasonal worker passing through, and right now he was chipping potatoes in the kitchen.

'I'll have one of your delicious lamb burgers, and a prawn cocktail for starters,' Jack said.

'I'll have the rocket salad, and seafood mornay for mains,' Rose replied.

'Lovely. Before I get started out the back, tell me how the new restaurant is coming along. I saw the write up in the paper yesterday, and there were some wonderful photos of the farm.'

'It's all pretty exciting, but about to get warp-speed hectic for me. I'll have to attend the rehearsal dinners, and make sure Terry says the right things to the press. I wish Jack could be there, but Terry has a history of poaching my boyfriends and can't be trusted.'

'I'd love to hear *that* story sometime. Can you imagine Ross if Jack went to work for the opposition? He'd go off the deep end. He's still holding a grudge you know. I heard him tell Marty during one of their drinking sessions he'd like to see Shorty *eat shit*.' Connie whispered the last two words. 'He thinks your brother has spies watching him.'

'Yes, he was rather rude to the photographer. I'm fairly sure he'll realize his mistake when he sees the pictures in the paper. Right now Terry doesn't have time to keep tabs on Ross, far too much schmoozing to be done. The guest list is looking promising for opening night.'

Once Connie had gone Rose looked at Jack and commented, 'You've been quiet. What's on your mind?'

'A couple of things. Number one: I'm afraid Ryan won't come back after the break. He's had a guts full of Ross. Number two: I'm sick of us having to sneak around like criminals, and three: Ross has been unusually mellow lately. I've got a bad feeling that he's planning something. You know how I said I'd tell you if I thought there was trouble coming? Well, there is. I can't say what just yet, but I'm close to finding out - and there's another matter, or two, but it can wait.'

'What are you saying? What could Ross do?'

'Contaminate the bay.'

'Would that make the oysters unsafe to eat, or just kill them?'

'I don't know yet. Potentially both. It depends on what he's cooking up, but it won't be good.'

'Oh crap. Just what I need. Stuff *Terry*. My name's on this job, and it's gaining high profile. I'm just back on the scene building a reputation. I'll be tarnished along with the company if anything should happen to the product. That's how business works. It won't matter that it wasn't part of my contract to know what happens on the farm, it's all association. Is there any way to stop Ross?'

'OK. I'll tell you what. Let's eat and get out of here. There's some things we need to discuss in private. Real private.'

'Oh my god, are you like an international spy or something?' Rose giggled at his seriousness. She might think it was a bit of a joke all this cloak and dagger talk in rural New Zealand, but Jack doubted she'd still be laughing when he explained it properly. So far she was concerned for her reputation, and maybe for Terry too, more than she let on, but Rose had no idea how messy this could get.

'No. Just national.'

He didn't smile.

On the drive home Jack was full of nerves, mind racing to put his words in the right order. Very shortly he would have to explain himself. If that went alright he would have to mention what he'd seen out at the homestead. Jack contemplated leaving it out, what Shorty did wasn't his main concern and people could be touchy when family were implicated but if he was off-loading then better to do it all in one go. There was even a remote chance that Rose might know some small piece of information that made it all fit together, though it was doubtful. This wasn't nothing, what they were about to discuss. It would shape their future. He was certain a future involving Rose was what he wanted, but first they needed to trust each other. It was time to find out.

Jack placed two glasses and a bottle of whisky on the table. He had asked Rose if they could go to his place. He needed the confidence of being on his own territory. If she chose to walk out it would be less awkward than Jack being asked to leave. Staring out the cabin window at the pohutukawa trees with their red flowers taking on a deeper colour as the sun dimmed, he gathered his thoughts while Rose waited attentively. He would start with the basic facts. Drawing a breath he began, 'My brother is an oyster farmer up north.' Rose lifted her eyebrows showing surprise, and he continued, 'Some of the farmers are worried that this falling out between Terry and Ross might cause problems for all of them. It's a small industry. Word gets around. Some threats were made. Josh asked me to come and look into it, find out what's going on here, and alert him if I needed to.'

'Wow. So you kind of *are* a spy. I can't believe you didn't tell me. Am I the only one who doesn't know, apart from Ross?' There was a peeved look about her mouth that Jack was wary of.

'Nope. The opposite. You're the first person to know. I think Connie suspects something, but I've been careful to keep it hush hush. Sorry I couldn't tell you before, but your brother isn't exactly blameless. Everyone knows how Ross was shafted. I needed to feel I could trust you not to involve him, at least until I know what is going on.'

'Fair enough, and you can, but I want to hear the rest. All of it.'

'Okay.' Jack took a gulp of whisky, letting the after-burn abate before continuing. 'No one thinks Ross got fair treatment, and they think he's mad enough to risk everything on revenge. This is what I've heard, okay? Five years ago he was a nobody who had a brilliant idea. He developed a device that could put triploid spat on a farm at one millimetre in size. That almost splits the cost of spat in quarters. Spat isn't cheap, and the bigger you buy it the more expensive it is. Most farmers buy 10 millimetre spat because it's big enough to go straight in the baskets. There are only one or two others buying at 4 millimetres, and no one else does one mill. Thanks to Ross, your brother is the only farmer able to grow from so small. It saves him thousands of dollars.'

'I can see why it's a big deal, and I understand the unfairness, but as the law stands what a person develops at work is the property of their employer. It's hard luck.'

'Yes, I believe Ross found that out, but not to give the person who has enriched your company something in return is pretty rough. Ross wanted to buy into what he was helping build up. Instead he was told he'd get nothing, not the manager's position, not a pay rise, not his name on the design, not a share in the right to patent or sell the design - no recognition what so ever.'

'I'm not surprised. Terry was never one to share his toys.'

'Then, Ross tried to start his own business farming single seed, making the transition over several years. Your brother cut him out of that too, leaving him no choice but to go stick farming when all his knowledge was in single seed.'

'But I heard he purchased a stick lease. How is Terry to blame for that?'

'He did, but usually council will accept a submission asking for an amendment to what a lease is used for. Terry obviously felt threatened at the idea of being in competition with Ross and used his contacts to have the submission declined, claiming a conflict of interests in a small catchment. So the answer is: Terry had everything to do with it. I suspect Ross has been waiting and doing a lot of thinking. He's clever, but Terry knows that. Me? I can run a farm because it's mostly rotation and easy maths, but Ross can probably tell you the name of everything in the water - *in Latin*. Word is he'll release a virus, but I'm not convinced. He puts everything into his work, and anyone who works for him has to do the same. Everything in the bay would be affected by a virus.'

'So, if he wanted to release a virus to wipe out Terry's stock, Ross would lose his too?'

'Not all of it. This new lease? He's shifting next year's harvest out there so they should be safe, but he'll lose some spat. He's accounted for that. We've laid out twice as many bundles, but that's not the point. The last virus went international, and that's why I think they're wrong. Fundamentally Ross is a good guy. I can't imagine him being responsible for ruining hundreds of other men's lives. He's just not that antisocial.'

'What other way is there to close down a farm, in the local sense?'

'That's what I've been trying to work out. There are a few things he could try.'

'Give me an example.'

'Okay, too much fresh water. More than twenty mills of rain and you can't harvest for two days from when it stops.'

'What's wrong with rain?'

'Nothing. It's the run-off from the land after heavy rain. The oysters filter the water, so dirty water means dirty oysters. If you live somewhere built up, lots of housing, or cattle, then you might get shut down after eight mills of rain and not reopen for three days. Where *we* are the rainfall can be more because it's relatively clean land.'

'So what's the main contaminant in the run-off?'

'Crap, of course. Human and animal waste. Leaky septic tanks, sewerage ponds...poo isn't bad for oysters, they get nice and fat on it, but poo fed oysters are bad for *us*. All oyster farmers have to pay for monthly water testing to check the number of fecal coliforms in the water stays below a certain number.'

'So why couldn't he just shit in the water?'

'He could, but where would he get it from? We're not talking about a dump at the coast every morning, it takes a bit more than that. You need a license to deal with waste, so even if he got The Poo Man in he'd need to store it somewhere.'

Jack sipped at the whisky in his glass. The Poo Man's slogan was 'Your business is our business' and he was known to dump a load about the place if he couldn't be bothered going all the way back to base when it was busy. He had a few choice spots which farmers had said he could use as long as no one from council saw him doing it; mostly down steep gullys that were too dangerous for grazing but easily reached by farm roads. Jack was surprised. Rose was coping with this news remarkably well; she was a bit tense but hadn't touched her drink. He could see all her attention was focused on the problem, and he had a picture of how she must throw herself into her work.

'Well, it's a better theory than Ross the Rainmaker. You haven't seen him secretly building an ark lately?' Jack didn't bother to answer, his thoughts were sending up little flares: *Over here! Pick me!* But Rose was talking again. 'Supposing he had somewhere to store it, couldn't he just collect it from his own septic? Him, his wife, three kids....I bet it doesn't take long to fill a barrel, and-'

Jack cut her off. His brain had sorted out the clues and it was like Guy Fawkes in there. He gabbled quickly, 'Holy shit, Rose. The *barrels*. I went in his shed - the one he rents off Dave. There wasn't much to see, except some old drums. The smell. I thought he might be keeping something to feed the host with, if there's a virus in the ponds. I have to go back in there and find out what's in the barrels, but I reckon you've cracked it. Raw sewerage makes sense. It's also the easiest option.'

'You sound happy about it. Forgive me for sounding selfish, but if it's true then I still have a problem with that. I know Terry isn't an angel, but I don't want to see everything he's built up ruined, and his reputation is what he lives for. If guests at the restaurant eat poisoned oysters he'll be finished in the food industry. The list of dignitaries is a page and a half long.'

'I think seeing some of the people who helped Terry crush his dreams go down with a bad case of the trots won't be much of a deterrent for Ross. No wonder he's been in such a bloody good mood lately. He must have been planning this anyway, then he hears about Tide to Table and, bingo!'

'Even if we're right what can you do about it? He'll fire you and deny everything, and do it anyway. I can't do anything about the restaurant going ahead, too late for that. So what, then? Is there enough proof to ask the authorities for help?'

'Possibly. I'll look into that in case, but there's another way: give Ross what he wants. Talk your brother into putting things right, bury the hatchet. There's always squabbles going on, deals going ass up, poaching the workers, pinching customers, stealing oysters off the rails of unused leases. If it's just a case of pay-back Terry won't get any help from the other growers. He needs to make good with him or take the risk.'

'And unless I want early retirement then that's my job, right? Wow, this sucks. Maybe I should ask Lucy if she needs an assistant. He's incredibly stubborn, you know.'

'Yep, probably how he's risen in the world, but if we're right, then I might have something you can hold over Terry as leverage.' Jack was almost enjoying this. Rose was a bit worked up, but in a fighting way. She hadn't gone all emotional and lost the plot like some women would.

'Finally some good news. I'll need every trick in the book. What have you got? Don't tell me it's got something to do with Nancy. The DNA tests proved he wasn't the father.' Jack looked at her with alarm. What on earth was she going on about? His whisky glass was half way to the table, but he kept it there in mid air. He had a hunch he might need it again soon.

Speaking slowly and carefully Jack said, 'No, it's not, but I would very much like to know what the heck you're on about.'

'Oh. I thought you knew the story. Sorry. I guess it's why I understand the way Terry shafted Ross over the intellectual property. You seemed to know everything else so I just assumed...' Jack lowered his head, looking at her intently from under his eyebrows.

'Don't they say there's always two sides to the story? Sounds like I only heard one of them.'

'Well, just before I left for London Terry started dating this woman. She was some sales rep he met at a party in the city. Terry's a bit unfortunate with women. I think he has to hire them. Anyway, he told me he was seeing this woman, a bit younger than him, her main attraction being that she genuinely liked him. Her name was Nancy. Then we lost touch. I had flown the coop, and wasn't talking to Terry. I'd been gone about a year when I had this long email from him. In it he said he was very happy, Nancy had agreed to marry him, and would I please try to make it back home for the wedding. So I wrote back saying I would come. The date was set for the following spring so I had some time to plan it. Skylar said she'd be there too, even though she can't stand Terry. I booked a ticket and three months later I get another mail to tell me the bride to be is expecting a baby so they pushed back the wedding date. The baby would be born in spring, and the wedding would be in summer. It wasn't until September that Skylar rang me to say the whole thing had been called off. Apparently Nancy had been spending time at the homestead alone, supposedly overseeing the renovations, and wandering down to the yard for company. George the caretaker had walked into the shed to find her kissing some worker and told Terry. Nancy said it was nothing, just a kiss. Apparently she was lonely with him gone all week. Terry said if that was true then he'd forgive her, but he wanted a DNA test once the baby was born and she couldn't stay on the farm unless he was there. Well, it turned out not to be his. I'm sure you've guessed who the worker was.'

Jack shook his head. What a bloody drama. There's Ross making out to everyone he's such a victim, and really he dug his own hole. Poking the boss's fiance. It wasn't surprising Ross had kept that quiet. Jack put down his empty glass and waggled Rose's inch of whisky at her but she shook her head. He swallowed it in one go. That's a fine way to make an enemy; one screws the other's woman, the other retaliates and takes his ideas off him.

'And you say George squealed? That makes sense. Probably jealous she didn't pick him. You know it was George's wife's idea to move somewhere isolated, I'll let you guess why. I wonder if Ross wasn't a bit put out having to keep Nancy. A moment of fun turns into a life changing event. He must have felt obliged after the DNA results. The punishment fits the crime alright. I always wondered why she puts up with his crap. Poor Nancy.'

'Poor Nancy? You could say she isn't exactly blameless either. So if it's nothing to do with her, your leverage, then what is it?' Jack missed her discomfort and returned to the story.

'It's to do with George, but I guess it's all connected. Last month, you remember when you took me out there? I got up early like I would for work, and I saw George out tinkering with Ross's farm. He was weakening the structures so everything comes loose.' Jack paused. He wanted to hear Rose's reaction, and what conclusions she'd come to on her own, but there was one more thing he wanted to clarify. 'What ever is going to happen, I'm with you in this.'

Rose smiled and clasped his hand, 'Thanks, Jack. I doubt George is acting alone. I bet Terry put him up to it. I might be able to use that. I won't tell him what Ross is planning, just that a reliable source tipped me off. Right? I'll say the plan is fool-proof, undetectable, and catastrophic. I'll threaten to leave unless he talks to Ross, then I'll tell him that someone's noticed what goes on before dawn. That should put the wind up him. You need to go back into the shed and check we're on the right track. I'm not doing all this for a few barrels of sheep dip.'

'Do you know something Rose? I just bloody love you.' Jack reached across the table and kissed her as spontaneously as he had the first time. She was a contradiction, vulnerable and strong at the same time. Rose smiled up at him. 'I'm glad you said that. When this mess is sorted out I've got a confession to make, but I think we've spilled enough guts for today.' She kissed him back, tasting the smokiness of whisky on his lips.

Bees were swarming over the pohutukawa flowers before the dew had even lifted. It was almost the height of summer. Another clear sky day. Jack left Smell with Rex since it was one of Betty's busy days, and the old dog was resting a lot. Rex liked company in any shape, and Smell was an easy companion to please. At first she had whined when Jack left, but regular treats throughout the day kept her distracted. With all the extra food and less exercise Jack expected her to put on some weight, but instead she continued to lose condition.

Ryan was changing. Lucy was willing to get on his level every Sunday, but she expected him to follow her lead in other areas. His interests had extended from horses, rugby, beer, and porn, to photography, art galleries, food groups beyond bacon, eggs, and pies, and colour charts for paint. This hadn't been a quick process, but the results were becoming obvious after just three months of courtship. A woman was a powerful force for change. This morning he couldn't shut up about yellow.

'Do you know how many shades of yellow paint there are to choose from? So far I've counted fifty. *Fifty*. We've managed to narrow it down to five test pots. Some of the names are pretty creative; Hahei Sunrise. Do you think someone takes a photo and then tries to make up the colour, or do you think they make the colour and try to match it with something?' Jack made a fart sound with his lips in response. Wouldn't it be great if all he had to think about was the colour of paint?

Jack had also observed recent changes in Tyrone, though the young man wasn't aware of it. They nick named him 'Motor-mouth' and he still was, but he was taking his work more seriously, and this pleased Ross. He was even allowed to drive the old barge occasionally. The job was no longer just a meal ticket, or to prove to his girlfriend he wasn't some good-for-nothing dole bludger, and since he was less annoying they all got on better.

When they picked him up for work the first thing he said was, 'Hey fullas! You know what Ross got planned for us today?' looking keenly at their faces. At work he had adjusted his pace from spasmodic to steady like Jack, and he wasn't done-in by lunchtime either. What Tyrone *had* noticed in himself were his physical changes. Four months ago he was tall and lean. Now he had started to thicken out. His arms, shoulders, and legs were gaining muscle mass, and when Ross told them to 'pull out the big guns' Tyrone would try to flex them all at once saying, 'Which ones, boss?' making them all laugh.

In the ute he tapped his hands on his thighs to a beat only he could hear, head bobbing slightly in time. 'Me an my missus went to the rugby on Saturday, eh. Ross said I should think about joining the team. Sharn thinks I should. Reckons it'll keep me out of mischief. What do you guys reckon?'

'Go for it, bro. You've just got to build up your stamina and you'll be an awesome player. The farm will help with that. They're a good bunch of lads at rugby. There's no downside. I'll even come and watch your game when you've had some practice,'

Ryan said.

'Yep, same here,' Jack nodded.

'Ty? Hey, bro? What did I say?' Ryan gave Jack an alarmed look, but Jack shook his head in response. Give the boy a minute. Tyrone rubbed his eyes with the heel of his hands and looked out the windscreen, not that Ryan or Jack were watching.

'I never had people encourage me to do stuff. My dad never stuck around, and mum had six of us to take care of. I really appreciate what you guys have taught me, eh.' Tyrone spoke to the dashboard, then his knees. Ryan patted him on the shoulder, and Jack said, 'No worries, mate. We're just passing the favour. You don't think myself and Ryan here were born this perfect, do ya? We climbed our own learning curves, and there were blokes who helped us. Maybe it's your dad, a mate, your boss...mum's are special, but only a man can show you the kind of man you should be.'

'Ooorr, that sounds gay as, but I know what you're meaning.'

To break the mood and get things back on normal ground, Tyrone lifted his ass half off the seat and farted, 'Ah, that's better.' They all laughed, cursed him and his ass, and wound the windows down as far as they'd go.

'There's an empty dog box on the back, Motor-mouth,' Ryan joked, and they all laughed again, the dregs of emotion releasing into the slip stream of air outside.

At work Ross was in a typical Monday morning mood, hungover and suffering nicotine withdrawals after a weekend of living it up. They all knew what to expect and no one mucked him about. Tyrone would save his jokes for later. He usually worked off his grump at the tide and mellowed by lunchtime.

Ross sent Ryan off with a flea in his ear over the state of the crates which should have been cleaned on Friday for this afternoon's grow-ons to go in. He'd forgotten he was the one who told Ryan to do them later, and never gave him time to. As they were changing into waders Jack said casually, 'I don't mind staying behind to wash crates. If I'm done before you're back I can get ahead on the bundles going out tomorrow. I'll stack them down at the dock.'

'Uh ha. I was going to suggest that,' Ross replied. Yes, it always worked better if Ross thought it was his idea. The crates were used to hold the grow-ons which had come off the sticks with the big oysters and needed longer to reach full size. Some farmers threw out the undersize oysters, some sent them to a processor for a small return, but Ross was tidy like that. With the yard to himself Jack washed a few crates, blasting them with the high pressure hose to get the dried mud, seaweed, and dead barnacles off. A dirty crate would impede the flow of water, collecting even more fouling and cutting back the food supply to the oysters.

Jack kept busy like that until the barge disappeared from view. Once it went round the corner he walked quickly to Ross's shed and took out the key. The padlock clicked open easily this time so Ross must have been in here not long ago.

He'd brought an empty plastic drink bottle with him; if they were wrong about the sewerage then he'd still need to have the ponds tested.

Once inside he could see three barrels had been added along the side wall, forming a second row in front of the first. There was that faint smell of slightly sweet rotten cabbage again, stronger as he neared the wall, or so he imagined. The lid on the closest barrel was loose and unscrewed easily. Sharp ammonia like a slap in the face singed his nostril hairs and opened the way for a waft of rotten eggs and sweet earthiness. Jack pulled his t-shirt over his mouth and nose, leaned in again, then threw his head back in disgust. Raw sewerage filled three quarters of the barrel. A small brown turd rose to the surface and rolled over like a lazy swimmer, pulling a used tampon with it by its string. Holding his breath Jack let his t-shirt slip and quickly replaced the lid; he had definitely seen enough, and it hadn't come from animals. Looking at the quantity of raw material lined up along the wall, and given Ross had a continual supply, closure could last indefinitely if he put it in the water before the testings were done each month. He could use the thick alkathene pipes to pump it from here to the bay at night and no one would be the wiser. He supposed he ought to check the contents of the other barrels but he couldn't bring himself to do it. Instead, he kicked the other two new ones and was satisfied when they didn't budge.

Taking deep breaths of cleaner air Jack went to the ponds to check nothing had changed there, and heard the crunch of an oyster shell behind him. Nancy stood outlined in the doorway, her silhouette unmistakeable.

'Oh, hi Jack! I thought it might have been Rossy. I saw the door ajar.'

'Oh, hi Nance. Sorry to disappoint, they're all out on the new lease just now. I was curious to see how the nursery was coming along.'

'Oh, you're not any kind of disappointment.' Nancy took a few steps towards him. Jack was trying to keep his cool. Lucky she hadn't come in two minutes ago and seen him looking in the barrels. He focused on slowing his breathing. If Nancy was aware of what Ross was up to, then this was it. His goose was cooked. He remembered what Ryan had said about all Nancy's money being tied up in the farm, so what she said next didn't make sense. 'You feel it too, don't you Jack.' It came out as a statement, which was lucky because Jack didn't know the answer. This was turning weird. The look she gave him made his toes curl. Her lips were slightly parted and her chest was rising and falling rapidly so that for a second Jack wondered if she was having some kind of a turn. Nancy closed the distance between them until her heaving chest almost touched his, and he realized she was excited. If she wasn't in on the plan, then what on earth was she up to? She spoke rapidly, like the words had been rehearsed and waiting impatiently to come out, misreading his apprehension for feelings similar to her own excitement. 'I've seen the way you look at me sometimes. It must be hard for you working for

Ross, knowing how he treats me. I know you wouldn't treat me like that, and I'm ready. I'm ready to give myself to you, Jack.'

She had caught him off guard, and he stood momentarily helpless as Nancy wrapped herself around him like an octopus. He stood woodenly, in his head wondering if this was what a bean pole felt like, except if Nancy was a bean it would be a Broad Bean. He began removing her limbs from his body one at a time and spoke quietly to her, considering his words carefully. 'Nancy, I know how you feel, and I admit there have been moments...' Her arms crept back around his waist.

'Don't worry, Ross will never find out, I promise. We'll find a way to meet,' and she giggled, suddenly happy.

Now for the extrication, Jack thought, using the oldest excuse in the book. 'That's very thoughtful of you Nancy, and I appreciate you making this easy for me, but there's something you don't know.'

He knew he had to handle this situation very carefully, and reminded himself to breathe slow and not panic as one soft hand slid into the waistband of his pants. His instincts told him to push her away, but he pulled her closer and put an arm around her shoulders. 'I thought I could hide my feelings but you've seen through me. I hate saying this, but it's too late for us, Nancy. I didn't think it could ever happen. I met someone recently and she's helped me deal with my feelings. Now it's serious, between me and my lady. I don't think it would be fair if I didn't give her a proper chance after all she's done for me.'

Nancy's arms slowly slid off him and she looked into his grey eyes, her smile faltering.

'I'm so sorry, Jack. I know I made you wait too long. I'm so busy all the time, and there was just never an opportunity.' She looked deflated, like an older version of herself.

'Hey, no Nancy, don't be hard on yourself. It's my fault as much as yours. Now I've found someone I care about, so be happy for me, okay? You'll always be my favourite Nancy.' He didn't know any other Nancy, so this statement held true. Jack felt it was time to leave, but she would need a minute to process what had just happened, he couldn't do a runner. It probably wasn't every day she went out on a limb and threw herself at another man; though you never could tell. He guided her through the door gently, and locked it behind them. Outside he felt sudden relief. It looked like he might get away with his trespassing. He turned to face her and put a hand on each substantial shoulder.

'I'd better get back, the others will be along soon. Still friends?' He smiled hopefully, trying to catch her eye. Nancy's cheeks were flushed dark pink and she was looking at her feet.

'Still friends,' she forced a smile, 'but if things don't work out...' she left the rest unsaid, and Jack nodded vigorously, eager to be away.

This had turned out so bizarre. Jack went back to work feeling puzzled, not sure if he should also feel guilty. That had been a tricky situation, but he was pleased with the way he'd handled it. He wondered if Nancy would mention seeing him in the shed, after what she had proposed. All this time she had been misreading his looks of concern and friendliness for tortured desire. Maybe he should warn Ryan, he could be next. Jack had lied to Nancy but the alternative was too mean; she was a bubbly and warm-hearted woman who had married a reserved and moody man who probably resented her. Wasn't that a tough enough life sentence? Besides, he didn't need a spurned woman causing trouble for him.

Chapter 10

Jack was waiting for Rose on her deck when she got home. He told her about everything that had happened in the shed. She was miffed about him giving Nancy such an easy let down, and didn't believe for one second that Nancy was the long suffering wife.

'I bet she's had loads of affairs. Just because she's all sweet and nice to everyone doesn't mean anything.'

'But you understand I had to play along, right?' Jack was quietly pleased with her reaction, reading into it a touch of possessiveness he hadn't seen before. He hoped it was an indication of the strength of her feelings, because now he knew that Ross wasn't planning widespread damage he was free to leave. Jack was past midlife in the biblical sense, he'd peaked and missed it, but there was enough of a downhill gradient ahead of him that if he got stuck in, he could cross the finish line in style. The only way to know if Rose would come for the ride was to ask. He zoned back in to what she was saying, something to do with Nancy.

'...understand, but I don't have to like it. Come inside, I need to eat something before replying to today's emails.'

Rose made a pot of tea and opened a packet of biscuits saying, 'I can't believe he's really storing shit in his shed.' She made a disgusted face. 'That means I have to tackle Terry, doesn't it? That won't go down well this week. If he does come to the table, so to speak, what should be on the menu? Bare in mind he'll want to relinquish as little as possible.'

'Well, crumbs won't be enough for Ross. We're talking a long starvation here. No doubt he's been dreaming of a roast with all the trimmings. Ok, cut the food analogies. The prospect not to cause untold damage has to outweigh the satisfaction of causing untold damage. I know Ross fairly well. He won't take less than he wanted in the first place, and he'll want a cherry on top. To the non gourmand that means a big, fat apology.'

'Oh come on! They both did wrong. Talking and selling is what I do for a living. If I pull this off then I'm bloody Bill Gates.'

'I suggest he offer him a partnership. Maybe not an equal share of things, but enough to seal the deal. Talk up the advantages. A brilliant manager, future advances in oyster culture, respect from the wider industry, the whole bay under one flag, and the shit storm will go away. If *that* doesn't get him thinking, talk up the disadvantages. A restaurant that can't serve its own oysters, a sister who hates him, a farm that goes bust, and everyone laughing behind his back while quietly cheering for the little guy. Either way, I'm free to go.' There. He had said it. Jack waited for her to react.

Rose was washing her hands in the sink but she stopped moving and he saw her back stiffen. Now it was out he'd better explain. She must have guessed he didn't plan on settling here once his job was done, but neither of them had raised questions about the future because the *right now* was kind of full-on.

'Rose? I came here for a reason and my part is done. There's nothing for me here - apart from you, that is. I'm needed back home. Joshua's ten years older than me...he wants me to take over the farm. He hopes I'll buy him out when he retires, and I love the work. I can't keep drifting round the country for ever. I'd like to settle down, be part of something permanent. I don't want the only evidence of my existence to be 'Jack waz ere' on the door of public toilets in Manawatu.'

'Don't try to make me laugh, Jack. Where do I fit into this?' Rose was facing him now, her face tight.

'With me. Marry me, Rose.' He stared at her in shock. Where the heck had that come from? He hadn't planned to say more than wanting to leave, and asking her to consider coming along. What he wanted to get across was simple; she was the only thing here that he didn't want to leave. This was the most risky, spontaneous moment of his life. He would be miserable if she wasn't part of his future. Too late he realized it was selfish and unfair only to think and act in his own interests. He hadn't considered any of the possibilities - like how Rose would feel about moving, or leaving her job, where they would live, if it was all too soon for them, or even if she wanted real commitment.

Rose had covered her face with her hands. When she lowered them he knew right away it wasn't good news. 'Jack. I love you, but I can't believe you're asking me this *now*. I have to think about what that would mean for me, but I can't, because on top of my enormous work load I'm doing damage control on my brother's fuck-ups!' Her voice had risen as she spoke and the last words came out squeaky. Rose was visibly upset and she threw her hands in the air as a final protest, eyes welling up.

'Ah, heck. Of course you need to think about it. I'm sorry.' Jack held her to his chest and stroked the top of her head. 'I'm an idiot. I didn't think it through. I only meant to say you could come with me, and I got carried away. Let's just forget it for now, okay? I'm not going anywhere without your answer, so take as long as you need.'

Rose nodded, getting a grip on her emotions. They parted a short while later, Jack feeling like he'd messed up a good thing. He wouldn't see Rose during the run up to the opening of Tide to Table, apart from a quick hello here and there. It might be a good idea to give her some space, and hopefully she'd come round. He didn't want to think about the alternative.

Even though it was only Monday he rang Joshua. 'I took a look in those drums today, Josh. You can call off the witch hunt, they're full of sewerage.'

'Really? Ha ha! Then you were right about Ross on all fronts. I knew you were the right man for the job. You might be a bit slow for some people, but you always do things properly. You going to let them sort it out and get back here? I could use a hand.'

'Ahh, yeah, well there's one thing I never do right. I screwed up with Rose today, big time.' Jack told his brother about his ill-timed proposal.

'I see. You'll wanna sort that out before you leave, eh? It'll be alright. Give her time to think it over. If she loves you it'll work out, and maybe you should, you know, make it up to her somehow. Buy some flowers...'

'Thanks, I might just do that. I've said I'll stay until it's all sorted out. I can't leave her to do it alone, and she's too mixed up in it professionally.'

Jack explained how Rose had agreed to try and talk her brother around to a reconciliation with Ross. Joshua agreed not to tell anyone about the situation, since it didn't concern anyone outside the bay. People would draw their own conclusions, 'When the shit hits...,' said Joshua, having a chuckle at his own joke.

The next day Jack and Ryan stopped at the pub for a beer after work. They even allowed Tyrone to come in with them, since it was his last ride in the ute. His license was waiting to be picked up from the police station. Tyrone spotted someone he'd met at rugby and went to say gidday.

'I'm handing in notice,' Ryan said when they had a table to themselves.

'Yeah, I thought that was coming. I'm impressed you lasted so long.'

'I just can't stand being ordered about anymore. It's like being in the army. If I was younger I wouldn't mind so much, but I'm not, and he's supposed to be a mate. He'll still have you and the young fella next year.'

'Not me, mate. My time here is almost up.'

'What?' Ryan's craggy face was a picture of

worry. 'If you've got something wrong with you, you know you can tell me. I'll stand by you, mate. It's not cancer is it?'

'Oh boy, you always pull the wrong end of the stick!' Jack laughed as Ryan relaxed back into his chair. 'I appreciate the concern, but I was just meaning I'm thinking of moving on in *this* world. Maybe a change of scene. At my age I don't need an arsehole on my case every minute of the day. I hope I've still got a few good years of work left, and there's a place for me up north with the old guy I told you about. If you come to visit I'll tell you a story you won't believe. Nothing's set in place, so it'd be good if you didn't mention it to anyone just yet. Rose knows, but I'm not sure how that's going to pan out. She's thinking it over.'

'No worries, mate. Mum's the word. So what will you do if Rose won't leave?'

'Maybe stick around, find other work.' Jack cradled his beer studying the foam patterns on its surface. 'Or maybe I'll go anyway and we'll see each other when poss.'

He didn't want to think about the 'what ifs' just yet. Turning the conversation back to Ryan he asked, 'So what will you do for a job?'

'You'll never guess. I've got the renovation bug. I think there's enough equity in the Blue Bach to take on another mortgage, buy another do-up. It's satisfying, you know? Fixing things, making it look good again. Lucy's a great boss. She's got that eye for detail, sees it all before it's done. She'll earn enough to cover the bills if we run into problems, and she can work from anywhere. Her old man's a real estate agent, so he'll tell us if we're making stupid mistakes. I'm doing a coat of paint in the kitchen tonight.'

Jack could have guessed, the way he'd been banging on about his paint charts and wood strippers since the renovations started. He finished his beer and made a quick getaway before Ryan could bore him to tears talking about skirting boards and scotia. Not that he wasn't thrilled for him, of course.

Jack went home, showered, and walked Smell. Alone. No lights showed in the cabin on the *Skylark*. Out in the harbour boats were drifting at anchor. There were so many it looked like an invasion fleet. The sun set the horizon on fire and port holes, like small moons, hovered above the water reflecting the light. It was dinner time, and cooking smells wafted towards the shore. Jack felt the hollow of an empty stomach and knew he should eat. Rose might not even come back tonight.

The moorings and docks along the shore were also full, and would remain so until late February. More vessels were arriving every day for the silly season. They hung back on the deeper moorings, their occupants rowing in and out in dinghys or motorized inflatables. There were all sorts here, from every country under the sun. Some even flew their flags.

Betty was organizing the next party, a big one for Christmas, since most people coming here would be far from their families. Those who had come to get away from it all, or spend Christmas alone would decline the invitation, but plenty would accept. Jack already had a list of jobs he was to help with. Nancy and Ross had agreed to let them have the live oyster bar they used at markets, which Jack would run.

He headed back home throwing sticks for Smell who loped along picking up the ones which fell in her path and leaving the rest, her enthusiasm for the game not what it used to be. Jack cooked himself dinner and took a lidded wok to Rose's deck with what was left in case she came home hungry. He knew she would be too tired or busy to eat properly, and it was his way of showing he cared while still giving her some space. Jack placed a note with heating instructions beside it, weighed down with a smooth stone he'd picked up on his walk.

Rose had promised to keep him informed on her progress with Terry. Hopefully her brother would grasp how serious the situation was and act fast. Once the sewerage went in the water it was game over. Water testings were done monthly by a laboratory, so all Ross had to do was contaminate the water sometime between the last testing and the opening of Tide to Table and a lot of people would be very sick come next Sunday. Damn it! Jack couldn't let it happen. As much as he wanted to walk away he couldn't do it. If Terry wasn't prepared to make Ross an offer, then Jack would have to find a way to stop it. It wasn't just the thought of Rose's career being dashed, it was his social conscience. Old people could die from that kind of food poisoning. There was no going back once you knew a thing like that. He swore and thumped his fist on the table, making Smell jump. He had to think of a back-up plan. Jack rested his head on the table, and remained that way for the best part of half an hour. Only one solution seemed solid, and it wasn't nice. 'Hello? Is Charles there?' Jack spoke into his mobile phone. 'Tell him it's Jack. Jack Sprat. We were at school together. He'll know who I am.' Jack had given the nickname he'd had as a teenager. It was a good name for a kid who spent all his spare time fishing off the beach, or eeling in the creek. A deep voice came on the line.

'Bloody hell! Is that you Jack?'

'Gidday Charlie, how you been?'

They'd been close friends back then, and kept in touch long after school finished, only losing touch when Charles got serious about a woman. Jack was ringing now because he needed information, and Charles was a cop.

'Honestly? Not so good really. Some little shit threw a rock through the driver's window and I went off the road. Wrote off the patrol car, and got sixteen stitches in my left leg. I'm on leave for another week. And you? Still fishing?'

'Something like that. At least you're alright. Did they catch him?'

'Nope. I've been driving down that road every night since I came out of hospital looking for the bugger. My wife says I've become obsessed.'

'Then let me take your mind off it. I came by some information and I need to know how the law can help.'

'I'm listening, but if it involves the abuse of women or children then I'll have to report it. You okay with that?'

'No worries. Say if someone fouled up the water, knowing that food was being taken out of there and sold for human consumption, would the police be any help?'

'I would say so. You'd need to have proof. What can you give us?'

'I can prove if the water's been recently contaminated, and I know where the stuff is kept. I even have a key.'

'Geez, is that it? We'd have to have a search warrant to take a look. They don't give them out like lollies.'

'What if it meant that some very important people, possibly the Chief of Police included, was going to get very sick from eating this food?'

'Are you talking about a public event? Because if that's the case then we can certainly look into it. I'll need more details, but if we do a search and find something, can you match it to what's in the water?'

'Yep. Better than that, I can tell you if there's any missing from where it's stored too.'

'That should be enough to make an arrest for intention to cause public harm. You want to tell me more, or are you just making inquires for now?'

'Just asking. There's still a good chance it'll be resolved, but in case it isn't, can I call you at work? It might be short notice. The window for contamination and consumption will be tight, between next Wednesday and Thursday before harvest. I'll have the people concerned take a water sample before the harvest. The lab will have results within an hour or so.'

'No worries, Jack. I'll do whatever I can to get some officers mobilized the same day if you need. We should catch up properly some time, but right now I've got to take a wee drive. I'd invite you to join me, but no doubt you're in the wop wops at the other end of the country.'

'Not so far from you really, but I've had a guts-full of detective work. Good luck Charlie, hope you find him tonight.' Jack hung up, pleased with hearing a familiar, friendly voice. Help was at hand. Having Ross arrested would be a last resort, but if he was stupid enough to put lives at risk then he deserved being locked up. No doubt Shorty would make sure it was plastered all over the papers, and Ross might find customers hard to come by after that. Rose would need to have Terry's men send a sample of sea water straight to the lab for urgent testing next week and somehow pass the results on to him. If the test came back positive he would ring Charles and set things in motion.

Jack saw the empty wok sitting on his deck when he came home from work on Wednesday. When he picked it up there was a note underneath.

Delicious! Meeting T tomorrow before rehearsal.

See you Friday?

X X Rose.

Jack scratched his head. Was two kisses a sign she wasn't still mad at him? Correspondence with women wasn't something he had delved into before. Sending your mum a postcard didn't count. Jack decided to drop in on Connie. The restaurant would be busy, it always was all through December, but he didn't feel like staying in with his own company. Luckily, he was early enough to be seated before the main dinner crowd arrived.

Connie came to greet him, but she couldn't stay long. Jack pulled Rose's note from his pocket. 'What do you make of that?'

'Well, she's meeting someone who's name starts with a T tomorrow, and she hopes to meet you on Friday. What's this about, Jack?'

'I did get *that* part. We had a bit of a tiff the other night. What does xx mean?'

'Ah, well it generally means everything is as normal. Nothing to worry about. Now I'm a busy woman tonight, so I'll not muck about. I just came over to tell you that somehow Nancy knows about your girlfriend. I swear it wasn't me. She was asking if I knew who she was. I told her you'd brought her here once or twice, and her name is Rose. That's all I said.'

'Thanks for that. I appreciate your discretion. It was me who told her. You *could* say she had me cornered. I hope it won't be an issue much longer.'

Connie didn't have time to interrogate him about what he meant with that sentiment, and Jack was relieved. She was a formidable person to keep a secret from. She had managed to pull the worms from his nose many times in the last year, and knew more details about him than any other person he'd gotten to know. She was especially keen to meet Joshua, should he ever stop by.

Jack took a polystyrene container filled with fresh pasta in creamy basil sauce home for Rose, and a foil bag of kitchen scraps for Smell. He left the container with another note, this one much simpler:

Connie sends her regards. See you Friday. X

He hesitated over making a second x, but decided not to. Two felt a bit...girly. Jack retraced the x making it bolder and larger, hoping that if you really *meant* one it sort of counted as two anyway.

On Thursday Ross yelled at Jack for missing an oyster with a broken shell. Ross was grading the harvest while the others culled and pre-graded, sorting the grow-ons from the rest. The final grade was the quality control part of the job, the final check before the oysters were put in bags or crates for delivery. Usually Ross preferred to do this himself, it was his product and ultimately he was responsible for making sure what went out was acceptable. It was unlike Jack to miss a fault like that, but his mind wasn't on the job. Rose would be running over what she would say to Terry in a few hours. Dragging his attention back to the job in front of him Jack tried harder to concentrate.

'Does everyone know why we don't sell an oyster with a broken shell?' Ross was in the mood to lecture. He'd started feeding Tyrone more information lately, treating him more like a long term investment than just a work machine, since he was joining the rugby team. Ryan and Jack knew the answer and didn't bother looking up from their work.

If things were done properly the harvest would be culled, graded, and put back on the lease for a few days to recover. Oysters were prone to shock from handling, and benefitted from a rest after being banged off sticks, washed in a drum, and whacked with blunt knives. Ross sometimes skipped this extra precaution. If there wasn't enough processed stock on the farm to fill the orders he sold them the same day they came off sticks. This was all good and well, since most of his customers used them the same day, but it meant he needed to be extra vigilant on the quality control.

Ross carried on his lesson. 'By this time tomorrow the fish will be dead and probably full of bacteria. If no one notices and they eat it, that's a customer you won't get back.' The offending oyster was held up for display. The crack in its shell was only two millimetres wide and would heal back out in the water. The water in the bay was so clean and rich that Jack had even put oysters back with six millimetre chunks of shell missing and seen them recover. Ross tossed it into the grow-on's basket and the lesson ended.

Ryan was waiting for the end of season to hand in his resignation. Jack had advised him not to make their last weeks unpleasant, and losing Ryan wouldn't go down well with Ross. It wouldn't cross his mind that the way he treated Ryan had anything to do with him leaving.

At knock off time he announced, 'Yo! Keep next

Saturday night free, boys. This year we're having a barbie at the yard for our work do. Food and drink on the business, so bring your girlfriends, those who have them, those who don't might get lucky! Nancy will bring her crew so there will be a few of us. And share a taxi if you want to get hammered. Trust me, it's a bit pricey getting here in a taxi at two am when the wife won't answer her phone.' Ross chuckled reliving some private moment. 'Don't worry, I used her shopping account to pay for it.'

Jack held back a groan. He was being asked to give up his Saturday and spend it at work, watching a bunch of people he didn't much like get pissed on cheap beer and wine. He wouldn't even get paid for it. The sooner he could quit, the better. 'Don't forget your Secret Santa present. You'll get a text from Nancy tonight telling you who you've got, and there's only one rule - it can't cost more than twenty bucks.'

Oh joy, another bottle of cheap spirits that other people would drink on the night, then. If there was one thing he'd learnt it was to follow the unspoken rule. Last Christmas every Secret Santa present had been alcohol, except Jack's gift to Louise, and a blow-up sheep which was undoubtably the work of Not So Secret Ross who enjoyed it more than anyone. There was no way he was making that mistake again. He knew Louise still held a grudge, and it wasn't only the present she resented.

Unlike the other Secret Santa's Jack had made an effort. It was his first Christmas here and he didn't know what to expect. In the chemist he grabbed the first womanly looking presenty thing he could see. It was one of those packets with a little cloth, and some sort of creams or lotions. He turned it over and checked the price on the back wasn't more than the rules allowed, and walked to the counter to pay. The pharmacy assistant had said, 'How nice, is it a gift for your grandmother?'

Jack had replied, 'No, for a colleague. Why did you think it was for my grandmother?'

'Oh, sorry. Ah, it's just that you chose the Violet Scented Pamper Pack with the talcum powder. It's very popular with the oldies?' Jack felt completely lost. He never came into these shops unless he had a doctors prescription, and his last visit to the doctor was ten years ago. He'd cut his finger with the tomahawk chopping kindling. It had needed stitches. For most cuts Jack used electrical tape - the type a sparky used to separate wires, but it hadn't been enough to stop the bleeding that time.

The chemist when he was a kid used to be nothing more than a few shelves of medical supplies and a counter. He looked about, bewildered by the amount of merchandise; this one even sold orthopedic jandals and fake leather handbags.

'Right,' he said to the assistant, scratching his head, 'do you think you could swap it for...something a younger woman might like?' Jack crossed his fingers.

'Of course, sir. Is this a romantic gift, or something less personal? Roughly what age is the person?'

'No, nothing romantic. A lady who works part

time for the oyster shop. My boss's wife is very keen on Secret Santa. The woman's maybe forty five? She looks fifty five, but I'd say it's the drinking. I wasn't sure what to get her, but every woman I know has a shelf full of those nice bathroom things, so here I am. I did think of getting her a decent bottle of wine but I don't think she needs encouragement to drink. Something that smells nice would be good; she's quite heavy on the cigarettes.'

Jack became aware he was thinking out loud and stopped talking. This was why he hated shopping, it was so embarrassing. There must be a shopping protocol, but he'd never learnt it. Now she was leading him back down the row of display shelves trying to show him something.

'Will this one do? It's honeysuckle and papaya, with a shower gel instead of talc. I believe the scent is quite strong.' She smiled her professional smile, perfect white teeth sneering at him. He'd given himself away with that speech, and now she knew he was out of his depth she would zone in for the kill. 'Would you like to try the tester?' Another fake smile. Jack recovered quickly, 'Yes, I would.' It seemed to be the correct response. He didn't want to rub the cream on, but the assistant had put a blob of it on his hand. It really smelt quite good, if a little overpowering. Jack nodded and the assistant gift wrapped the packet.

'Will there be anything else, sir?'

'Do you sell electrical tape?'

'Ah, I don't think so. What is it for?'

'Never mind. How much do I owe you?'

'Twenty nine dollars ninety, and we have a special deal today. Because you have spent more than twenty dollars in our beauty range you can choose any key-ring for three dollars.'

Jack knew he was beaten and chose the key-ring closest to him, paid for his purchases, and left before she could sell him something else he didn't need. As he was nearing the exit she called out, 'I'm sure Aunty Lou will enjoy your gift.'

Great, just what he needed. Wait till that bit of gossip got around. He'd be as popular as the guy who stepped in dog turd before getting on the bus. The key ring turned out to be a plastic square with the words *Keep Calm And Wear High Heels* embedded in it. When he presented it to Connie she thought it was hilarious, but not nearly as funny as what he'd said to the assistant about her aunt. The joke was lost on Jack.

Louise had been disappointed not to get a bottle of something, but she didn't hear about what he'd said, about her being a heavy drinker who stank of cigarettes, until sometime later. She hadn't said a word to him since.

On the way home from work Jack stopped at the bottle store to grab a box of beer for his fridge. The specials poster advertised a 750ml bottle of Midnight Moonshine, 45% for $19.99 and Jack bought one. There, job done. May they drink to stupid oblivion. He didn't care who got it, and he hoped a little nastily that it tasted as horrible as it sounded. Back in the ute Ryan had a laughing fit when Jack showed him. 'Ever tried that stuff?' Ryan wasn't sure if Jack was being intentionally cruel or just ignorant.

'No, don't plan to.'

'Well, I hope you're not *my* Secret Santa. It's like lolly water, but gets you mean drunk. Then you have a most mind-blowing hangover, after the third glass.'

'Perfect. If I do get you I'll swap with Ty, okay? Now you're safe, how 'bout a beer at your place?'

Rose wouldn't need dinner left out tonight, she would be wining and dining at the hottest new restaurant in town. Tonight was the rehearsal dinner and Jack needed a distraction from going over and over the possible outcomes from her meeting with Terry. Betty had Smell at her house today, and besides, he'd only be an hour late.

'Okay. You can tell me what you think of the work so far,' Ryan agreed.

From outside the bach actually looked worse than before. Ryan had sandblasted the flaking paint, showing up the white undercoat, and patched the rotten boards with recycled ones that had a pink undercoat. Adding to the pastel pink, blue, and white, sections of board had been painted in different shades of pale yellow, one of them presumably 'Hahei Sunrise.' It looked like the house made of candy the witch lived in.

Lucy heard them arrive and opened the door. She was dressed in a vibrant red skirt and blouse, with matching red heels and her long hair flying about in the evening breeze.

'Not bad, eh?' Ryan congratulated himself. Jack

wasn't sure if he meant the progress on the house or his dolled-up girlfriend, but probably the latter. Lucy evaded Ryan's attempt to grab her for a quick cuddle.

'Nice to see you too - but stay back! You're filthy, and I leave in two minutes. Hi Jack.' She leaned in and carefully pecked him on the cheek.

'And there's me thinking you'd dressed up for me. Oh well, come on Jack, let's drown our sorrows.'

Jack saw Ryan head up the door step behind his girlfriend and pinch her bottom as she passed inside. 'Ryan Fulman! That's no way to treat a lady,' but from the way she smiled over her shoulder Jack could see she wasn't displeased. At least this relationship was on solid ground.

He needed a way to show Rose how much she meant to him, and slowly the ideas were coming. He would see her tomorrow, and then head up north for the weekend. It would be refreshing to get away, blow out the cobwebs, but his main motive was more essential. There was something he needed to ask Joshua in person, and it couldn't wait.

Ryan carried Lucy's photographic equipment to the car for her before closing the door and taking beers from the fridge. They sat down on the cracked, brown leather couches they had helped Lucy move here not long ago, and said nothing. In the silence they could hear the slam of a car door, the cooling of the tin roof, the children across the street squealing. It was important to enjoy that first beer and give your mind and body a small respite from the day. The men understood this and hovered protectively over the moment, Ryan trying to stifle a belch he couldn't hold in.

Four minutes passed. Ryan took two more beers from the fridge and the spell was broken with the sound of cans cracking open. Jack was wondering if Rose would mention his proposal to Lucy tonight at the rehearsal dinner. He didn't want Ryan to hear it from Lucy first, but then he didn't want to piss Rose off if she was keeping it quiet. Jack hadn't thought to check with Rose if it was an event they would discuss with others, and now he was uncertain. See? Women brought complications, which is why the one you chose should be worth the doubt and confusion she brought to your simple existence. He decided to phrase it hypothetically and see what happened. 'You and Lucy are getting on pretty well. I think she's a stabilizing influence on you.'

'Yep. She's the one for me.'

'I was thinking, once all the restaurant hoo harr has finished, I might ask Rose to make a decent man out of me.'

'What, again? Don't you have to wait for an answer now?'

'So you heard? Huh.'

'I heard she didn't take it too well.' Jack shook his head.

'I knew it was wrong the second after I said it. It just slipped out, you know? But I've got a plan. This time I'll do it properly.'

No wonder he was a bit spaced out at work. His mind was full of Plan B's for everything.

'Yeah? If you need a hand setting it up, I'm your

man.' Ryan thumped his chest.

'Sure? I might take you up on that. I'll let you know next week.' Jack finished off his beer and stood to go. 'Cheers, mate. See you in the morning.'

Jack was in bed. He no longer used the hammock in case Rose spent the night, and he'd made Smell a new bed from an old sofa squab, befitting of a canine pensioner. His phone beeped signaling an incoming message. He hoped it was Rose with a goodnight message, maybe some of those nice x's, but it was just Nancy to say who he had to buy a present for - Ross. Jack had a good laugh at that and fell asleep easily. Natural justice had such a calming effect.

The end of the day couldn't come soon enough for Jack, but they did finish early. Unfortunately for half the staff, the other half wanted to go fishing.

'Come on, boys, let's have a fish. We've earned it,' said Ross.

'Choice! Kaimoana for tea.' Tyrone loved fishing as much as Ross. There was no easy way Ryan or Jack could wriggle out of it. It was two o'clock and technically they were paid to be here until four. If the boss wanted to fish, then they would all fish. Ryan grumbled to Jack about what he could be doing on his house instead, but he was wasting his breath.

It was ironic that the two who had no interest in fishing were the only ones to catch anything. Perhaps it was because they sat so still, forgetting the lines in the water, hypnotized by the flashing sunlight bouncing off the tiny wavelets. After two minutes of nothing happening Ross and Tyrone would wind up the slack, flex the rod, or reel it all the way back in to check the bait and cast out in another direction. For them it was a sport, excitement, not a chance to relax. Who knows when they would have given up if Jack and Ryan hadn't handed over their catch. If fresh fish was the price to pay, then they were willing.

Gravel tinkled under the ute as they left the yard, bumping in and out of potholes. Tyrone had stayed behind to fillet the fish and drink beer with Ross.

The road needed grading again. Ryan was just starting on his second beer, and tried to time his guzzles between the bumps so it didn't spill all down his front. He didn't care about his clothes, but a man didn't waste beer. Jack had only had one to be polite. He didn't want to be accused of beer snobbery, though he knew what Ross liked was the same as him, and different altogether from what the business bought. He had drunk it quickly, letting out an 'Ahhh' for good measure, and said he was off home.

According to Ryan who had been woken at midnight by Lucy, the trial run for Tide to Table had been a success. Everything had gone smoothly and the staff had been congratulated by Terry. There had been drinks afterwards, but neither her or Rose had stayed. Jack was envious of Ryan as he imagined Lucy coming home to slip into bed alongside her man. Rose hadn't come home at all, let alone been in his bed. He almost rang her this morning, but it would feel weird talking on the phone. They hadn't talked since the night he'd blurted out his offer of marriage.

Jack wasn't in the mood to have company this evening. It was later than usual and he was desperate to see Rose. Ryan didn't mind him turning down a Friday night swill; he was raring to go on ripping up the lino tonight before the industrial sander arrived tomorrow.

Jack was full of nerves when he saw the red Peugeot in the resident's parking lot. It had been four days since he'd seen Rose; the longest they'd been apart since they met. He hoped there was time to tidy himself up before he saw her.

After collecting Smell from Betty's he headed straight for the shower. A tiny gas califont heated water from the tank on the roof and squirted it out the smallest shower head ever made. Washing all the dry mud off his body was a laborious process, but it was better than waiting in line for the public shower.

Rubbing his hair dry, Jack heard a knock on the door and Rose let herself in. They embraced wordlessly, their bodies seeking out the solid reality of each other.

'I've missed you.' Jack kissed the top of her brown hair.

'Me too. I feel like I've been to another planet and back this week, and it's not over yet.'

'I'm dying to know how your meeting went, but what do you say we take Smell for a quick walk first, and then I'll cook while you talk.' Smell barked once on hearing 'walk,' and Rose laughed, breaking the intensity of the moment. 'Can't say no to that, can I Smell?'

Daylight would last another four hours and the sun was still hot. It was good to be out with Rose, even the dog looked happier. Jack held her hand and talked about Ryan, work, and who he'd seen that week, but he stayed away from anything personal. Rose had slept over at the office last night, in a small room with a single bed and bathroom attached. After her 8 am meeting with the editor of a magazine who wanted to run a story on the restaurant, she had driven home and worked on her laptop, not even bothering to change her clothes from last night until lunch time. Jack could see the black half circles under her eyes and knew she was exhausted.

'Thanks for feeding me, Jack. That was so thoughtful of you. I would have lived on coffee and biscuits otherwise.' She smiled at his weathered face, darkly tanned except for the top half of his forehead where his cap usually sat. They were back on Jack's boat, and he had insisted on Rose taking the bench seat and relaxing while he busied himself in the kitchen.

'Shall I begin?' she asked. Jack nodded. 'Ok. As expected Terry wasn't at all pleased with the news that his farm is under attack. At first he wanted to fire me if I didn't tell him who my source was, and then he wanted to come out here and kill Ross. Luckily, I know how to talk him out of a rage. Then he said he'd have someone watching his farm day and night. I pointed out that he would need to monitor the whole bay, and that Ross could easily contaminate the water while he was working on his lease in broad daylight and no one would know. Then he said he'd rather buy his oysters somewhere else than let Ross put one over him. Finally, I got him to see he had no choice but to make peace with Ross or give up the farm. That was when I mentioned that I knew what George was doing, and if he doesn't make good then I'll tell.'

Rose paused to pull off her stockings and Jack felt his attention wander before he remembered she hadn't yet told him the outcome. Rose rolled her stockings into a small tan sausage and slipped them in her pocket before she continued. 'Terry's agreed to ring Ross tonight. He knows Ross will deny everything, so he's going to pretend he has finally come to his senses and apologize for the way things ended between them. If Ross accepts the apology he will offer him a position as manager, and a merger of the two farms. If Ross says no then he'll have to buy oysters from somewhere else to supply the restaurant and think of something else.' Jack put down the vegetable knife and said, 'That's a big relief. I've been going crazy thinking how to help if you couldn't talk him round. Does Terry have any idea how lucky he is to have you as a sister?'

'Yes. He did apologize after dinner last night. I wouldn't be surprised if he decided to go back on his word, but this whole mess is his problem from now on. I have requested an extra water testing for the day before we open, just to play it safe. It's expensive, but I won't have my name in the mud if Terry fails to win Ross over.'

'You think of everything. I was prepared to bring the cops in if you weren't successful. I don't like Ross the boss, but I've nothing against the man personally. On the other hand, I can't have sick people on my conscience.'

'I think you're off the hook. I also couldn't take the chance; people can die from food poisoning. I've lined up another supplier, a lovely man from up north named Joshua.' Jack laughed. She was so sharp he felt like a pin-cushion.

They ate slowly savoring the company more than the dinner, and when there was only one topic left unmentioned, Jack got there first. 'I am sorry I startled you the other night, Rose, and I would like to withdraw my proposal for now, because I don't want you stressing out about it. Let's just get to the end of this year and see how we feel when things settle down.'

'I'm sorry too,' she shrugged. 'I'm touched you asked, but I agree, now's not the time. What I said...I mean it. I do love you.'

'I like hearing you say that.' Jack, a man who defined the saying, 'an even keel,' was almost tearing up. He blinked twice and forced a smile. 'I'll be away this weekend. I need to see Josh. I'd take you with me but I know you're busy. Another time perhaps.'

Rose sighed. 'I'm working like a fiend right up until Christmas.'

'Will you be joining the Christmas celebrations here?' Jack was doing his best to sound casual but there was an uncomfortable knot in his guts.

'Of *course*. Skylar is in Oz on some cabaret circuit and Terry's crowd is not my scene, so I don't really have a family to spend it with. I can visit Mum in the rest home on Boxing day, but she won't have a clue who I am. She hasn't recognized anyone for three years, apparently. I always try to visit when I'm having a bad day so that I feel depressed beforehand. That way it doesn't come as such a downer. I feel so guilty for not being here the last years before she lost it, but I never imagined she would end up demented by sixty. Sometimes she calls me 'Patty,' after her dead sister Patricia.'

'Want me to come? Maybe you just never had the

right kind of cheering-up afterwards.' Jack grabbed her and tickled her until she was squirming on her knees and squealing, and despite her best intentions to work late into the night she let Jack take her to bed.

Smell must have known where they were going. She was allowed in the cab with Jack as a treat and she was trying to behave, sitting still on her haunches. As they got closer she whined and put her head out the window to catch the country scents. At the turnoff where a cow paddock used to be, a digger was parked for the weekend. White pegs marked out a quarter acre section and a house site had been leveled, a rectangle of yellow clay. In the tiny village a new shop had opened selling home-wares and gifts. It was seventy minutes from here to the city, and as city prices grew people were moving further north looking for cheap land and new opportunities. There was a small school which had been here a hundred years. Closed down for the last twenty it looked to be functioning again. Towns like this were benefitting from a bad economy; a reverse of the migration that had seen them abandoned by all but the elderly, and those with farms.

The ute slowed as Jack neared the old house, a hillside planted in olives with a metal gate set into a stone entrance flanked Joshua's messy yard. Out front was a large shed where the oysters were processed, and various farming paraphernalia was stacked along the fence beside it. Jack wondered how the new gentry liked living next to a scruffy old place like this. Joshua stepped off the porch of the old timber villa and came to meet Jack. 'I thought you might turn up soon.' He clapped Jack on the back and stooped down to ruffle Smell's ears. 'Good to see you, Sprat.'

'It's good to be here. I just wish I wasn't leaving again so soon.' Jack stretched, feeling the muscles in his back pulling. He wasn't accustomed to making long drives through city traffic.

'Let's not worry about tomorrow. Come on, breakfast's waiting.'

Inside, the house was in half light. It was only nine in the morning and this had always been a dark house; not in a spooky way, in a warm cosy way, like a bedroom at night with a small lamp, it told you you were safe within its walls, the world shut out. The rooms were large with high studs up to wood-paneled ceilings, and nothing had been altered since it was built. Some of the furnishings had been in the family five generations, coming over on ships from Ireland.

Jack's family had always worked the ocean with nets, lines, and crayfish pots. Joshua had built up his father's oyster lease from a semi-exploited two hectares, to a fully loaded ten hectares. He currently employed two men to help and worked hard himself. When Jack came back there would be four, a more reasonable number. The maintenance work was running behind schedule.

Joshua made a pot of tea while Jack watched him. In the last year he had turned grey, no longer salt and pepper sprinkled. He was two years shy of fifty. His shoulders were still broad and he retained a solid strength, but he complained of stiffness in his wrists and elbows in winter. The sea aged a man faster than the land, throwing the sun at you from above and below. The constant immersion in cold salt water, a feisty wind, and heavy lifting didn't go easy on a body.

'I've been to see a friend of Diane's. She does acupuncture. Apparently she can keep me going for another ten years if I stop overworking myself. The last time I stuck a needle in my arm it was half the price and a lot more fun, but that's age for you, but I'm guessing you came here for more than a look at my pretty face,' Joshua said, placing a mug in front of Jack.

'You'd be right then. I have a favour to ask, but tell me about how the farm's doing first, and I'll tell you how the local drama is coming along.'

News and stories were traded back and forth across the table as they ate a late breakfast of toast and hard boiled eggs. Sometimes it was funny, sometimes serious, and always with the ease of two brothers who think highly of each other. One had never let the other down. Their parents were no longer alive, the old man passing away two years ago in his sleep; his wife a long time before. Joshua had been married for fifteen years, but there were no children. His wife lived down the road, now married to a dairy farmer. Her youngest child was still in primary school. Once the plates were empty Joshua cut to the chase. 'I'm guessing your coming home has some connection to a woman called Rose, am I right?' Jack nodded. 'You know, it's not genetic, Jack. There's no reason why you shouldn't be carrying a loaded gun, so to speak. Though at your age it wouldn't pay to muck around.'

When Joshua's wife had left him it was with his blessing, though it almost broke him to do it. He hadn't seen Diane for a few years after that, she knew he needed time to heal and lick his wounds, but they had been good friends a long time now. Joshua even played an uncle's role to her children, and went duck shooting every May with her husband.

'That's not exactly why I'm here,' Jack said getting down to his point at last. 'Of course I've wondered if I would have your difficulties, but I would like to get the wife bit sorted first. I'm planning to ask Rose to marry me again, but properly this time. Whether we have children is anybody's guess, but I think a ring might help my chances.'

'It's right here. It's been waiting for you.' Joshua went to an oak cabinet and slid open a drawer. His hand scrabbled against the back of the drawer and emerged holding another drawer, a miniature of the first. The miniature drawer only held one object, a black velvet pouch pulled closed with a gold ribbon. This he passed to Jack who put it into his pocket and smiled at Joshua.

Joshua was right to think Jack worried about his ability to father children. It was Jack who helped his brother through the bad years after Diane left, encouraging him to put more effort into the farm as a way of moving forward. There was also Jack's sadness losing Diane as a sister; they had been part of a family and he missed the way she made the simple things fun. She was a lively person and a natural with kids, a bitter-sweet pleasure to see her in that role with someone else.

Spending the night in his own room, it felt strange sleeping in a house again. It was such a luxury to have all this space to wonder around in. To go from the bedroom to the bathroom seemed to take ages. There were so many comforts he didn't realize he'd been missing. Jack loved being on the water, but there was nothing like home. His bed closed around him like the hug of an old friend - or maybe he was just getting soft in his maturity? This thought didn't bother him the way it once would have. Finding a bed too comfortable was a young man's crime.

He woke to the smell of bacon frying and threw on his clothes. From the wardrobe he took three pairs of socks, pulled on a pair, and then tossed them all back when he saw they had holes. After a big breakfast he put his stuff on the tray of the ute and lifted Smell Hound into the cab. It was tempting to leave her here where she felt at home. Smell was getting slower by the day, and her legs looked stiff. In the end he decided against it; she didn't like being separated from him. He hugged Joshua goodbye in the driveway, keen to be away before the Sunday traffic made a mechanical snake down the highway.

'See you for Christmas. And don't bring anything, I've got it all.'

'If you're sure. Diane's invited me to spend the day with them, but I do feel a bit like The Matchstick Girl, watching them all playing happy families together.'

'Well, you make a damn ugly girl. Can't have you licking the windows and scaring the kids, can we?' They both laughed at the thought.

'Hooroo!' and Jack was gone, kicking up dust on his way back out to the main road in the Sunday morning heat.

There was another reason for not hanging about today. Jack was determined to buy some new clothes. It had been on the cards for months, and he would need all the self confidence he could get to ask Rose a second time to marry him. He trawled along the main street checking out the window displays. The street-wear looked too young, the sensible shops looked too fuddy duddy. Finally he found something in between. The sign said, *Mission Possible*, which he hoped was the case.

Inside the shop a whole wall was lined with mannequins dressed in order of extremely casual (shorts and singlet), all the way to the dinner jackets at the end. The clothes were up to date but simple, with discrete details that indicated they were more than cheap chain store garb. This was definitely his kind of place. He walked up to the counter where a man was leaning, reading a novel. 'Yeah, gidday. I'll have what he's having, and what he's having,' Jack said pointing at two of the middle dummies.

'Good choice. Two smart casuals coming right up. Those come in navy or cream, and the other style in faded red or brown.'

'I'll take one of each colour.'

'And you'd better try the pants on for size. You'd be a 32? While I'm out back getting your size take a look at what you need in the way of undergarments over here.'

They sold plain boxers, undies, and socks in every colour and Jack filled the counter space with packets of each, enough to last the next twelve months at least. His work socks he would buy from the farming shop next time he went for a sack of dog biscuits. He was in and out of Mission Possible in twenty minutes with two bags of new clothes and a smile. He'd be back here the next time for sure.

There was nothing to stop Jack leaving his job now that he knew Ross wasn't planning a widespread attack on the aquaculture industry. Jack would drop the bomb at the Christmas work do, after Ross had a few drinks in him. He would be in full Ross the Good Guy mode, competing against himself for Boss of the Year award. With an audience present he should keep things civil, but Jack planned on keeping a clear head just in case, not so much for himself but for Ryan's sake.

On Monday Jack told Ryan his plan, and Ryan agreed it would make a satisfying end to things. If you could kill two birds with one stone, you could also make a very thorough job of one bird with two stones. Put the boot in, so to speak.

'You and Lucy coming to the Christmas party down at the wharf?' he asked.

'Yeah, we'll be there. We're spending the morning with her folks, but we should be back in the afternoon. Need a hand setting up?'

'I think we've got it covered, but there is something you could help me with. I'm running the live oyster bar and I might need a hand shucking. Are you up for that? It'll run for about two hours.'

'Sure thing. *I'm not the oyster shucker I'm the oyster shucker's son, I'm only shucking oysters till the oyster shucker comes!*' He belly laughed, tickled with his remake of the old tongue twister.

Ross was in an especially good mood that morning, and when Ryan asked him how he was, he replied, 'Bunch of fluffy ducks!'

Jack was the only one with a clue to why this might be. Ross even let Jack make the coffee, stepping aside with a flourish. 'Last week, men! But don't think you can slack off. If we finish our work here then we'll be giving Shorty a hand. He's got a fancy restaurant opening on Saturday so he needs help with the harvest if we've got time.' Ryan and Tyrone looked confused, but Ross was smiling at Jack in an unsettling way.

'But, I thought yous hated each other, boss,' Tyrone frowned. 'Why'd you want to help him?'

'Nah, hate's a bit of a strong word for it. Anyway, it was all a misunderstanding. Shorty rang me to apologize. Said he realized what an asset I was, how things hadn't been running smoothly since I left, and would I think about coming back. He's going to be too busy to oversee production, so he wants to make me manager. Maybe even a partner in the long term.'

'So did you say you'd do it?' Ryan had recovered from the shock, and was waiting for a punchline. It had to be a joke.

'What do you think, mate? I told him to stick his oysters where the sun don't shine and suck my balls while he's down there.' Ross threw his head back and laughed.

Ryan wasn't sure if it was safe to join in, there was something manic about the way Ross was laughing. Jack continued to watch, his face carefully relaxed. Ross must suspect something but he didn't want to confirm it for him. Tyrone's eyes widened, showing the whites all around, 'Huuu! You *really* say that?' Ross just shook his head.

'No, you dumb ass. Of course I accepted his apology. I said it would be great to be back in single seed production. No one would turn down that kind of offer. He's got one of the most high tech farms with the best equipment you can buy. They've got machines imported from France to grade the oysters, automatic washers, and you've seen their barges. If something breaks they don't have to wait for the next quarter for a replacement; but they still aren't as good as us, and Shorty knows it. Shorty doesn't know how to lead his men like I do.'

Ross's smile was smug, and Ryan finally found a joke he was sure of and sniggered away, flicking Jack a look. No one denied that Ross was a top farmer with excellent strategy and above average results, but when it came to managing employees...there was a growing list of people who could testify against that.

'What about us, boss?' Tyrone was looking uncomfortable, not sure where this left him. He was just getting the hang of this work, and he'd told all his mates the boss would help him get his skipper's ticket next year.

'Don't worry your pretty head, you'll still have a job - in fact, you've done three months so you're due a pay rise. That should buy you a few more eggs. You're going to earn it today. Does anyone know what day it is?' Tyrone's eyebrows lifted and he grinned happily. He'd never stayed in a job long enough to get a pay rise. Just wait till he told the missus!

'It's Monday?' Tyrone suggested. What kind of trick question was that?

'It's not just any Monday. It's Sump Monday!' Ross shouted at them. Jack groaned. Why oh why couldn't he have left it for after the holidays when Jack would be gone. Tyrone and Ryan looked puzzled. 'Come on, bring a spade each. Put your boots on but not the waders. You'll never get them clean again.'

At least this year the job would go quickly with all of them helping. Ross was even joining in, smearing sunscreen over his face and neck as they walked round to the back of the shed where the yard ended at the foot of the hill.

'Are you serious? We have to move this muck?' Tyrone had one arm over his nose. Ryan was already digging, but the stuff was so sloppy it would almost be easier with a bucket.

'Think of it as man's work. Put some hairs on

your chest.'

'I've just remembered, I'm allergic to mud. If it touches me I ahh, I, like, get this rash?' Tyrone finished lamely, but he couldn't keep a straight face and giggled. Ryan threw a handful at his legs where it made a wet splat noise, running down into his boot. Jack went and got all the buckets he could find and waded into the mud. When Ryan took a shovel out, Jack came after and scooped up the liquid that pooled there. Ross and Tyrone worked the same way, trying to go faster with an eye on the others, cracking jokes about what a 'sloppy job' Jack and Ryan were doing.

By smoko a large circle of dark brown sludge was spread a metre out from the sump hole. Jack knew by the time it was finished the mud would be piled so high it would look like a thermal crater. Except Rotorua smelt *much* better than this. At lunch they were hungry but it was difficult to eat with the smell clinging to them, especially their hands. Each time food was raised towards the mouth the smell put them off taking a bite. Each man had a way to get around the problem; Jack ate quickly, Ryan used his spare hand to hold his nose, and Tyrone put his food on a plate and ate without hands while Ryan made noises like a small terrier for him. 'That's right, lick your plate clean. Good dog.'

At the end of the afternoon they were half way there. The stuff in the bottom layers was slimier than the top with a stickiness not normally associated with mud. It was all over them when Ross called it a day. Jack knew there was no point changing his clothes and getting another set dirty, but he couldn't get in the ute as he was and the same went for Ryan. They both stripped down to undies and hosed off their arms, legs, and gumboots outside before hopping in, naked apart from undies and wet boots. 'Smell you later!' Ross called.

Ryan was lucky to have a short walk from the car to his front door, but Jack had the car park and shoreline to cross. A mother with her children on the swings stared at him with her mouth open, and turned her child's head away. He must look like a swamp monster, Jack thought. He took a very long shower in the public cubical, his towel still turning from white to grey as he dried himself off. Luckily Rose was staying several nights in the city this week.

Tuesday was Sump Tuesday, and closely resembled Sump Monday, except for lunchtime when Tyrone pulled a pair of rubber gloves from his bag and put them on before eating. Ryan also had a new method of attack; special foaming soap in a bottle, which he shared with Jack.

'Lucy wouldn't let me in bed until I had a second shower last night. She still moaned - and not the good way. I reckon this stuff will help.' Jack reckoned it did. There was tea tree oil in the soap strong enough to make his eyes water. I'll have to ask Mr Chin to get me some, he decided. Be good for washing Smell Hound after one of her adventures. Except come to think of it, she wasn't going far nowadays. Could it be there was more than old age slowing her down? Jack had an attack of guilt; he'd never taken her to the vet. What if she had some sort of dog virus? She was a hardy mongrel of unidentifiable breeds who had never been sick. A farmer had found her on his boundary line coming out of the scrub behind his farm, a skinny and hungry pup. He had been on the brink of shooting her when she lay down and looked at him so sadly that he couldn't do it. Smell hadn't resisted when the farmer picked her up and carried her home, but he couldn't keep her. He had as many dogs as he needed. Jack saw an add pinned to the notice board outside the pub, and rang him. She was about two months old but looked younger from malnutrition. It was such a sorry sight Jack couldn't say no, even though he'd wanted something from a water-loving breed.

'Wouldn't worry about that,' the farmer laughed, 'she's bound to have something in her bloodline that fits. She's a Bitsa, *bitsa* everything.'

Jack fattened her up on cream with eggs beaten into it before treating her for worms. By the time she was four months old you'd never seen a healthier dog, and she'd stayed that way until now.

Jack went back to shoveling muck, and Ryan took a turn on the bucket. After work all their mud crusted clothes were hung over a fence to dry. Ross wanted to burn them, but wet mud was incredibly difficult to light. He would let the garments dry out and burn them in a few days.

As it turned out they didn't have time to help Shorty. On Wednesday they did a special harvest for the weekend orders which would be delivered earlier than usual. Thursday they culled and graded and

Jack made the deliveries after work. This plan freed up the workers for Friday afternoon to help Nancy set up for Saturday's staff party. The yard was to be transformed into a tropical paradise. How Nancy hoped to carry this out was beyond Jack, but no doubt it would require a stretch of the imagination from the attendees.

Rose was busy again on Thursday night and Jack didn't mind. He'd come to see this time as a breather. Whether or not things panned out the way he wanted he ought to be ready for them. Somehow a pile of objects of minimal value that weren't worth the space they took up had accumulated on the boat and he began the task of sorting through them. For disbursement amongst the wharf community he made one pile; a tennis ball, two can openers, an old wallet, a pack of cards, and other semi useful things. The next box of bits and bobs was soon sorted into keepers and chuck-outs, and the latter he gave to Betty for the charity shop. She received them gratefully and ushered him inside. 'So, a little birdy tells me we might meet some of your family soon.' Betty insisted on feeding him a plate of curry and rice, partly to make him stay and chat, and partly because she didn't like wastage.

'Ah, I imagine the little birdy also doggy-sits and cuts hair for a living. Yeah, I was telling Rex my brother will be here for Christmas. We usually spend it together if I'm in town, and I'd like him to meet you all. Besides, he's great at shucking oysters.'

'Had some practice, has he? How does he make a living up north?'

'Well, he used to do a bit of firewood, but these days he just grows oysters.'

'Jack, you always surprise me. I suppose there's a reason you're working for Ross and not your brother?'

'There was, Betty, but not for much longer. I'm quitting. Joshua can tell you all about it when he gets here.'

'Oh? Then I'm sure we'll have lots to talk about, wont we?'

'Can you keep a secret? Especially not tell Rex?'

'Of course! Tell aunt Betty,' she patted her neatly curled hair in mock vanity.

'I need help to organize a few small details for the night. I'm planning to ask Rose if she'll marry me.'

'That's wonderful news!' Jack glanced up at her sharply. The excitement sounded forced.

'Heard about my first attempt, did you?'

'Oh come on Jack, you know what this town's like. But I promise to keep this one a secret. I'd love to help, and I am genuinely thrilled for you both. Isn't it amazing how quickly life can change? I bet you didn't think you would meet someone like Rose here. A damn sight better than that wet rag Lara. Oops! Did I just say that out loud? My tongue runs away with me sometimes, must be the age.'

Jack noted that she didn't look contrite at all, and he laughed and shook his head at her. He didn't expect to meet someone like Rose anywhere. He didn't think such a combination of determination, honesty, intelligence, humour, and looks even existed in one woman. His past experiences with girlfriends indicated that two out of five virtues ain't bad, but it always was after about the third month.

'So what will you do for work if you quit the farm?'

'That all depends...on Rose. If she agrees, then we'll go up north. Joshua's missing me on the farm and I'm sick of moving about. If not, then maybe I'll look for other work here. I won't be slaving my ass off for Ross, you can bet your bottom dollar on that. Not Shorty either. They're in cahoots again.'

'We'll be sad to lose you both, but I hope she goes with you all the same. I do love a happy ending.' Betty took his plate and dumped it in the plastic tub, poured boiling water over it, and made a pot of tea. Jack would miss this too.

Friday's atmosphere was cheerful and relaxed at the yard, and Nancy gave everyone jobs to help set up for tomorrow. Nancy must have benefitted from Ross's change in circumstances. Some of his good temper must have been extended her way, and maybe that's all she needed from him to be happy with her lot. It was almost like Tyrone, Ryan, and Jack didn't exist when Ross was in sight. Her smiles were all for him that day, and though Ross maintained his nonchalance towards her it must have been an effort to do so, for several times he looked away grinning, his eyes glazing over in daydream.

Jack was currently helping Nancy put up decorations inside the shed, stapling multi-coloured cloths and palm leaves to the walls while she held them in place. Ryan was covering the lights in bits of cellophane, so they would cast reds and oranges around the room. According to Nancy this would give the effect of a tropical sunset. 'Do we get to meet this new girlfriend of yours tomorrow, Jack? Connie said she seems nice.'

It was the first time Nancy had tried to talk to him on a personal level since their moment in the shed, when he discovered the contents of the barrels. There was nothing to suggest she felt uncomfortable with him bringing a girlfriend, and Jack was keen to be seen with Rose after keeping her a secret so long.

'She's been busy, but I'll ask her tonight,' he replied.

'There's someone I'd like to bring along too,' Ryan piped up from his position on the ladder.

'Oow, you never said you had a girlfriend, Ryan! You're a secretive bunch, eh? Louise will be disappointed, she's had her eye on you. Between you and me, Lou tends to have strange ideas about her own desirability, though I firmly believe there's someone for each of us. I just don't think Lou is for *you*. I keep suggesting she try the local RSA. Plenty of veterans there with no qualms about dating an older lady and her bottle of white wine, eh? Her and Dad get along great, but I'm kind of glad she keeps turning him down. They'd only encourage each other to over-indulge.' Nancy rolled her eyes. Her attempts to make a responsible grandfather out of her dad had never got far. 'What's her name then, your friend?'

'Lucy,' Ryan said quickly. 'She's my girlfriend,' he added for good measure. Jack laughed knowing that

Ryan was terrified at the thought of being preyed upon by Louise.

'Well, Lucy is very welcome. Tell her to wear something festive.'

Nancy had the Christmas fever something chronic. Ross had been told to bring a load of sand in the tractor's bucket to dump on the floor inside. Jack thought it was a waste of time when they could sit on the beach a few metres away and watch a real sunset, but he kept his thoughts to himself. If nothing else he supposed the sand would soak up any spillages. Ross dumped the sand and turned the engine off, leaving the tractor in the shed's entrance. 'Hell's bells, Nance. Did you have to do a number on my gear? Is nothing sacred?' The tractor was wrapped from end to end with strings of tinsel in matching red. Nancy was delighted with Ross's reaction and laughed loudly. 'See boys, this is the sort of trouble a wife brings,' Ross said shaking his head and starting the motor up again.

Once the decorations were all in place Jack began chopping pineapples and oranges, dropping them into an oversize steel pot. They would soak overnight in five litres of rum, and be the base for a large quantity of tropical punch. He had time to think that 'punch' was a very apt name for the concoction and run through a list of other beverages with befitting names. Did whisky whisk you away? Did wine make you whine? Under these fickle thoughts were the dark knots of his future; the scene which would play out with Ross tomorrow when they quit, his proposal to Rose; but he was also aware that he had no control over the outcomes and left these thoughts alone.

Tyrone had been sent to drag the barbecue over and clean it, something that the barbecue had never experienced before by the look of it. 'Yeah, that's right, give me all the stink jobs,' he complained, scraping grease from the hotplate.

'You should be used to it by now,' Ryan grinned. He was helping unload two picnic tables from the ute and place them near the barbecue end to end. Nancy dumped a load of paper plates and cups on the bench inside and began to rake the sand Ross delivered into an even covering over the concrete floor.

Jack finished the punch and rigged up the stereo Ross had left on the floor but couldn't get it working. Eventually he gave up and called Ross to take a look. 'Oh, I forgot I still had this in my pocket.' Ross pulled out a cable and connected it, and Meatloaf launched an aural assault.

With all the main tasks completed a final end of season clean up began, but mostly because Ross loved a good burn-off. All the rubbish from the house and the yard was dumped in the middle of the paddock where it would burn well into the night. This included irregular objects such as broken plastic crates, broken toys, tyres, empty tin cans, dirty clothes from cleaning the sump, batteries, glass bottles, and an old bicycle that was rusting slowing into the long grass behind the shed. Ross's theory was that anything would burn if you could get the fire hot enough. He also believed that a fire was more environmentally friendly than landfill or recycling because it got rid of everything very quickly. The dump was a lingering process where stuff took up space for years and years, required transportation, or a factory full of machines to process it, and was unhygienic. Basically, he was doing the world a favour by not sending rubbish to the dump. If only he could make everyone come round to his way of seeing the issue there would be no need for rubbish dumps and mountains of unsorted bottles or stinking rubbish. Jack thought the high fees charged by the dump might be skewing his vision.

This ancient farm practice of the quarterly burn-off did require several litres of petrol. Poured over it at frequent intervals it assisted the non-flammable items to at least look like they were burning. After watching the haphazard way Ross had of sloshing the petrol from an open can no one was keen to stand too near him. The potential for a flame to run back up the stream of fuel wasn't only highly possible, it actually happened. Ross jumped backwards sending another slosh of petrol into the air and the flame ripped upwards and away from the canister. He stubbed out the toe of his leather boot which had been doused in the process and grinned like a mad man. Jack had seen him playing with fire before and guessed it was some kind of test, him against the fire, wits against nature. They finished dragging over the last items; a single mattress with the stuffing coming out, and the safety net off the kid's trampoline. Jack had heard Nancy ask suspiciously where the safety net was, but by then Ross had already bundled it into a big cardboard box and he wasn't about to give it up.

Ross was content to stand in the paddock throwing things on the blaze while he worked up a thirst, but when the pile got low he went searching for more. The old outboard motor for example, which should have been sent in for repairs, made an impressive explosion, its casing shooting up into the sky and landing in the nearest paddock where it startled a grazing sheep. Soon he would pull up a chair and open a beer like an old man enjoying a winter fire while the black clouds of chemical laden smoke swirled up and over the bay. Nancy would relax, knowing the deck chairs and pot plants would be spared the inferno this season.

That Friday night the town was buzzing. The first of the holiday crowd had already taken up residence in the baches, and all the shops were open late for trade. As a rule Jack didn't do presents, but by chance he had seen a book in a shop window that Betty would like. As a precaution he had dragged Rose out with him and she had agreed to help. 'I can't believe a big, strong man like you is afraid of a little old book seller!' she said incredulously. 'It's that one, isn't it?' she pointed to the window display. Jack nodded, feeling a bit daft. 'Watch and learn.'

Rose walked briskly into the shop, towing Jack by one hand. She picked up the book and placed it on the counter, and waited for the woman to serve her. Under her breath so that only Jack could hear she instructed, 'Don't look around the shop. Keep your eyes focused above the counter or she'll think you might buy something else if she waits a bit.' Jack did as he was told, trying not to fidget. Rose folded her arms and cleared her throat. The seller hurried over. 'Sorry to keep you waiting. A present is it? I have others I could show you on this subject if you're interested.'

'I would like it gift wrapped please,' Rose smiled.

'Certainly,' the seller acquiesced. 'Do you need a little card on the front? There's a selection on the counter if you'd like to choose one.' Rose did not move or reply. She waited until the wrapped package was placed in front of her and said, 'How much do I owe you?' She handed over her card and paid, smiled again, thanked the woman, and walked straight out the door. Once outside she handed the book to Jack who was laughing. 'And that is how you buy a book.' Rose linked her arm through his as they walked.

'Very professional. Dinner's on me. What do you say we get some pizza and eat on the boat?' Rose was pleased to accept. They sat in two fold out chairs on the deck of the *Skylark* and ate, feeding the crusts to Smell. 'She's not looking too good, Jack.' Rose looked at Smell who lay at their feet. 'Maybe you should take her to the vet. I know she's old, but six months ago she was still a lively dog.'

He had come to the same conclusion and already booked her in for a check-up next week. Maybe she needed mineral supplements or something. She had been resting the best part of most days while he was gone so it couldn't be over-work.

'As it happens she's booked in with the vet for Monday. I'll be a free man next week after quitting the job tomorrow. How would you like to be my date for the work do? It'll be awful, but Ryan and Lucy will be there.'

'Why not? I can finally meet the man who's bested my brother. It could be fun! And I'm not needed for the opening of Tide to Table, although Terry did try and set me up with one of his cronies. I told him about you to get him off my case. An oyster farmer from up north. He knows better than to ask to meet you.'

'Did the water testing come back clean?'

'Yep, not a thing above normal. So what's this party going to be like?'

'The theme is Tropical Island. More dress down than dress up. I could help you get started on your costume,' Jack wiggled his eyebrows. He wanted his future to be full of moments like this; sharing pizza in the evening sun with Rose, his dog at his feet, and nothing to do for the rest of the day. For this to happen one of them would have to make a big change, bend to the needs of the other person. Jack didn't know how he would make a living if Rose chose to stay, he just knew it wouldn't be working for Ross. Aside from fishing, driving boats, and oyster farming, he was a 38 year old unskilled labourer.

Rose sensed he had turned to introspection and pulled him back to the present. She slid the straps of her dress off her shoulders. 'Is this dress down enough?' Jack smiled and shook his head, 'No, you'll have to do better than that.' Rose tugged on the skirt, pulling the dress down to reveal the top of her breasts, 'And this?'

'Now you're talking,' Jack grinned wider, his eyes dancing with mischief, 'but I think we'd better go inside for a private viewing of the collection.' He kicked aside the empty pizza boxes and led her eagerly to the cabin.

Chapter 12

The four of them were crammed into Lucy's small hatchback heading for the farm. Ryan had sold his old car for scrap a few months ago and Sonny had a mate leaving the country who had agreed on a good price for Ryan if he could wait until the day before he flew out to take the car.

The men each held a bottle shaped Christmas present, and wore their best shorts and t-shirts - less stained or ripped than the ones they normally wore to work. Jack was saving his new clothes for Christmas. It had taken the women all afternoon to decide what to wear. Every time they put on an outfit the men said, 'No.'

'Seriously? A white miniskirt and a low-cut top is too dressy? Are they all Jehovah's Witness or something?' Lucy was incredulous.

'Maybe it's the way you wear it,' offered Jack. They both looked too good for a shed party. The other women would feel awkward and outclassed, the husbands and boyfriends would stare, and once you added alcohol to the mix it could end up all wrong.

'What about those shorts you wear around the house?' Ryan suggested.

'You mean the ones I *paint* in? They have paint on them,' Lucy rolled her eyes.

They were at Ryan's pink-white-yellow-blue bach because Rose had returned from Europe with one suitcase of old clothes, and everything else she'd bought since was too officey. Jack only owned one box of clothes, and still thought it was too many, but Lucy had insisted on loaning Rose something to wear.

Finally they were ready. Rose was wearing a knee length denim dress, and Lucy had opted for a thin cotton jumpsuit. They would blend in perfectly. In honor of the island theme they both wore hibiscus flowers in their hair and lipstick the same shade of bright pink.

It was six o'clock when they drove up to the yard. Music was blasting out of the shed and guests were gathered outside; men around Ross and the barbecue, women at a picnic table with glasses of punch. Kids were poking sticks in the embers of yesterday's fire in the paddock and chasing each other with the blackened ends.

Nancy saw them arrive and came over. 'Brace yourself,' Ryan put a proprietary arm around Lucy's shoulders, and hoped Louise was watching. Nancy made a fuss over the flowers they gave her and draped strings of polyester flowers around each of their necks in mock island welcome. She led them over to the crowd and left them to make their own introductions.

Most of the conversations were loudly punctuated with swearing and raucous laughter. Some had been drinking since after lunch and gave no more than a quick nod to the newcomers before delving back into heated discussions on what so and so had said to whats-her-name, and what *she* did after that. Louise, on her way out of the shed with a glass of punch, tried to maneuver herself between Lucy and Ryan from behind but Ryan's arm didn't lift to allow her in, if anything he tightened his grip. The co-joined couple turned about like siamese twins to face her. Louise wasn't deterred and started up her usual banter. Lucy did her best not to get fed up with the smutty jokes and suggestive looks which she was cut out of. After the first five minutes Jack saw her try to disengage herself from Ryan but he tightened his grip on her waist. Rose's phone beeped from a denim pocket. 'Lucy says if I don't bring her a litre of very strong drink she's going to start singing. Oh dear. I'd best do as she asks.'

'Get her some punch. I'll guarantee it's potent enough.' Jack led her into the shed.

Tyrone had cut off his long hair that morning and was self consciously stroking his head and sipping a beer. Apparently short was better on a rugby field. His girlfriend was excited to be here and chatted to everyone about how great this place was. Jack marveled that a person could spend years living somewhere and have no idea what was just down the road.

Ross was surprised to see the nosey photographer with Ryan and did a double take. Lucy stepped up to him and stuck out her hand. 'I'm Lucy. We haven't been properly introduced, although I have a good shot of you on the water. I can email you a copy if you're interested. I'm a freelance photographer. If you like my work I can come and do some portraits of your family. My fees are quite high, but you can't beat a quality family portrait on your wall.' Ross coloured slightly.

'Yeah, sorry about the other week. Bit of a misunderstanding. Were those your photos in the paper? Very nice.' He let go of the hand he'd been shaking.

'Yes, and thank you, but it's not difficult getting a good picture out here.' She indicated the hills and sea, settling into an evening pastel. Ross nodded in agreement, eager to redeem himself.

'Nancy's the one to talk to about a family photo. I think it's about time we did one. Give her your card.'

Lucy wasn't trying to embarrass him into a photo shoot, this was just what she said to people. She was a business woman who never missed a chance to ply her trade. When Rose stepped forward Ross smiled, 'And you must be Rose. Miss Rose Shawe.'

'That's right, but I don't remember having met you before.' Rose was puzzled. She certainly wouldn't have known his face in a crowd.

'No, we haven't met. I started working for Shorty just after you left the country. Apparently you weren't speaking to him at the time. The man I lease this land from said he knew your family, still keeps in touch with your uncle. Accountant in the city isn't he? Dave likes to frequent the pub, and mentioned seeing you there with Jack. I just put two and two together. Nice to finally meet you.' He shook her hand too. 'What would you ladies like to drink? There's plenty of punch.'

Jack was puzzled about what Ross had said. It sounded as if he'd known he and Rose were an item long before they'd come out of hiding. He couldn't make his mind up if this was significant or not. It was odd that Ross had said nothing of it, but then he never gave much away.

A meal of blackened barbecue meat, and salads of pasta, potatoes, or lettuce and tomato was eaten on the knees outside, space at the tables being limited. Plenty of tomato sauce added flavor to those foods of a bland nature, and once the majority were satisfied the drinking began again properly. Alcohol consumed as aperitif didn't count, that was just to lay a good foundation down. The keg of beer was already empty.

Nancy and other elected parents had taken the children to bed when the sun went down, and left a babysitter in charge. The music was cranked up and the punch was flowing. A game of coconut bowling was started on a strip of raked sand inside the shed. Since many of the contestants were two sheets to the wind the competition was quickly whittled down to two teams of serious players. Dirty tactics were brought into play with sneaky kicks and distractions from both teams, but this only increased the amount of fun being had. To much applause and cat calls the winners took their prize, and were encouraged to demonstrate how to put rum to good use with onlookers chanting '*drink, drink, drink, drink.*' Jack had thrown his coconut wide after the third turn, not wanting to end the night blind drunk. He still had to find the right moment to tell Ross he wouldn't be back next year. This sort of party wasn't his scene at all. Lucy and Ryan didn't mind mixing with the others, but Rose was trying bravely to maintain a smile she didn't feel. They watched as Ross played air guitar in the centre of the dance floor while Nancy gyrated around him, her hair coming loose.

'You know, Terry and Ross have a lot in common. They both want to rise in the world, and they're both cunning bastards. Terry has the advantage of more money,' Rose whispered to Jack, 'but Ross has the advantage of air guitar.'

After the excitement of competition had died off, the burlap sack in the corner was dragged through the sand clinking into the middle of the room. Secret Santa presents were handed out by Ross, who said, 'My wife's a ho ho ho. Merry Christmas!' and had to pass the job onto someone who could read the names.

When he unwrapped his bottle of Moonshine, Ross tried not to look completely disgusted but the grimace was easily readable. Ryan sniggered. More than a few people were having trouble speaking clearly now, and Santa's gifts weren't making them any smarter. Jack got a bottle of wine which he made a show of hiding under his coat for later. Santa had splashed out. The sticker on the bottle said $11.95.

The first casualty was discovered under the picnic table snoring on his back. It was Nancy's father. Had it been anyone else it's unlikely he would have remained unmolested. Nancy went to fetch the grey army surplus blanket from the first aid cupboard to put over him, and learnt that Ross had thrown it on the fire yesterday.

'What the hell, Ross!'

'Ah, that old rag? Only good for a dog blanket! Full of moth-holes.'

Nancy knew this was an outrageous lie. She had purchased and washed it herself only three months ago before the safety inspection, but there was no point contradicting him.

Jack was keeping tabs on Ross, and reckoned he was past the point of tipsy and well on the way to drunk. Now would be a good moment to catch him, before he could go looking for the cat. His favourite party trick was a demonstration of cat bagpipes, a difficult instrument to master. It involves a cat held tightly to the musician's chest, one cat foot in the mouth, and a contraction and expansion of the cat's rear legs. If the cat is of a fragile temperament the music is considered better. Ross and Nancy's cat had become extremely nervous and disappeared under the house any time guests arrived.

Ross was currently standing by the bench talking to someone's husband. Jack waited close by. When the other man was pulled onto the dance floor by his wife, Jack gave Ryan a signal with his eyebrows, and told Rose they'd be off soon in low tones. Lucy was more difficult to round up, being the only one of their group who was carefree and drunk. Rose had nominated herself their sober driver. She looked tired and bored.

The two blokes cornered Ross and thanked him for the eventful evening. 'My pleasure, boys. Good effort this year.' He held them by the shoulders and shook them playfully. 'We make a good team, eh!'

'It's been interesting, alright, but I won't be back

next year Ross,' Ryan said. 'I always said I'd do it to help out until I knew what to do next, and now I've got plans.' Ross rocked back on his heels unsteadily and Jack leaped into the silence before he could recover. 'Same for me. I won't be back either. You'll have plenty of new workers with Shorty on board so I don't think you'll miss us.' Ross looked from one to the other.

'Are you pulling my leg? No?' he shook his head in case plain English needed back-up. They stared at the floor shaking their heads too. This could be where it got dicey. 'Oh. I see. Well, I'm disappointed in both of ya's. I had big plans for you, you know? Maybe even let you buy into the farm - but you, you were always a bit slow, Ryan. Like the way you play rugby, not desperate enough to win. You never did have the edge.' It was a cheap shot, but it got a reaction. Ryan moved forward a fraction, his neck tendons straining.

'That's right Ross, it's a bloody *game*, for *fun*. Like working here was just a *job*. You're so caught up in fighting your way through life that you can't see the people around you just want to enjoy it. I don't think I've ever enjoyed a job *less*. You busted my balls for an extra bag of oysters, and you still think we're *mates*? Why do you think no one ever stays?'

Ross was having difficulty understanding Ryan. He frowned, puzzled. Jack wondered if any past employee had ever admitted why they were leaving. Making excuses and going quietly was the easy way, especially if you planned on socializing later in the same small town. 'Argh, just forget it,' Ryan turned abruptly and walked off before Ross could respond. He'd been close to swinging a punch a minute ago, and for what? He was outta here. He'd said what needed to be said.

Ross looked up at Jack, patting the air in dismissal. 'He's a bit out of sorts tonight. I don't know what he's on about, but you, well, you served your purpose, Jack. Been in my shed lately?' Ross grinned. 'Hard to get that key off Dave was it?'

Jack nodded thoughtfully, letting the meaning sink in. He should have wondered about that. 'Dave said you've been very generous, buying his beer at the pub every week. He wanted to hang on to the key a bit longer, but I told him it wasn't fair to take advantage of you like that. Very stern, I was. Yeah, Nancy told me you wanted to get a look in there and I got a bit nervous. Then I found out about you and Shorty's sister! I mean, what are the odds of that? Ol' George the caretaker told Dave that Rose was back, and Dave said he'd seen you together. All I had to do was let you in the shed and you and Rose did the rest.'

'You took a risk,' Jack eyeballed him.

'Yeah, it looked that way, until I hear he's opening a restaurant while I'm saving up the Moro bars. That's when I knew I had the advantage.'

Now he was laughing so hard his words came out in separate syllables, 'ad-varn-tige,' so that for once he wasn't mumbling. Jack got the joke, only it wasn't that funny. Ross looked at him with genuine affection, little tears showing at the corners of his eyes.

A weary frustration came over Jack. He'd been played. So Nancy had told Ross about the pump breaking down he'd faked. In that case he'd underestimated how much the right hand told the left. As for Dave, it stood to reason he would do Ross a favour because Ross paid him for the use of the cottage and sheds. As a shepherd he didn't do very well, and maybe he'd over extended himself financially and it paid to keep his tenant sweet.

If it weren't for meeting Rose his time here could be classed as a bad joke. There was not much point in blaming Ross, he'd just turned things to his *advarntige*. The man was impervious to his own faults or the trouble he put others through. The best thing Jack could do now was walk away and forget it, but he wanted to know one thing.

'That's real clever Ross, but when were you planning on dumping your waste?'

'Right before the next water testings of course! What? You don't think I'd do it any other time, do ya? Hell, that could make people seriously ill. Obviously the *potential* to ruin Shorty's party helped, but I'm not the bastard you think I am. I just wanted to stop a few months of harvest next door, be a pain in the ass. It's almost a shame I can't still do it, but business is business.'

'I hope that's the case. I never thought you were a bad guy, just kinda messed up. Sounds like you and Shorty are made for each other. I hope it works out for you both.' Jack wanted to leave, but Ross was enjoying himself too much to let him go. 'Come on Jack, have another drink. No hard feelings, okay?

Best bloody worker I ever had. Let's celebrate! I should give you a fuckin' medal for helping me get one over Shorty. Except it was my brilliant plan, so I think I'll reward *myself* with another drink as well. Whoa!' he exclaimed as he ladled punch over his hand, ice cubes scattering over the bench. Ross corrected his aim, tipping the last inch of punch into a plastic cup before plunging the ladle in again for another scoop. Jack took the ladle out of his slack grasp and refilled Ross's cup before saying, 'If that's all you were wanting to do, why did you wait so long? You could have had your laugh any time.'

'Oh. No, no, no. That was plan B - the *merde*, if you'll pardon my French. Plan A was a bit more complicated. You remember the ponds? That nursery? Well, the new fashion in oysters is to create a recognizable product, right? Terry always wanted a black marking on his shells, like a T. I thought it would be funny as fuck to develop those suckers and whack a trademark on it. Took ages to find the right breeders, and in the end I did get half a dozen spat with black markings, but the T's all had this tail. They looked like J's.'

'Did they now? Maybe one day we'll talk about that, but not tonight. I'm off.'

He didn't bother saying goodnight to anyone. If he never saw them again he couldn't care less. Maybe in the future he'd look back and feel differently, but at this moment he was sick to the back teeth of this place.

Jack walked out of the shed to find the others waiting in the car. Rose turned the ignition on the moment his legs were in.

'What kept you?' Ryan asked.

'Nothing. He just wanted to wish me luck.' Jack wasn't going to repeat what Ross had said to anyone. The main thing was, he knew whatever happened here in the bay, it would stay here in the bay, and that was good enough for him.

Joshua arrived in his beat-up Land Rover on Christmas Eve in the afternoon. It looked like the sort of car Fast Billy would warrant. Old boat ramp wars evident along it's dented panels, and an elbow of polished driftwood for a door handle. The sight of it made Jack smile with fondness, for it's driver and for the car itself, so much a part of his history. He'd learnt to drive in that old tub.

After inspecting the houseboat with Jack, a cold drink in his hand, Joshua declared it was time for a swim to cool off. The day was overcast and muggy, the heat making everyone feel sticky and lethargic. 'Come on Jack, water's lovely!' he called, floating on his back away from the boats. Jack had been on dry land a whole week, an occurrence that only happened to oyster farmers for a short time each year. Jack waded out to where it was deeper, feeling the sand and mud, soft and cool under his feet. Joshua was right, the water slipped over his skin like satin. He'd had a dressing gown like that once with a dragon embroidered on the back. They floated together moving slowly through the water, happy to be on holiday and have each other's company.

This was how Rose found them when she arrived home from shopping in the city. She dumped her bags inside and looked out the cabin window to see two heads bobbing towards the shore, one silver the other light brown. They talked as they paddled in, and Rose wondered if Jack had told him about Smell. She quickly stuffed presents in a cupboard and took off her shoes, walking down the plank to meet them.

'Now who's this beauty, Jack?' Joshua nudged a dripping Jack and smiled at Rose.

'Josh, this is Rose. Rose, my brother Joshua.' Rose greeted Joshua with a small wave, and went to kiss Jack who wrapped his wet body over hers and rubbed his hair into her neck while she gasped and wriggled, trying to dislodge him. When he let go her dress was splotched with water, but in this heat she didn't mind. 'I'm going to do a few jobs on the boat and let you two have a catch up. Come over for dinner at six.' She kissed Jack on the mouth, smiled at Joshua, and left.

They sat on the grass step with their feet in the sand and let the air dry them. There was a delay before Joshua spoke, and from the way he watched Rose retreating to her boat Jack guessed his thoughts pertained to her. She was also foremost in Jack's mind because there wasn't much time left to acquaint Joshua with his plan; Christmas was tomorrow.

'Made any progress then?' Joshua asked, lifting his chin at Rose's departing back but looking at Jack. It was a way of speaking openly yet with discretion, something they both did from habit.

'I wouldn't exactly call it progress but I've been busy working on it. Are you up for giving me a hand with a few details tomorrow night? You can have a front row seat and watch me publicly humiliate myself.'

'You can count on me, but how can you be embarrassed in front of your own brother? Haven't I seen you do it all before?'

'Not quite. You haven't seen this one.'

'Oh, is this the significant event involving Herculean amounts of courage and a dirty knee?'

'Yes to the courage, not sure about the knee. I'm just going to go with the moment on that one.' Jack grinned in a strained manner. His stomach was already cramping with nerves just thinking about it.

'For God's sake, lighten up would ya? She'll say yes. You'd have to be blind to miss the way she melts into you.' Joshua shoved Jack's shoulder playfully and Jack cracked a real smile. This felt like the most wonderful and awful idea he'd ever had. He couldn't imagine how it would all work out, but he had to try. After his first bungled attempt he was determined to make this occasion more memorable for Rose. If he waited till they had a chance to talk things over, the romance, the grand gesture of it would be lost, and he wanted her to have that. She deserved it. In his mind's eye he got as far as presenting the ring and saying the right words, but he couldn't picture what came next. He was able to pinpoint his anxiety to that exact future moment, his eyes locked to Rose's eyes, before the picture was stopped, like a movie paused mid scene. 'And anyway, what's the worst that can happen?' Joshua said callously. Jack laughed, understanding that Joshua enjoyed to see Jack squirm a little. 'You bastard,' he shook his head with faked incredulity and then hauled the other man to his feet.

Rose slapped up a quick meal of cold chicken, salad with hard boiled eggs, and a loaf of French bread. The brothers found her reading a magazine, the table laid but covered with a cloth to keep the flies away. Rose studied them as they set down a plate of cheese and crackers, and a bottle of wine. There was an obvious similarity in their features that marked them as closely related, but their colouring was different. Joshua's eyes were brown where Jack's were greeny-grey, and his hair must have also been a darker shade of brown before it turned the deep silver of old knives. Though both were weather beaten, skin tanned and leathery, she could see that they would still be handsome well into old age.

The houseboat windows were open to catch the cool evening air coming off the water. A breeze had picked up after six o'clock, ruffling the muslin under-curtains. The sounds from other parties on other boats came in gusts and made it seem as if the whole country was happy tonight. Some of the boats were decorated with strings of solar powered fairy lights, making them look like miniature floating palaces.

As they tucked into the simple summer meal Joshua told Rose a bit about himself and life in the north. Jack knew he was trying to give Rose an idea of what it might be like to live there, without being too blatant about it; the long sandy beaches whipped by the salty wind, giant kauri forests, the water so fresh it made the skin tingle. Rose was content to listen, but after a dessert of fruit salad and yoghurt drizzled with honey from a local hive, she turned to Jack. 'Does he know about Smell?'

'Yes. I told him right after our swim. The vet will keep her until Josh goes home the day after Boxing Day. I'll go up with him and see her buried.' Rose nodded, and there was silence while everyone reflected on the kind of dog Smell had been for them. To Joshua she was an extension of his family, to Rose she had been an extension of Jack, and to Jack she has been his number one companion through thick and thin. Her loss had been a shock.

The vet had told Jack on Monday that Smell Hound had cancer. Jack wanted to treat it but it was too far advanced, and her body too old to withstand the treatment. Her heart rate was fast, a sign she was in pain. Jack had brought her home and spent time just sitting stroking her, talking to her, sleeping with her on the end of the bed, and letting her ride in the cab every time he went out. He had to lift her in and out, and she had stopped eating. He even tried feeding her from his dinner plate, but she just sniffed at the food and lay back down.

Last night Jack had taken her back to the vet. She whimpered when he moved her and lost control of her bladder. The vet left them alone in a room for five minutes, even though it was late and his last customers were waiting. Jack pulled himself together when the vet came back, rubbed a hand over his wet face and nodded for the injection that would end Smell's suffering.

'Can I come with you?' Rose asked. 'I'd like to be there when you bury her.'

'Yes. That would be perfect,' Jack said.

'My home is your home, Rose,' Joshua added. Jack sure hoped it would be, but he put that thought on the back burner. He would know soon enough.

Joshua spent the night on Jack's boat, except it really belonged to Joshua. He usually kept it moored near the farm as a bolt hole when the world crowded him. During summer when work temporarily stopped he would escape the crowds that flocked to the coast from the city by heading further north to places accessible only by boat. There was a lady up there who conveniently stayed in a little bach near the shore and took her holidays at the same time as him. Hers was the only house, separated from civilization by a large farm. The farm had been sold by her grandparents with the small waterfront held back for their children, and a right to use the farm tracks for access. In a few days she would be waiting there, by unspoken arrangement. They had not exchanged numbers over the previous two summers. Her husband had passed away three years ago, and she wasn't ready for more than what they had and Joshua was content to wait. Maybe, just maybe, if things turned out well he would be able to meet her again soon. If not, then he hoped she would understand. He couldn't throw his brother out, could he?

Jack was glad of an excuse to be on Rose's boat for the night. He wouldn't keep looking round to see where Smell was, and remember she wasn't here anymore. The timing might strike people as strange if they recalled the Lara episode. His dog had died and he was about to propose, as if Lara had been right about his over attachment to an animal. If Jack went home affianced there would be tongues wagging there too, a fact of small town life, judgments were dished out two a penny whatever you did.

They were awake early on Christmas morning, but tarried in bed until the sun beating on the roof made the room too stuffy and hot. Jack put some beans and sausages on to cook and called out to Joshua, who was up on deck sipping a coffee. It was too hot for a fry-up and Rose took her muesli outside, not at all pleased with the smell. Jack wasn't hungry himself but this might be the only meal he was able to eat today.

'Morning Sleepyheads!' Joshua greeted them from the beach. 'Should I bring the pot of coffee over?' He made his way from one boat to the other, a towel draped around his neck and his hair still wet from an early morning swim. The tide was edging out now, and the clouds of the day before had lifted. Under the pohutukawa trees along the grassy slopes a crimson carpet of dying flower petals carpeted the ground. There were kisses and wishes of a merry Christmas all round, and Rose gave them both a present. For Joshua a fisherman's multi-tool of the highest quality with glossy wooden handles, and for

Jack a folding pocket-knife hand forged by a local knife maker. The men were very taken with their gifts and wanted to set about using them but felt bashful because they had nothing to offer in return. 'We've got you a little something too,' said Joshua, 'but you'll have to wait for later to see it. Jack's orders.' He tapped the side of his nose to imply a secret. Jack shrugged apologetically.

'With Jack's fear of shops I wasn't expecting anything, unless it's hair ties from the 4square,' Rose said with a sideways glance at Jack.

'Nice try. You can't trick me into giving away clues, miss, so just stop right there,' Jack laughed. 'You'll have to wait and see.'

After breakfast they all went to help with the party preparations on the domain. There was a gathering of a small group of those permanent residents without early celebrations to attend, and everyone knew each other well. They were all keen to meet Joshua and came to shake hands; he felt as though he was joining old friends, so much had Jack told him about them all. He was assigned to tea and coffee duty with Betty; it had been decided to have a morning tea break together to save time.

While they filled the urns and opened packets of biscuits Joshua revealed to Betty that it was his fault Jack had ended up here, and went on to explain. Jack had warned him that Betty was curious, and there was no reason not to let her in on it now. Once he had finished she put her hands on her hips, saying, 'That scallywag! He could have trusted me with his secret. I wouldn't have told a soul.' One of the reasons she put up with Rex was his penchant for a good gossip. As the person responsible for making sure the wharf ran smoothly she considered it her business to know the details of the lives being lived around her, and Rex had a talent for putting people at ease. He made no secret of his vagrant past and rather than looking down upon him people held him in higher esteem for raising himself above it, and felt he was the sort of man who would hear you out without judgement.

This trickle of information meant Betty could make sure the wharf didn't become a hide out for druggies and criminals, or regress to former standards. On the other hand she could offer assistance where needed. Many a resident had been helped by her hearing of their problems. The idea of organizing an alternative hang-out for drunks had come to nothing after the fire to Rex's boat because she was so angry they could turn on him, and her natural largesse was instead bestowed upon those closest.

There was an element of competition between Betty and Rex regarding the collecting of information; Rex thought he had the monopoly on secrets, so Betty found it satisfying to know things he didn't and keep them to herself.

Right at this moment Betty was the only other person apart from Joshua who knew that Jack would propose to Rose in the very near future. He had asked them both to do a few small favours, and work it out between them. Together they went over the plan, heads and voices lowered over the tea things. It was all in the timing and the detail, and Betty wanted it to be perfect for the couple.

Sixty-odd guests were expected tonight, and an extra tent had been raised to accommodate them all. Plenty of the holiday boats had accepted the invitation and the wharfies had all invited various friends.

After taking a lunch break Jack helped gather folding chairs from the boats who had them, and arrange them under the larger of the two tents. The smaller tent was set up for food and drinks, of which there was plenty. Every one was bringing something. A pig had been roasting on the spit since earlier in the day, sending up wisps of steam so rich and tantalizing you could almost get full just breathing it in.

Ross and Nancy arrived to deliver the oyster bar; an impressive slab of macrocarpa with oyster shells inlaid along the top, and a panel at the front with the farm logo. Jack put the bins of live oysters under the counter in a neat stack where they could be easily reached when the rush started. There were about fifty dozen live oysters ready to be shucked. When they were done setting up Joshua came over and greeted the pair. 'Gidday. That's a good looking set up you've got there. You must be Ross, and you must be Nancy. I've been hearing a lot about you from Jack here. My name's Joshua.' Ross was looking from Jack to Joshua suspiciously.

'Gidday. Have we met before?' Ross asked.

'I'd say you've seen me at the Oyster Farmer's conference on several occasions. I'm Jack's brother in case the penny hasn't dropped. I run a farm up north. One of the bigger ones.' He was standing with his legs slightly apart and his arms crossed in front of him, at ease but not exactly friendly.

'Well, that's a surprise. Jack never mentioned you,' Ross's face did look the picture of surprise. Nancy gave Jack a curious look, spotted Rose outside, and left the men to talk.

Jack could see Ross's mind scrabbling to put pieces in place, watching his wife walk away to buy himself a moment, his smile forced. Joshua continued, 'Let's just say it was for the best. We're all happy to hear that you and Shorty made up, but make no mistake - if you play dirty make sure you're in the right. As the saying goes - shit sticks.' It was an acknowledgement of what had happened and a warning. Ross was smart enough to read between the lines. He wasn't aware until now that he had been under wider observation, and Jack guessed he was feeling a bit exposed all of a sudden. 'Look, don't take it personally, we have to protect our interests in this business,' Joshua's tone had become less aggressive and more confidential, inviting Ross to state his position.

'Don't worry, I've got a conscience. What happens in the bay stays in the bay. You have my word on that. Now I know why Jack was so good at the work. I thought he didn't stumble enough in the mud, but some of us are more graceful than others. Maybe I can buy you a beer at the next conference, prove I'm not a monster.'

'I'll look forward to that,' Joshua stuck his hand

out and they shook, 'but from now on if you've got an issue, mind what threats you make. Some of us can't afford to ignore them.' Both men were forthright and sincere in their communications. Joshua excused himself and Ross squared up to Jack. 'Merry Christmas, fella. So that was it, eh? You weren't there on honest terms. Well, that explains why you didn't make much fuss. I never would have picked you for a sneak. So enlighten me; what did they think I was going to do that needed a watch dog?'

'A virus. Most of the farmers are just ordinary blokes, but you've got a degree in marine science. I think it makes them edgy, you're not playing at the same level. My guts said you weren't the sort, but you acted so weird about the shed I stuck around to make sure.'

'A virus, eh? Hmm. No, not my style. I've got a hunch how the last one happened, but so does every other farmer from here to Timbuktu. Sure I can't tempt you to stay? There'll be a reshuffle next year. I had you in mind for the assistant manager's position.' Jack baulked. This man had skin as tough as an old bush pig to think they could wipe the slates clean and carry on. Jack hesitated, considering his reply, but in the end he couldn't stir up enough energy; he was saving it for tonight. Ryan had said it all anyway so what was the point?

'Sorry Ross, the coffee's just not up to standard. Ring me when you get a percolator, or better yet, an expresso machine.' Ross laughed and took it to mean Jack wasn't inclined to disclose his real reason for leaving, and went to round-up his gossiping wife.

Luckily, Ross hadn't asked Jack what he planned to do next because the answer was hanging by a thread like a milk tooth, waiting for Jack to give it a last tug. The smell of roasting pig made him hungry but his stomach was tense. He made for the toilets again.

At five o'clock the band began setting up in the big tent where the dancing would be. A bunch of young locals had agreed to play from 8 p.m. until midnight for a modest sum, if dinner and drinks were included. No one had heard them play yet, but they were the only performers who could be rustled up to work on Christmas Day. Rex knew the father of the drummer who let them do band practice in his garage, and talked them into the gig in exchange for a free haircut. Ryan and Lucy were with Rose on the boat and Jack went to fetch them all; dinner was about to kick off, and he needed extra help shucking. Joshua was busy shucking a few for the band who would eat first and start with some quiet numbers while the rest of the crowd ate, and plenty of guests would want oysters as an appetizer in a minute.

'Wow! Look at *you*,' Rose stared at Jack, her eyes all lit up. She hadn't seen him in the new duds. 'Did you go clothes shopping all by yourself?'

'Of course. Nothing to it,' he winked at her. He was clean shaven and well turned out; nervous as hell and feeling good simultaneously. They joined the party under the canvas as people began arriving, and Jack donned an apron to preserve his good clothes.

'Looks like a mean spread,' Ryan rubbed his stomach as they passed tables laid out with a Christmas feast.

Behind the oyster bar the three men shucked as people came up with plates, greedy for oysters. The band tuned their instruments; two guitars, a banjo, and a violin, and began a slow instrumental. Shell after shell was opened, cleaned of fish, and discarded. Some people obviously didn't mind the slightly metallic tang of an oyster about to spawn, and Jack waited hopefully for Rose to come and ask for some. They were down to the last bin, and the music had revved up a notch, the lead vocalist singing a sweet and melancholy tune.

As the first diners finished their meal Rose came up to the bar. Jack had known she would but the relief was huge. Lucy was close behind, and they each carried a plate heaped with food for their hungry men. Jack's heart beat faster. Rose looked radiant tonight in a long cream dress covered in small red poppies. Her hair had grown longer since they'd met, and now it curled gently over the top of her shoulders.

'Good evening handsome oyster farmer, I'd like to sample your wares if you have any left,' Rose giggled, handing Jack his dinner.

He was pleased to see her looking happy and relaxed, she had been so stressed the last weeks. Some people got a kick out of high pressure work but Rose wasn't one of them. Playing along with her he said, 'Certainly Madame, I have saved you the best one.' Reaching beneath the counter he took a big oyster from its hiding place, and winking at Joshua, placed it on the counter. Joshua flapped a tea towel vigorously as if shaking out crumbs and the band played three more chords, the volume dropping a little each time. Betty appeared at the end of the bar with a tray of clean glasses, setting them down carefully. Jack slid his knife into the shell of the perfect specimen he had selected for Rose. Someone nearby made shushing noises and the chatter stopped at the same time the last chord of music faded. As Jack prized up the lid of the shell there was total silence. He offered Rose the bottom half of the oyster shell, and she sucked her breath in quickly. As she stared at the gold ring in its bed of cotton wool Jack came round the counter and spoke loud and clear, before she had time to look up. Joshua had cleared him a path, and stood like a sentinel at his back. 'Rose, I would like it very much if you agreed to marry me. What do you say?'

Jack's hands were trembling at his sides, his palms turned upwards. The guests had fanned out around them, stunned to witness such an unexpected declaration. Everyone watched them, not a body moved. Rose picked up the ring. It was twenty four carat gold with roses carved either side of a large sapphire. The ring had belonged to Joshua and Jack's mother and her grandmother before her.

'It's a beautiful ring, Jack. I'd be honored to wear it. So, yes, I'll marry you.' She launched herself at him and he crouched to catch her, arms wide open. Noise erupted from all around them and the drummer hit three beats to open a song. Rex and

Ryan popped open bottles of champagne kept for this moment, and glasses were handed to the celebrated couple. 'Wait!' Rose held up her hand, the ring catching the light. 'I can't drink this. I'm pregnant.'

Joshua did his best to steady Jack from behind as he bent at the knees and took half a step forwards. Rose looked intently at Jack, waiting for a reaction. Three seconds passed and he was still dumbstruck, but got his legs under him again. A big smile spread out on his face and he belted out, 'Bloody hell! I'm gonna be a dad? That's some Christmas present.' Thrusting his untasted champagne into Ryan's hand he wrapped his arms round Rose and rocked her against him. Right this second he wished they were alone. He wanted to see her bare stomach, observe it closely for changes, feel the skin that hid his child, but this moment was for Rose.

The last piece of news rippled out to the guests around them and the congratulations doubled, were repeated all over again, and then the cheering began as words failed to have enough power to express the excitement. The mood of jubilation was infectious, and even the strangers in the crowd were hugging each other just to be a part of it. An onlooker would think they were all swingers warming up for the night.

'I can hardly believe my ears. Tell me again,' Jack demanded of Rose.

'I will if you promise not to pass out.' Jack grinned like a maniac.

'You sure know how to surprise a fella.'

'Then that sorta makes us even, doesn't it?' Rose quipped.

Ryan butted in, 'Now, now, you two. Plenty of time to squabble later. We're not quite done with the announcements yet - and Jack, you are such a *prick*! How am I supposed to compete with *that*? Lucy'll never have me now.'

Lucy was side-on to the engaged couple, busy catching the moment on film. This would make a great prelude to a wedding album. Maybe she could start a new trend; couples could hire her to record their proposals, but that could be awkward if the answer was no.

Betty came forward with a gift for Jack and Rose. Inside a small leather case was a key. They looked at Betty, wondering what the key was for.

'You see, I wanted to give you something you could both enjoy together. This key belongs to my motorbike. It hasn't been out of the shed for about ten years. My husband and I used to go all over the country on that bike. It was our treat to ourselves on our first anniversary. I tried to keep riding after he died, but it made me feel so alone, and Rex is hopeless on it. I hope you'll get as much pleasure from it as we did - if it still goes! We can get it out tomorrow and have a look.'

They thanked Betty for such an extraordinary gift, and promised to make good use of it. Sonny was quick to add that he'd be happy to check it was running smoothly and give it a tune up.

Jack had already seen the bike. What inquisitive person wouldn't take a peek under a motorbike shaped tarp? It was at the back of the shed across the road where the trestle tables were stored, under a canvas soaked in oil to prevent rust. He had assumed it belonged to the man who owned the shed, and probably so did everyone else. 'I'm afraid it makes our present look a bit mean in comparison,' Jack said, handing her the book in its wrapping.

'I wasn't expecting anything, so how can I be disappointed?' She unwrapped the book, carefully folding the paper and slipping it between the back pages for reusing another day. The book was an old first edition of Aunt Daisy's Recipes and Helpful Home Hints. It was signed by the author on the first leaf. Betty closed it and hugged it to her chest. It was a rare book and quite valuable. She could remember her mother using it until it fell apart at the spine. 'Just my sort of cooking,' she laughed. 'Do you know, there might even be that recipe in here for converting your old carpet into lino. It's bound to come back in fashion, homemade lino.'

Rex was doing the rounds, hugging each person in turn whether he knew them or not. Now he wrapped his arms around Betty, his face wet with tears but smiling. She patted his back, making soothing sounds. The drink often brought out his maudlin side.

Then it was Joshua's turn. 'Ah, this one's a bit tricky. I know you haven't had time to sort out your lives, but think of it as an open offer.' He extracted a key from his pocket and presented it palm up to the couple. 'The family home is yours when you want it. An old bachelor like me has no use of four bedrooms. It needs a family in it again. Bring it to life, fill it with little feet and laughter.'

'We couldn't take your house, Josh,' said Rose with a firm shake of her head. 'It's very kind, but I'm sure we can find somewhere to live.'

'Nah, it's Jack's house as much as mine, and it's too late. I've already had plans drawn up for a smaller dwelling down the back. I hope you won't mind having me as a neighbour, but there's plenty of room. I can show you the plans next week when you come to visit.' He offered Rose the key and she took it humbly. Jack hugged his brother, and Rose buried her face in his shoulder.

It had been a night full of emotions; the excitement, the nervousness, the joy, and now the humbling gratitude for so much love. 'Hey Rose, I think you just won the jackpot!' Ryan slapped Jack on the back and laughed, and Rose went from teary to laughing with no pause between, momentarily doing both at once.

It was the best Christmas party the wharf had ever hosted, and it continued right through until the morning and even the next day. After the band finished those with guitars strummed and sang until they were too tired or drunk to continue. Plenty of guests fell asleep on chairs or under tables, being in no mood to row back out to bed. Ryan and Lucy crashed in Jack's double bed at five am, leaving the hammock for Joshua, if he made it to bed.

On the deck of the *Miss Terry Rose Skylark*, Jack and Rose saw in the dawn with a plate of pavlova covered in fresh strawberries and cream. Like lovers do, even the older ones in especially romantic moments, they took turns feeding each other with the spoon. Rose fed Jack the last mouthful and licked the spoon clean.

'You know Jack, I've got a good feeling about today. I think after a nap we should make some plans.'

'Hmm...' said Jack, and smiled in his sleep. Rose pulled the blanket around them and curled up in the crook of his outstretched arm. In seconds she was out like a light.

Chapter 13

Two weeks later and all of their gear was loaded onto the tray of the ute. There'd been a wee send off the night before, and much hugging and squeezing goodbye. They would see them all at the wedding in six months, but it was the end of daily life together.

Connie had offered to do the catering, and Lucy the photos, so the wedding plans were already underway. The *Skylark* would stay here a while longer. Ryan and Lucy had asked to have a loan of it while they installed a new bathroom and kitchen at the bach.

Jack and Rose were leaving early to avoid any more fanfare. Once Jack had checked the straps holding the tarp over the load, they were off. It felt like going on an adventure with your best mate who just happened to have a great pair of...well, lots of great pairs of everything that came in pairs, and a few interesting solo bits as well.

'There's one more stop on the way,' Jack patted Rose on the knee and pulled into the car park outside the 4square. From under his bag on the tray of the ute he took a large flat package. He had spent several hours wondering how to say goodbye to Chin, and a few more putting it together. Wrapped inside brown paper was an old piece of wood he found washed up on the beach. It had been painted white once, and was worn smooth at the edges, showing the bleached wood underneath the paint. Jack had glued his coloured plastic letters on it.

There had been more over the past months, and after an hour of moving them about they finally conveyed the message Jack wanted. On the paper wrapping Jack wrote, 'Dear Chin, I won't be back for a while so I just wanted to say...' Glued on the board were the letters: CHEERS MATE.

He checked if Chin was in the shop but there were no lights on inside. He left the package propped against the door frame and got back in the ute.

Joshua was just back from his annual holiday and had made the trip back down to give a hand. He pulled on a pair of leather gloves and jacket, pushing the motorbike out of its long resting place. Sonny had stripped it back and replaced rubber valves which had crumbled, oiled every moving part, and put it back together again. The bike gleamed like a wet sea lion in the dawn light, a solid machine in glossy black. He caught up to Jack's ute as it pulled onto the main road towards the city.

After five minutes in convoy Joshua was unable to hold back the humming metal under him. It had been waiting for the open road a long time and he hadn't felt this exhilarated since last week when his boat moored in a little bay up north. This time his thrills didn't depend on another person. He raised a hand in the air as he overtook the ute, and then gave her some more throttle. Jack and Rose laughed. Same old Joshua, Jack thought. Always the daredevil. They might just have to share their new toy. Since they had a way to go, Jack told Rose about the time Joshua had ridden his bicycle along the railing of the local bridge as a dare from his mates. The sides were concrete, a foot wide, and the bridge wasn't a long one. Even so, Jack had tried to talk him down. Joshua was certain he could do it, and there was a bag of lollies owed to him if he did. Joshua made a good start and would have made it all the way, if a car hadn't come along and tooted its horn making him lose concentration. The bike and teenage boy had wobbled and fallen into the drink separately. After two days of diving from the banks to find it they gave up, and Joshua went without a bike until Mum forgave him and bought a new one next Christmas. Jack felt so sorry for Joshua that he used his week's pocket money to by lollies for him.

About twenty kilometres after the turnoff Jack spotted a man standing on the roadside trying to hitch a lift. He was short and stocky, in black stubbies with a huge grin on a likeable rogue's face. Something in this combination of features struck a note with Jack and he pulled up. Rose put down her window.

'Where you heading?' Jack asked the man.

'Don't know,' he smiled. 'Just finished a job. Anything happening where you're heading?'

'Could be,' Jack nodded, 'I'll have to ask the boss. Jump in, we can talk about it on the way.'

About the author:

Hailey is married to an oyster farmer. Oysters have invaded her life. To learn more about their farm go to their facebook page: Monsieur Oyster.